漢魏六朝 林明理
古今抒情詩三百首
漢英對照

Parallel Reading of 300 Ancient and Modern Chinese Lyrical Poems:
Han, Wei and Six Dynasties（Chinese-English）

■ 著者：林明理　Author：Dr. Lin Ming-Li
■ 譯者：張智中　Translator：Professor Zhang Zhizhong

天空數位圖書出版

著者簡介
About the Author & Poet

　　學者詩人林明理博士〈1961-〉，臺灣雲林縣人，法學碩士、榮譽文學博士。她曾任教於大學，是位詩人評論家，擅長繪畫及攝影，著有詩集、散文、詩歌評論等文學專著37本書，包括在義大利合著的譯詩集4本。其詩作被翻譯成法語、西班牙語、義大利語、俄語及英文等多種，作品發表於報刊及學術期刊等已達兩千四百餘篇。中國學刊物包括《南京師範大學文學院學報》等多篇。

　　Dr. Lin Mingli (1961-), poet and scholar, born in Yunlin County, Taiwan, master of law, honorary Ph. D. in literature. She once taught at a university and is a poetry critic, and she is good at painting and photography. She is the author of 37 literary books, including poetry collections, prose, and poetry reviews, as well as a collection of translated poems co-authored and published in Italy. Her poems have been translated into French, Spanish, Italian, Russian and English, etc., and over 2,400 poems and articles have been published in newspapers and academic journals.

©林明理專書 monograph、義大利出版的中英譯詩合著
Chinese-English Poetry Co-author published in Italy
© Lin Ming-Li's monographs and co-authored Chinese-English Poetry collections published in Italy

1. 《秋收的黃昏》*The evening of autumn*。高雄市：春暉出版社，2008。ISBN 978-986-695-045-2
2. 《夜櫻—林明理詩畫集》*Cherry Blossoms at Night*。高雄市：春暉出版社，2009。ISBN 978-986-695-068-9
3. 《新詩的意象與內涵—當代詩家作品賞析》*The Imagery and Connetation of New Poetry —A Collection of Critical Poetry Analysis*。臺北市：文津出版社，2010。ISBN 978-957-688-913-0
4. 《藝術與自然的融合—當代詩文評論集》*The Fusion Of Art and Nature*。臺北市：文史哲出版社，2011。ISBN 978-957-549-966-2
5. 《山楂樹》*Hawthorn Poems* by Lin Mingli（林明理詩集）。臺北市：文史哲出版社，2011。ISBN 978-957-549-975-4
6. 《回憶的沙漏》*Sandglass Of Memory*（中英對照譯詩集）英譯：吳鈞。臺北市：秀威出版社，2012。ISBN 978-986-221-900-3
7. 《湧動著一泓清泉—現代詩文評論》*A Gushing Spring-A Collection Of Comments On Modern Literary Works*。臺北市：文史哲出版社，2012。ISBN 978-986-314-024-5
8. 《清雨塘》*Clear Rain Pond*（中英對照譯詩集）英譯：吳鈞。臺北市：文史哲出版社，2012。ISBN 978-986-314-076-4
9. 《用詩藝開拓美—林明理讀詩》*Developing Beauty Though The Art Of Poetry—Lin Mingli On Poetry*。臺北市：秀威出版社，2013。ISBN 978-986-326-059-2
10. 《海頌—林明理詩文集》*Hymn To the Ocean*（poems and Essays）。臺北市：文史哲出版社，2013。ISBN 978-986-314-119-8
11. 《林明理報刊評論 1990-2000》*Published Commentaries 1990-2000*。文史哲出版社，2013。ISBN 978-986-314-155-6
12. 《行走中的歌者—林明理談詩》*The Walking singer —Ming-Li Lin On Poetry*。臺北市：文史哲出版社，2013。ISBN 978-986-314-156-3
13. 《山居歲月》*Days in the Mountains*（中英對照譯詩集）英譯：吳鈞。臺北市：文史哲出版社，2015。ISBN 978-986-314-252-2

14. 《夏之吟》*Summer Songs*（中英法譯詩集）。英譯：馬為義（筆名：非馬）（Dr. William Marr）。法譯：阿薩納斯·薩拉西（Athanase Vantchev de Thracy）。法國巴黎：索倫縈拉文化學院（The Cultural Institute of Solenzara），2015。ISBN 978-2-37356-020-6
15. 《默喚》*Silent Call*（中英法譯詩集）。英譯：諾頓·霍奇斯（Norton Hodges）。法譯：阿薩納斯·薩拉西（Athanase Vantchev de Thracy）。法國巴黎：索倫縈拉文化學院（The Cultural Institute of Solenzara），2016。ISBN 978-2-37356-022-0
16. 《林明理散文集》*Lin Ming Li's Collected essays*。臺北市：文史哲出版社，2016。ISBN 978-986-314-291-1
17. 《名家現代詩賞析》*Appreciation of the work of Famous Modern Poets*。臺北市：文史哲出版社，2016。ISBN 978-986-314-302-4
18. 《我的歌 *My Song*》，法譯：Athanase Vantchev de Thracy 中法譯詩集。臺北市：文史哲出版社，2017。ISBN 978-986-314-359-8
19. 《諦聽 *Listen*》，中英對照詩集，英譯：馬為義（筆名：非馬）（Dr. William Marr），臺北市：文史哲出版社，2018。ISBN 978-986-314-401-4
20. 《現代詩賞析》，*Appreciation of the work of Modern Poets*，臺北市：文史哲出版社，2018。ISBN 978-986-314-412-0
21. 《原野之聲》*Voice of the Wilderness*，英譯：馬為義（筆名：非馬）（Dr. William Marr），臺北市：文史哲出版社，2019。ISBN 978-986-314-453-3
22. 《思念在彼方　散文暨新詩》，*Longing over the other side*（prose and poetry），臺北市：文史哲出版社，2020。ISBN 978-986-314-505-9
23. 《甜蜜的記憶（散文暨新詩）》，*Sweet memories*（prose and poetry），臺北市：文史哲出版社，2021。ISBN 978-986-314-555-4
24. 《詩河（詩評、散文暨新詩）》，*The Poetic River*（Poetry review, prose and poetry），臺北市：文史哲出版社，2022。ISBN 978-986-314-603-2
25. 《庫爾特·F·斯瓦泰克，林明理，喬凡尼·坎皮西詩選》（中英對照）*Carmina Selecta (Selected Poems) by Kurt F. Svatek, Lin Mingli, Giovanni Campisi*，義大利：Edizioni Universum（埃迪采恩尼大學），宇宙出版社，2023.01。
26. 《紀念達夫尼斯和克洛伊》（中英對照）詩選 *In memory of Daphnis and Chloe*，作者：Renza Agnelli，Sara Ciampi，Lin Mingli 林明理，義大利：Edizioni Universum（埃迪采恩尼大學），宇宙出版社，書封面，林明理畫作（聖母大殿），2023.02。
27. 《詩林明理古今抒情詩一六○首》（漢英對照）*Parallel Reading of 160 Classical and New Chinese Lyrical Poems (Chinese-English)*，英譯：張智中，臺北市：文史哲出版社，2023.04。ISBN 978-986-314-637-7

28. 《愛的讚歌》(詩評、散文暨新詩)*Hymn Of Love*(Poetry review, prose and poetry)，臺北市：文史哲出版社，2023.05。ISBN 978-986-314-638-4

29. 《埃內斯托·卡漢，薩拉·錢皮，林明理和平詩選》（義英對照）(Italian-English)，*Carmina Selecta (Selected Poems) by Ernesto Kahan, Sara Ciampi, Lin Mingli Peace-Pace*，義大利：Edizioni Universum（埃迪采恩尼大學），宇宙出版社，2023.11。ISBN 978-889-980-379-7

30. 《祈禱與工作》，中英義詩集，"Ora Et Labora" Trilogia di Autori Trilingue: Italiano, Cinese, Inglese 作者的三語三部曲：義大利語、中文、英語 *Trilingual Trilogy of Authors: Italian, Chinese, English*，作者：奧內拉·卡布奇尼 Ornella Cappuccini，非馬 William Marr，林明理 Lin Mingli，義大利，宇宙出版社，2024.06。

31. 《名家抒情詩評賞》(漢英對照) *Appraisal of Lyric Poems by Famous Artists*，張智中教授英譯，臺北市：文史哲出版社，2024.06。ISBN 978-986-314-675-9

32. 《山的沉默》*Silence of the Mountains*，散文集，臺北市：文史哲出版社，2024.09。ISBN 978-986-314-685-8

33. 《宋詩明理接千載——古今抒情詩三百首》(漢英對照) *Parallel Reading of 300 Ancient and Modern Chinese Lyrical Poems (Chinese-English)*，臺中市：天空數位圖書出版，2024.10，ISBN 978-626-7576-00-7

34. 《元詩明理接千載——古今抒情詩三百首》(漢英對照) *Parallel Reading of 300 Ancient and Modern Chinese Lyrical Poems (Chinese-English) :Jin, Yuan, and Ming Dynasties*，臺中市：天空數位圖書出版，2024.11，ISBN 978-626-7576-02-1，ISBN 978-626-7576-03-8（彩圖版）

35. 《清詩明理思千載——古今抒情詩三百首》(漢英對照) *Parallel Reading of 300 Ancient and Modern Chinese Lyrical Poems: Qing Dynasty (Chinese-English)*，臺中市：天空數位圖書出版，2025.01，ISBN 978-626-7576-08-3，ISBN 978-626-7576-09-0（彩圖版）

36. 《唐詩明理接千載——古今抒情詩三百首》(漢英對照) *Parallel Reading of 300 Ancient and Modern Chinese Lyrical Poems: Tang Dynasty (Chinese-English)*，臺中市：天空數位圖書出版，2025.02，ISBN 978-626-7576-10-6

37. 《漢魏六朝接明理——古今抒情詩三百首》(漢英對照) *Parallel Reading of 300 Ancient and Modern Chinese Lyrical Poems: Han, Wei and Six Dynasties (Chinese-English)*，臺中市：天空出版社，2025.03，ISBN 978-626-7576-12-0，ISBN 978-626-7576-11-3（彩圖版）。

譯者簡介
About the Author & Translator

　　張智中，天津市南開大學外國語學院教授、博士研究生導師、翻譯系主任，中國翻譯協會理事，中國英漢語比較研究會典籍英譯專業委員會副會長，天津師範大學跨文化與世界文學研究院兼職教授，世界漢學·文學中國研究會理事兼英文秘書長，天津市比較文學學會理事，第五屆天津市人民政府學位委員會評議組成員、專業學位教育指導委員會委員，國家社科基金專案通訊評審專家和結項鑒定專家，天津外國語大學中央文獻翻譯研究基地兼職研究員，《國際詩歌翻譯》季刊客座總編，《世界漢學》英文主編，《中國當代詩歌導讀》編委會成員，中國當代詩歌獎評委等。已出版編、譯、著120餘部，發表學術論文130餘篇，曾獲翻譯與科研多種獎項。漢詩英譯多走向國外，獲國際著名詩人和翻譯家的廣泛好評。譯詩觀：但為傳神，不拘其形，散文筆法，詩意內容；將漢詩英譯提高到英詩的高度。

　　Zhang Zhizhong is professor, doctoral supervisor and dean of the Translation Department of the School of Foreign Studies, Nankai University which is located in Tianjin; meanwhile, he is director of Translators' Association of China, vice chairman of the Committee for English Translation of Chinese Classics of the Association for Comparative Studies of English and Chinese, part-time professor of Cross-Culture & World Literature Academy of Tianjin Normal University, director and English secretary-general of World Sinology Literary China Seminar, director of Tianjin Comparative Literature Society, member of Tianjin Municipal Government Academic Degree Committee, member of Tianjin Municipal Government Professional Degree Education Guiding Committee, expert for the approval and evaluation of projects funded by the National Social Science Foundation of China, part-time researcher at the Central Literature Translation Research Base of Tianjin Foreign Studies University, guest editor of *Rendition of International Poetry*, English editor-in-chief of *World Sinology*, member of the editing board of *Guided Reading Series in Contemporary Chinese Poetry*, and member of the Board for Contemporary Chinese Poetry Prizes. He has published more than 120 books and 130 academic papers, and he has won a host of prizes in translation and academic research. His English translation of Chinese poetry is widely acclaimed throughout the world, and is favorably reviewed by international poets and translators. His view on poetry translation: spirit over form, prose enjambment to rewrite Chinese poetry into sterling English poetry.

序言一

〈當序前詩〉

譯筆神遊總是詩！

妙筆神思畫花開。

古今本是兩世代！

譯妙合筆續千載。

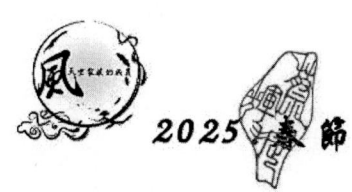

2025 春節

---

1. 本序乃總結作者前《唐詩明理接千載》等一系列的詩作；其中之"妙筆"，即代表寫作之筆，繪畫之筆；而"盡"字則表示，不管是詩、評論或繪畫等，作者都有很好的表現，以讚美作者妙筆生花。

A Poem as Preface

Divine translation entails
divine poetry, when the author
writes like an angel. Ancient
poetry and modern poetry are

two genres of poetry; through
felicitous writing and wonderful
translating, the poetic spirit
runs for thousands of years.

By Tsai Huei-Ching

The Spring Festival of 2025

序言二
Preface

〈七律　為序有感〉[2]

王守義

馳越千年今古誦，

歌吟譯筆鑄輪迴。

漢詩延展及當代，

明理詩接至漢巍。

翻譯起橋迎繆姒，

真誠伸手挽幽微。

人生雖短癡情久，

凡夢詩魂盡作陪。

---

[2] 我曾為譯家張智中博士英譯的當代詩人林明理以己詩對應古詩由漢至清系列中之唐詩卷作序《譯筆神遊牽古今》。

Inspired Upon Reading Lin's Poetry and Zhang's Translation[3]

Wang Shouyi

Ancient poetry and modern poetry,
through thousands of years, whose
translation entails transformation —
all for incarnation, to retain in another

language the poetic spirit and poetic soul.
Thousands of years of Chinese poetry,
from Han dynasty to the contemporary era,
Lin Ming-Li continues to write in the same

vein. Translation, as a bridge, welcomes
Muse; the translator, with a sincere heart,
labors out of love to reproduce the original
nuances. Masterful poets through dynasties,

in spite of the short span of life, leave us
classics out of passion of love for poetry.

---

[3] I have been invited to write a preface titled *A Translator's Roaming Pen Connects the Ancient and the Present*, for *Parallel Reading of 300 Ancient and Modern Chinese Lyrical Poems: Tang Dynasty (Chinese-English)*, one of the "the series of parallel reading of Chinese poems through thousands of years", authored by Lin Ming-Li and translated into English by Zhang Zhizhong.

序言三
Preface

它們都在那裡等妳
——給明理

知道妳喜愛
山谷
溪流
濕地
步道
香蒲、蓮花、蘆葦、水蘊草
山樹、小米園、青草與野鳥
森林的呼吸
沉默的綠蔭
雛鳥的輕啼
蟲聲唧唧
遠空高歌的鷹
山豬與飛鼠
湛藍的潭水
古老的故事
牆頭的彩繪雕塑藝術
豐收祭部落的歌舞
天真小孩的歡叫
歷盡滄桑老人的微笑

它們每天都在那裡
張開手
等著妳

They Are All Waiting For You There
— To Lin Ming-Li

I know you love

valleys

streams

wetlands

trails

cattails, lotus flowers, reeds, and aquatic grasses

mountain trees, millet gardens, green grass, and wild birds

the breath of the forest

silent green shade

the light cry of chicks

the chirping of insects

eagles singing in the distant sky

mountain pigs and flying mice

the deep blue pool water

ancient stories

painted sculptures on the wall

the song and dance of the Harvest Festival Tribe

the cheering of innocent children

the smile of an elderly person who has gone through the vicissitudes of life

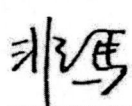

譯者導言
Introduction by the Translator

　　學者詩人林明理從她自己所感覺到的與對漢魏六朝詩閱讀的經驗回憶裡進行篩選、組合，欲使其創作的詩歌加在編譯的漢魏六朝詩作之後，以期望讀者更貼近地感覺和瞭解詩美的世界。而我認為，中國新詩與古詩的最大區別之一，是從聽覺藝術走向了視覺藝術。古詩是口頭可以朗誦的，新詩則是內心體會和感覺的。若能讓古詩和新詩研究同步相輔相成，讓翻譯詩歌的涵義變得更生動活潑，以趨使學生對欣賞詩歌與研讀上產生了更大的興趣，這是此書最重要的價值，也可以加深閱讀時的感性和體悟，這也是我的期許。

張智中
2025 年 3 月 8 日
於南開大學外國語學院翻譯系

　　Lin Ming-Li, as a scholar-poet of Taiwan, is a great lover of poetry, and she selects her own poems to be paired up with the quatrains by Chinese poets of Han, Wei and Six Dynasties, which have similar themes or sentiments, in order for readers to appreciate more thoroughly the beauty of poetry. It is my belief that one of the most glaring differences between ancient Chinese poetry and modern Chinese poetry lies in the shift from auditory arts to visual arts: when ancient Chinese poetry is to be declaimed, modern Chinese poetry is to be felt and savored in the heart. If the reading and translation of both ancient Chinese poems and modern Chinese poems can be undertaken simultaneously, the understanding of poetry will be deepened, and poetry translation will be more flexible through enlivening — and the readers' interest in poetry, hopefully, will be greatly heightened.

Zhang Zhizhong
March 8, 2025
Translation Department of the School of Foreign Studies,
Nankai University

目錄
Table of Contents

1. 垓下歌（先秦・項羽）A Song Composed at Gaixia, or Waterloo (Xiang Yu, pre-Qin period)
   在風中，愛妳（林明理）To Love You in the Wind (Lin Ming-Li)·············· 32
2. 和項王歌（兩漢・虞姬）In Reply to Xiang Yu (Lady Yu, Western and Eastern Han dynasties)
   她飛向天邊，旋舞如縷煙（林明理）She Flies to the Horizon, Dancing Like a Wisp of Smoke (Lin Ming-Li)·············· 34
3. 菟絲（先秦・無名氏）Cuscuta Chinensis (Anonymous, pre-Qin period)
   我不能忘懷妳憂鬱的眼睛（林明理）I Cannot Forget Your Melancholy Eyes (Lin Ming-Li)·············· 35
4. 枯魚過河泣（漢・樂府詩）Dirge of a Dried Fish (Anonymous, Han dynasty)
   把和平帶回來（林明理）To Bring Peace Back (Lin Ming-Li)·············· 37
5. 七步詩（兩漢・曹植）Written Within Seven Steps (Cao Zhi, Western and Eastern Han dynasties)
   因為有了愛（林明理）With Love (Lin Ming-Li)·············· 38
6. 酌貪泉詩（魏晉・吳隱之）A Greedy Mouth of Spring (Wu Yinzhi, Wei and Jin dynasties)
   我的心是一條小河（林明理）My Heart Is a Small River (Lin Ming-Li)····· 40
7. 思吳江歌（魏晉・張翰）Longing for the Wujiang River (Zhang Han, Wei and Jin dynasties)
   揚子江，你活在我的心裡（林明理）Yangtze River, You Live in My Heart (Lin Ming-Li)·············· 41
8. 神情詩（東晉・顧愷之）The Four Fair Seasons (Gu Kaizhi, Eastern Jin dynasty)
   在時間的繪影中（林明理）In the Shadow of Time (Lin Ming-Li)·············· 43
9. 華光殿侍宴賦競病韻（南北朝・曹景宗）At the Victory Banquet (Cao Jingzong, Northern and Southern dynasties)
   心頭閃亮起的名字（林明理）The Name Shining in the Heart (Lin Ming-Li)··· 45
10. 玉階怨（南北朝・謝朓）Plaint of Jade Steps (Xie Tiao, Northern and Southern dynasties)
    當思念變成一片雲（林明理）When Missing Turns Into a Cloud (Lin Ming-Li)··· 46
11. 王孫遊（南北朝・謝朓）Too Late, Your Return (Xie Tiao, Northern and Southern dynasties)
    我欲召喚在北國山村，等你（林明理）I Want to Summon in the North Country Mountain Village, Waiting for You (Lin Ming-Li)·············· 48

12. 子夜歌二首（其一）（南北朝・蕭衍）Midnight Songs (No.1) (Xiao Yan, Northern and Southern dynasties)
妳是畫卷裡走出來的史詩神話（林明理）You Are an Epic Myth Walking Out of the Scroll (Lin Ming-Li)·················· 50

13. 子夜歌二首（其二）（南北朝・蕭衍）Midnight Songs (No. 2) (Xiao Yan, Northern and Southern dynasties)
剪影（林明理）The Silhouette (Lin Ming-Li)·················· 52

14. 別詩（南北朝・范雲）Separations (Fan Yun, Northern and Southern dynasties)
你來自飛雪遙遠的虛幻（林明理）You Come From the Faraway Illusion of Snow (Lin Ming-Li)·················· 53

15. 相送（南北朝・何遜）Fare You Well (He Xun, Northern and Southern dynasties)
你的憂鬱是片片雪花的哀音（林明理）Your Melancholy Is the Sad Sound of Snowflakes (Lin Ming-Li)·················· 55

16. 長安聽百舌（南北朝・韋鼎）A Chinese Blackbird (Wei Ding, Northern and Southern dynasties）
再別金陵城（林明理）Saying Good-bye to Jinling City Again (Lin Ming-Li)··· 57

17. 入關故人別（南北朝・王褒）Farewell to a Friend (Wang Bao, Northern and Southern dynasties)
在望不盡的海岸之前（林明理）Before the Endless Shore (Lin Ming-Li)····· 58

18. 重別周尚書（南北朝・庾信）Once More Farewell to Secretary Zhou (Yu Xin, Northern and Southern dynasties)
走在歸途的寂靜中（林明理）Walking in the Silence of the Journey Home (Lin Ming-Li)·················· 60

19. 春江花月夜二首（其一）（隋・楊廣）Spring River & Flowery Moonlit Night (No. 1) (Yang Guang, Sui dynasty)
橋下閃爍的波影（林明理）The Flickering Shadow Under the Bridge (Lin Ming-Li)·················· 62

20. 江陵女歌（隋・楊廣）A Riverside Girl's Song (Yang Guang, Sui dynasty)
倘若再有相聚之時（林明理）If There Is Another Meeting (Lin Ming-Li)····· 63

21. 春江花月夜二首（其二）（隋・楊廣）Spring River & Flowery Moonlit Night (No. 2) (Yang Guang, Sui dynasty)
我步入富春江的奇山異水（林明理）I Step Into the Spectacular Mountains of the Fuchun River (Lin Ming-Li)·················· 65

22. 野望（隋・楊廣）View of Nature (Yang Guang, Sui dynasty)
看灰面鵟鷹消逝（林明理）Seeing Butastur Indicus Disappearing (Lin Ming-Li)·················· 67

23. 子夜歌（其一）（魏晉·無名氏）Midnight Songs (No. 1) (Anonymous, Wei and Jin dynasties)
    背對河南漫天飛雪的天空（林明理）Your Back Against a Skyful of Snow in Henan (Lin Ming-Li) ·· 69

24. 子夜四時歌·春歌（魏晉·無名氏）Midnight Songs Through the Four Seasons (Spring Song) (Anonymous, Wei and Jin dynasties)
    愛，在深不可測中發光閃爍（林明理）Love Is Shining in the Unfathomable Depth (Lin Ming-Li) ·· 71

25. 子夜四時歌·夏歌（魏晉·無名氏）Midnight Songs Through the Four Seasons (Summer Song) (Anonymous, Wei and Jin dynasties)
    曾經（林明理）Once (Lin Ming-Li) ··· 73

26. 子夜四時歌·秋歌（魏晉·無名氏）Midnight Songs Through the Four Seasons (Autumn Song) (Anonymous, Wei and Jin dynasties)
    每當秋風吹起（林明理）When the Autumn Wind Is Blowing (Lin Ming-Li) ··· 74

27. 子夜四時歌·冬歌（魏晉·無名氏）Midnight Songs Through the Four Seasons (Winter Song) (Anonymous, Wei and Jin dynasties)
    你的歌聲純淨如雪（林明理）Your Singing Voice Is Pure Like Snow (Lin Ming-Li) ·· 76

28. 東陽溪中贈答二首（其一）（南北朝·謝靈運）Two Poems of Social Intercourse and Response (No. 1) (Xie Lingyun, Northern and Southern dynasties)
    縱然剎那（林明理）Even for a Moment (Lin Ming-Li) ························ 78

29. 東陽溪中贈答二首（其二）（南北朝·謝靈運）Two Poems of Social Intercourse and Response (No. 2) (Xie Lingyun, Northern and Southern dynasties)
    不是春天的一場雨（林明理）Not a Fall of Spring Rain (Lin Ming-Li) ········ 79

30. 詔問山中何所有，賦詩以答（南北朝·陶弘景）In Reply to a Question (Tao Hongjing, Northern and Southern dynasties)
    在雪山西稜上，想你（林明理）Atop the Xue Mountain, to Miss You (Lin Ming-Li) ·· 80

31. 寄行人（南北朝·鮑令暉）To a Roamer (Bao Linghui, Northern and Southern dynasties)
    你的話語似珊瑚礁上的回聲（林明理）Your Words Echo on a Coral Reef (Lin Ming-Li) ·· 82

32. 山中雜詩三首（其一）（南北朝·吳均）Thee Miscellaneous Poems in the Mountain (No. 1) (Wu Jun, Northern and Southern dynasties)
    我愛晨露中的白馬寺（林明理）I Love White Horse Temple in the Morning Dew (Lin Ming-Li) ·· 83

33. 山中雜詩三首（其二）（南北朝・吳均）Three Miscellaneous Poems in the Mountain (No. 2) (Wu Jun, Northern and Southern dynasties)
    憶陽明山公園（林明理）Remembering Yangmingshan Park (Lin Ming-Li)⋯ 85

34. 山中雜詩三首（其三）（南北朝・吳均）Three Miscellaneous Poems in the Mountain (No. 3) (Wu Jun, Northern and Southern dynasties)
    聽那朱鸝圓潤的笛音（林明理）Listen to the Mellow Fluting of Orioles (Lin Ming-Li)⋯⋯⋯⋯⋯⋯⋯⋯⋯⋯⋯⋯⋯⋯⋯⋯⋯⋯⋯⋯⋯⋯ 87

35. 於長安歸還揚州，九月九日行薇山亭賦韻（隋・江總）Composed on the Double Ninth Festival (Jiang Zong, Sui dynasty)
    每當秋風吹皺了雲朵（林明理）When the Autumn Wind Ruffles the Clouds (Lin Ming-Li)⋯⋯⋯⋯⋯⋯⋯⋯⋯⋯⋯⋯⋯⋯⋯⋯⋯⋯⋯⋯⋯⋯ 89

36. 餞別自解（隋・樂昌公主）A Farewell Dinner (Princess Lechang, Sui dynasty)
    歲月讓我再次聽到了你的呼喚（林明理）Time Let Me Hear Your Call Again (Lin Ming-Li)⋯⋯⋯⋯⋯⋯⋯⋯⋯⋯⋯⋯⋯⋯⋯⋯⋯ 90

37. 人日思歸（南北朝・薛道衡）Longing to Return (Xue Daoheng, Northern and Southern dynasties)
    葛根塔拉草原之戀（林明理）Love of Gegen Tara Prairie (Lin Ming-Li)⋯⋯⋯ 92

38. 懊儂歌（南北朝・無名氏）The Song of Annoyance (Anonymous, Northern and Southern dynasties)
    黃河，你慢慢將時光留下來（林明理）Yellow River, Please Retain Time Slowly (Lin Ming-Li)⋯⋯⋯⋯⋯⋯⋯⋯⋯⋯⋯⋯⋯⋯⋯⋯⋯⋯⋯⋯ 94

39. 送別詩（隋朝・無名氏）A Farewell Poem (Anonymous, Sui dynasty)
    那穀雨前夕搖曳的燈火（林明理）The Flickering Lights on the Eve of the Grain Rain (Lin Ming-Li)⋯⋯⋯⋯⋯⋯⋯⋯⋯⋯⋯⋯⋯⋯⋯⋯⋯⋯ 96

40. 古豔歌（兩漢・無名氏）An Ancient Love Song (Anonymous, Western and Eastern Han dynasties)
    在綠梢的木麻黃間（林明理）In the Green Tops of the Casuarina (Lin Ming-Li)⋯⋯⋯⋯⋯⋯⋯⋯⋯⋯⋯⋯⋯⋯⋯⋯⋯⋯⋯⋯⋯⋯⋯⋯ 97

41. 古歌（兩漢・無名氏）An Ancient Song (Anonymous, Western and Eastern Han dynasties）
    在我故鄉的田野（林明理）In the Field of My Hometown (Lin Ming-Li)⋯⋯ 99

42. 采葵花（兩漢・無名氏）Plucking Sunflowers (Anonymous, Western and Eastern Han dynasties)
    亞城雪景（林明理）The Snowscape of Atlanta (Lin Ming-Li)⋯⋯⋯⋯⋯⋯ 101

43. 秋氣（西晉・傅玄）Autumnal Air (Fu Xuan, Western Jin dynasty)
    山寺秋雨（林明理）The Autumn Rain of a Mountain Temple (Lin Ming-Li)・ 102

44. 日南（西晉・張華）Wild Girls (Zhang Hua, Western Jin dynasty)
    歲晚（林明理）Late Into the Year (Lin Ming-Li) ················ 104

45. 大道曲（東晉・謝尚）A Thoroughfare (Xie Shang, Eastern Jin dynasty)
    想念的季節（林明理）The Memorable Season (Lin Ming-Li) ········ 106

46. 情人碧玉歌二首（其一）（東晉・孫綽）To My Love (No. 1) (Sun Chuo, Eastern Jin dynasty)
    致吾友——Prof. Ernesto Kahan（林明理）To My Friend, Professor Ernesto Kahan (Lin Ming-Li) ·· 108

47. 采菊（東晉・袁宏）Picking Chrysanthemums (Yuan Hong, Eastern Jin dynasty)
    這是個鳥聲躍動的茶園（林明理）This Is a Tea Garden Alive With Birds' Chirping (Lin Ming-Li) ·· 109

48. 松（東晉・袁宏）The Pine Tree (Yuan Hong, Eastern Jin dynasty)
    山的跫音（林明理）The Sound of Mountains (Lin Ming-Li) ········ 111

49. 桃葉歌三首（其一）（東晉・王獻之）Ode to the Peach Leaf (No. 1) (Wang Xianzhi, Eastern Jin dynasty)
    沒有人能搖動我的記憶（林明理）Nobody Can Shake My Memory (Lin Ming-Li) ·· 113

50. 同生曲二首（其一）（魏晉・無名氏）Songs of Living Together (No. 1) (Anonymous, Wei and Jin dynasties)
    儘管人生如露（林明理）Though Life Is Like Dew (Lin Ming-Li) ········ 114

51. 同生曲二首（其二）（魏晉・無名氏）Songs of Living Together (No. 2) (Anonymous, Wei and Jin dynasties)
    誰能再見北去的風（林明理）Who Can See the North Wind Again (Lin Ming-Li) ·· 116

52. 三洲歌三首（其一）（南北朝・無名氏）Sanzhou Songs (No. 1) (Anonymous, Northern and Southern dynasties)
    風中絮語（林明理）Whispering in the Wind (Lin Ming-Li) ············ 118

53. 三洲歌三首（其二）（南北朝・無名氏）Sanzhou Songs (No. 2) (Anonymous, Northern and Southern dynasties)
    遠方的思念（林明理）Longing From Afar (Lin Ming-Li) ············ 119

54. 三洲歌三首（其三）（南北朝・無名氏）Sanzhou Songs (No. 3) (Anonymous, Northern and Southern dynasties)
    大地在陽光中為我哼唱（林明理）The Earth Sings to Me in the Sun (Lin Ming-Li) ·· 121

55. 青陽度三首（其一）（南北朝・無名氏）The Spring Ferry (No. 1) (Anonymous, Northern and Southern dynasties)
    邀旅歷下亭（林明理）Touring the Lixia Pavilion (Lin Ming-Li) ········ 122

56. 青陽度三首（其二）（南北朝・無名氏）The Spring Ferry (No. 2) (Anonymous, Northern and Southern dynasties)
    默喚（林明理）Silent Calling (Lin Ming-Li)··················124
57. 青陽度三首（其三）（南北朝・無名氏）The Spring Ferry (No. 3) (Anonymous, Northern and Southern dynasties)
    四月的回憶（林明理）The Memories of April (Lin Ming-Li)··················126
58. 來羅四首（其一）（魏晉・無名氏）Four Come-on Poems (No. 1) (Anonymous, Wei and Jin dynasties)
    樸素的生活（林明理）A Plain Life (Lin Ming-Li)··················127
59. 來羅四首（其二）（魏晉・無名氏）Four Come-on Poems (No. 2) (Anonymous, Wei and Jin dynasties)
    儘管我在地球的另一端（林明理）Though I'm on the Other Side of the Earth (Lin Ming-Li)··················129
60. 來羅四首（其三）（魏晉・無名氏）Four Come-on Poems (No. 3) (Anonymous, Wei and Jin dynasties)
    誠然我已明白（林明理）Of Course I See (Lin Ming-Li)··················131
61. 來羅四首（其四）（魏晉・無名氏）Four Come-on Poems (No. 4) (Anonymous, Wei and Jin dynasties)
    當歲月漸漸飛去（林明理）When the Years Slowly Fly Away (Lin Ming-Li)··133
62. 贈范曄詩（南北朝・陸凱）A Poem Dedicated to Fan Ye (Lu Kai, Northern and Southern dynasties)
    贈友人－山東大學耿建華教授（林明理）To My Friend Geng Jianhua, Professor of Shandong University (Lin Ming-Li)··················134
63. 秋思引（南北朝・湯惠休）Autumnal Thoughts (Tang Huixiu, Northern and Southern dynasties)
    聽微風吹過竹林（林明理）Listen to the Breeze Blowing Through the Bamboo Forest (Lin Ming-Li)··················136
64. 詠梧桐詩（南北朝・沈約）Ode to the Parasol Tree (Shen Yue, Northern and Southern dynasties)
    禪就是這樣簡單（林明理）So Simple Is Zen (Lin Ming-Li)··················137
65. 斷句（南北朝・劉昶）A Fragment (Liu Chang, Northern and Southern dynasties)
    秋暮（林明理）The Close of Autumn (Lin Ming-Li)··················139
66. 別詩（南北朝・張融）A Farewell Poem (Zhang Rong, Northern and Southern dynasties)
    煙台黃昏的和歌（林明理）A Song at Dusk in Yantai (Lin Ming-Li)··········140

67. 遊太平山（南北朝‧孔稚珪）Touring the Taiping Mountain (Kong Zhigui, Northern and Southern dynasties)
    與天山相會（林明理）Meeting With Tianshan Mountain (Lin Ming-Li) ····· 142

68. 春詩二首（其一）（南北朝‧王儉）Two Poems About Spring (No. 1) (Wang Jian, Northern and Southern dynasties)
    雨中的回憶（林明理）Memories in the Rain (Lin Ming-Li) ················ 144

69. 春詩二首（其二）（南北朝‧王儉）Two Poems About Spring (No. 2) (Wang Jian, Northern and Southern dynasties)
    悼——空拍大師齊柏林（林明理）The Master Photographer from the Air: in memory of Mr. Qi Bolin (Lin Ming-Li) ················ 145

70. 和約法師臨友人詩（南北朝‧陶弘景）In Reply to a Friend (Tao Hongjing, Northern and Southern dynasties)
    寫給天津之歌（林明理）A Song for Tianjin (Lin Ming-Li) ················ 147

71. 贈王儉詩（南北朝‧王僧祐）A Poem Dedicated to Wang Jian (Wang Shengyou, Northern and Southern dynasties)
    西藏，你來自不可思議的遠方（林明理）Xizang, You Come From an Incredible Distance (Lin Ming-Li) ················ 148

72. 阻雪連句遙贈和（南北朝‧謝朓）Blocked By Snow (Xie Tiao, Northern and Southern dynasties)
    雪的臆測（林明理）Snow Speculation (Lin Ming-Li) ················ 151

73. 阻雪連句遙贈和（南北朝‧江革）Blocked By Snow (Jiang Ge, Northern and Southern dynasties）
    與黑龍江對話（林明理）Dialogue with Heilongjiang (Lin Ming-Li)········· 153

74. 阻雪連句遙贈和（南北朝‧王融）Blocked By Snow (Wang Rong, Northern and Southern dynasties)
    牧歸（林明理）Back From Herding (Lin Ming-Li) ················ 154

75. 阻雪連句遙贈和（南北朝‧王僧孺）Blocked By Snow (Wang Sengru, Northern and Southern dynasties)
    溪橋（林明理）The Creek Bridge (Lin Ming-Li) ················ 156

76. 阻雪連句遙贈和（南北朝‧謝昊）Blocked By Snow (Xie Hao, Northern and Southern dynasties)
    山居歲月（林明理）Years in the Mountain (Lin Ming-Li) ················ 158

77. 阻雪連句遙贈和（南北朝‧劉繪）Blocked By Snow (Liu Hui, Northern and Southern dynasties)
    緬懷山寺之音（林明理）Memory of the Sound of the Mountains Temple (Lin Ming-Li) ················ 159

78. 阻雪連句遙贈和（南北朝・沈約）Blocked By Snow (Shen Yue, Northern and Southern dynasties)
蘆花飛白的時候（林明理）When the Reeds Are White (Lin Ming-Li)……… 161

79. 春思（南北朝・王僧孺）Longing in Spring (Wang Sengru, Northern and Southern dynasties)
在濱海的渡輪上（林明理）On the Seaside Ferryboat (Lin Ming-Li)……… 162

80. 江皋曲（南北朝・王融）Melody of Riverside Marsh (Wang Rong, Northern and Southern dynasties)
倘若你明白（林明理）If You See (Lin Ming-Li)……………………… 164

81. 思公子（南北朝・王融）The Longing of the Princes (Wang Rong, Northern and Southern dynasties)
風就是從那兒吹起的……（林明理）That Is Where the Wind Blows… (Lin Ming-Li)……………………………………………………… 165

82. 後園作回文詩（南北朝・王融）A Palindromic Poem (Wang Rong. Northern and Southern dynasties）
木棉花開在步道的光亮中（林明理）The Silk Cotton Flowers Are Blooming in the Light of the Trail (Lin Ming-Li)………………………… 167

83. 估客樂四首（其一）（南北朝・釋寶月）Joy of the Businessmen (No. 1) (Shi Baoyue, Northern and Southern dynasties)
春之聲（林明理）The Voice of Spring (Lin Ming-Li)………………… 169

84. 估客樂四首（其二）（南北朝・釋寶月）Joy of the Businessmen (No. 2) (Shi Baoyue, Northern and Southern dynasties)
黃昏的潮波—to Athanase Vantchev de Thracy（林明理）Tidal Wave at Dusk: to Athanase Vantchev de Thracy (Lin Ming-Li)………………… 170

85. 估客樂四首（其三）（南北朝・釋寶月）Joy of the Businessmen (No. 3) (Shi Baoyue, Northern and Southern dynasties)
遠方的綠島（林明理）Green Island in the Distance (Lin Ming-Li) ……… 171

86. 估客樂四首（其四）（南北朝・釋寶月）Joy of the Businessmen (No. 4) (Shi Baoyue, Northern and Southern dynasties)
寫給鞏義之歌（林明理）A Song for Gongyi (Lin Ming-Li) ……………… 173

87. 望雪詩（南北朝・虞羲）Watching Snow (Yu Xi, Northern and Southern dynasties)
故鄉之月依舊明燦（林明理）Still Bright Is the Hometown Moon (Lin Ming-Li)……………………………………………………… 175

88. 邊城思（南北朝・何遜）Pining in the Border Town (He Xun, Northern and Southern dynasties)
回憶似細雨彈奏的音符（林明理）Memories Are Like the Notes Played by a Drizzle (Lin Ming-Li)…………………………………………… 177

89. 為人妾怨（南北朝・何遜）Complaint of Being a Concubine (He Xun, Northern and Southern dynasties)
暮春的石梯坪（林明理）Shitiping in Late Spring (Lin Ming-Li) ············ 179

90. 詠春風詩（南北朝・何遜）Ode to Spring Wind (He Xun, Northern and Southern dynasties)
在山角轉彎處（林明理）At the Corner of the Mountain (Lin Ming-Li) ······ 181

91. 擬古聯句（南北朝・何遜）After the Ancient Quatrain (He Xun, Northern and Southern dynasties)
當月光漫舞時（林明理）When the Moonlight Is Slowly Dancing (Lin Ming-Li) ·· 182

92. 月中飛螢詩（南北朝・紀少瑜）The Firefly Flying Through the Moon (Ji Shaoyu, Northern and Southern dynasties)
愛的讚歌（林明理）The Hymn of Love (Lin Ming-Li) ···················· 184

93. 詠長信宮中草（南北朝・庾肩吾）Ode to Grass in the Palace (Yu Jianwu, Northern and Southern dynasties)
每當思念如蝶翩然而來（林明理）Whenever Yearning Comes Lightly Like Butterflies (Lin Ming-Li) ··· 186

94. 春別詩四首（其一）（南北朝・蕭子顯）Bidding Adieu to Spring (No. 1) (Xiao Zixian, Northern and Southern dynasties)
當黃昏的淡雲飄來（林明理）When the Evening Pale Clouds Come Here (Lin Ming-Li) ·· 187

95. 春別詩四首（其四）（南北朝・蕭子顯）Bidding Adieu to Spring (No. 4) (Xiao Zixian, Northern and Southern dynasties)
藍色的眼淚（林明理）Blue Tears (Lin Ming-Li) ···························· 189

96. 詠鵲（南北朝・蕭紀）Ode to the Magpies (Xiao Ji, Northern and Southern dynasties)
枷鎖（林明理）The Fetters (Lin Ming-Li) ···································· 191

97. 思公子（南北朝・邢邵）Longing for the Prince (Xing Shao, Northern and Southern dynasties)
再會吧，溪橋（林明理）See You, Brook Bridge (Lin Ming-Li) ············· 192

98. 蜀道難（其一）（南北朝・蕭綱）Hard Is the Road to the Southwest (No. 1) (Xiao Gang, Northern and Southern dynasties)
黃昏在烏山頭水庫（林明理）Dusk in Wushantou Reservoir (Lin Ming-Li) ··· 193

99. 蜀道難（其二）（南北朝・蕭綱）Hard Is the Road to the Southwest (No. 2) (Xiao Gang, Northern and Southern dynasties)
在每個山水之間（林明理）Between Each Mountain and Water (Lin Ming-Li) ·· 194

100. 春江曲（南北朝・蕭綱）Ditty of the Spring River (Xiao Gang, Northern and Southern dynasties)
  在似夢非夢的幸福之中（林明理）In Dream-Like Happiness (Lin Ming-Li) ·· 196
101. 金閨思二首（其一）（南北朝・蕭綱）Pining in a Golden Mansion (No. 1) (Xiao Gang, Northern and Southern dynasties)
  月橘（林明理）Murraya Paniculata (Lin Ming-Li) ················· 198
102. 金閨思二首（其二）（南北朝・蕭綱）Pining in a Golden Mansion (No. 2) (Xiao Gang, Northern and Southern dynasties)
  悼－2011.02.22紐西蘭強震的罹難者（林明理）Mourning the Victims of the Powerful Earthquake in New Zealand on February 22, 2011 (Lin Ming-Li)···· 199
103. 望月望（南北朝・蕭綱）Gazing at the Moon (Xiao Gang, Northern and Southern dynasties)
  夏風吹拂福爾摩沙（林明理）The Summer Wind Blows in Formosa (Lin Ming-Li)··········· 201
104. 夏日詩（南北朝・徐悱）A Summer Poem (Xu Peng, Northern and Southern dynasties)
  南灣的記憶（林明理）Memory of the South Bay (Lin Ming-Li) ·········· 203
105. 出江陵縣還詩二首（其一）（南北朝・蕭繹）Out of Jiangling County (No. 1) (Xiao Yi, Northern and Southern dynasties)
  我寧可遐想（林明理）I Would Rather Daydream (Lin Ming-Li) ·········· 205
106. 詠細雨詩（南北朝・蕭繹）A Fine Drizzle (Xiao Yi, Northern and Southern dynasties)
  一棵極美的聖誕樹（林明理）A Most Beautiful Christmas Tree (Lin Ming-Li)··········· 207
107. 望春詩（南北朝・蕭繹）Watching Spring (Xiao Yi, Northern and Southern dynasties)
  正月賞梅（林明理）Admiring Plum Blossoms in January (Lin Ming-Li) ···· 208
108. 詠梅詩（南北朝・蕭繹）Ode to Plum Blossoms (Xiao Yi, Northern and Southern dynasties)
  富岡漁港冥想（林明理）Meditation at Tomioka Fishing Port (Lin Ming-Li)·· 209
109. 陌上桑（隋朝・無名氏）Mulberry Trees of the Path (Anonymous, Sui dynasty)
  多良村的心影（林明理）The Heart Shadow of Duoliang Village (Lin Ming-Li)··········· 211
110. 紫騮馬歌辭（南北朝・無名氏）Song of the Purple Steed (Anonymous, Northern and Southern dynasties)
  重遊南鯤鯓（林明理）Nan Kun Shen Revisited (Lin Ming-Li)············ 213

目錄

111. 折楊柳歌辭五首（其一）（南北朝・無名氏）Song of Breaking the Willows (No. 1) (Anonymous, Northern and Southern dynasties)
    倒影（林明理）Inverted Image (Lin Ming-Li)··················215
112. 折楊柳歌辭五首（其二）（南北朝・無名氏）Song of Breaking the Willows (No. 2) (Anonymous, Northern and Southern dynasties)
    雲豹頌（林明理）Ode to Clouded Leopard (Lin Ming-Li)··············217
113. 折楊柳歌辭五首（其三）（南北朝・無名氏）Song of Breaking the Willows (No. 3) (Anonymous, Northern and Southern dynasties)
    追憶－鐵道詩人　錦連（林明理）In Memory of Jin Lian, a Railway Poet (Lin Ming-Li)··················218
114. 折楊柳歌辭五首（其四）（南北朝・無名氏）Song of Breaking the Willows (No. 4) (Anonymous, Northern and Southern dynasties)
    傳說，拉瑪他・星星是英雄（林明理）Legend Has It That Istanda Lamata Sing Sing Is a Hero (Lin Ming-Li)··············221
115. 折楊柳歌辭五首（其五）（南北朝・無名氏）Song of Breaking the Willows (No. 5) (Anonymous, Northern and Southern dynasties)
    芍藥（林明理）The Chinese Peony (Lin Ming-Li)··············222
116. 折楊柳枝詞（南北朝・無名氏）A Song of Breaking the Willows (Anonymous, Northern and Southern dynasties)
    金池塘（林明理）The Golden Pond (Lin Ming-Li)··············224
117. 秋詩（南北朝・陽休之）A Poem on Autumn (Yang Xiuzhi, Northern and Southern dynasties)
    你在哪？孩子（林明理）Where Are You? My Child (Lin Ming-Li)·······225
118. 感琵琶弦（南北朝・馮小憐）A Farewell Poem (Anonymous, Northern and Southern dynasties)
    四月的夜風（林明理）The Night Wind of April (Lin Ming-Li)··········227
119. 寄王琳（南北朝・庾信）To Wang Lin, a Famous General (Yu Xin, Northern and Southern dynasties)
    夏風吹起的夜晚（林明理）The Night When Summer Wind Blows (Lin Ming-Li)··················229
120. 和庾四（南北朝・庾信）In Reply to Yu Si (Yu Xin, Northern and Southern dynasties)
    光點（林明理）The Luminous Spot (Lin Ming-Li)··············231
121. 和侃法師三絕詩（其三）（南北朝・庾信）In Reply to a Master-Monk (No. 3) (Yu Xin, Northern and Southern dynasties)
    記憶中的三條崙漁港（林明理）San-Tiau-Luen Fishing Harbor in My Memory (Lin Ming-Li)··················232

122. 行途賦得四更應詔詩（南北朝・庾信）A Named Composition (Yu Xin, Northern and Southern dynasties)
珍珠的水田（林明理）The Paddy Field of Pearls (Lin Ming-Li) ············ 234

123. 秋夜望單飛雁（南北朝・庾信）Watching the Solo Flight of a Wild Goose Through an Autumn Night (Yu Xin, Northern and Southern dynasties)
臺東糖廠印象（林明理）Impression of Taitung Sugar Factory (Lin Ming-Li)··· 236

124. 代人傷往詩二首（其一）（南北朝・庾信）Lament for the Past (No. 1) (Yu Xin, Northern and Southern dynasties)
一個難忘的瞬間（林明理）An Unforgettable Moment (Lin Ming-Li) ······ 237

125. 和王褒詠摘菊（南北朝・宇文毓）Plucking Chrysanthemums (Yu Wenyu, Northern and Southern dynasties)
記夢（林明理）The Memory of a Dream (Lin Ming-Li) ················ 239

126. 破鏡詩（南北朝・徐德言）A Poem of the Broken Mirror (Xu Deyan, Northern and Southern dynasties)
致小說家——鄭念（林明理）To Novelist: Zheng Nian (Lin Ming-Li) ······ 241

127. 哭魯廣達（南北朝・江總）Lament for Lu Guangda (Jiang Zong, Northern and Southern dynasties)
青藤花（林明理）Sinomenia Flowers (Lin Ming-Li) ···················· 242

128. 夏晚詩（南北朝・薛道衡）Late Summer (Xue Daoheng, Northern and Southern dynasties)
寫給卡法薩巴（林明理）To Kfar Saba, Israel (Lin Ming-Li) ············· 244

129. 三洲歌（南北朝・陳叔寶）The Song of Sanzhou (Chen Shubao, Northern and Southern dynasties)
我偏愛牢記詩詞（林明理）I Prefer Memorizing Poetry (Lin Ming-Li) ······ 245

130. 戲贈沈後（南北朝・陳叔寶）A Parody (Chen Shubao, Northern and Southern dynasties)
如風往事（林明理）Gone With the Wind (Lin Ming-Li) ·················· 247

131. 自君之出矣六首（其一）（南北朝・陳叔寶）Since You Left Me (No. 1) (Chen Shubao, Northern and Southern dynasties)
古老的驛站（林明理）An Age-Old Post (Lin Ming-Li)··················· 248

132. 敦煌樂二首（其一）（隋朝・王胄）The Melody of Dunhuang (No. 1) (Wang Zhou, Sui dynasty)
那些回味時代的光影（林明理）The Light & Shadow of the Times with Lingering Aftertaste (Lin Ming-Li) ·································· 250

133. 敦煌樂二首（其二）（隋朝・王胄）The Melody of Dunhuang (No. 2) (Wang Zhou, Sui dynasty)
詩觀（林明理）My View on Poetry (Lin Ming-Li) ······················· 252

134. 寄夫詩（南北朝・陳少女）To My Husband (Chen Shaonü, Northern and Southern dynasties)
憶台南水道博物館（林明理）Remembering Tainan Waterway Museum (Lin Ming-Li) ···253

135. 拔蒲二首（其一）（南北朝・無名氏）Plucking Cattails (No. 1) (Anonymous, Northern and Southern dynasties)
航行者（林明理）The Navigator (Lin Ming-Li) ···254

136. 拔蒲二首（其二）（南北朝・無名氏）Plucking Cattails (No. 2) (Anonymous, Northern and Southern dynasties)
我不能忘卻（林明理）I Cannot Forget (Lin Ming-Li) ···256

137. 作蠶絲二首（其一）（南北朝・無名氏）Producing the Cocoon Silk (No. 1) (Anonymous, Northern and Southern dynasties)
跟著風的腳步（林明理）Follow the Steps of Wind (Lin Ming-Li) ···········258

138. 入關詩（隋朝・虞世基）Upon Entering the Pass (Yu Shiji, Sui dynasty)
給 Giovanni G. Campisi（林明理）To Giovanni G. Campisi (Lin Ming-Li) ··259

139. 送別秦王學士江益詩（隋朝・劉夢予）Seeing a Friend Off (Liu Mengyu, Sui dynasty)
寒星（林明理）The Cold Stars (Lin Ming-Li) ···260

140. 因故人歸作詩（隋朝・蘇蟬翼）Upon the Returning of an Old Friend (Su Chanyi, Sui dynasty)
靈魂靜留在一塊礁岩上（林明理）The Soul Rests on a Rock (Lin Ming-Li) ···262

141. 寄阮郎詩（隋朝・張碧蘭）To My Darling Boy (Zhang Bilan, Sui dynasty)
致黃櫨樹（林明理）To the Cotinus Tree (Lin Ming-Li) ·························263

142. 自感詩三首（其一）（隋朝・侯夫人）The Moving Moments (No. 1) (Mrs. Hou, Sui dynasty)
葬禮（林明理）The Funeral (Lin Ming-Li) ···265

143. 自感詩三首（其二）（隋朝・侯夫人）The Moving Moments (No. 2) (Mrs. Hou, Sui dynasty)
赤崁樓懷古（林明理）Remembering the Past in Chihkan Tower (Lin Ming-Li) ···266

144. 自感詩三首（其三）（隋朝・侯夫人）The Moving Moments (No. 3) (Mrs. Hou, Sui dynasty)
寫作也是一種快樂（林明理）Writing Is Also a Pleasure (Lin Ming-Li) ······268

145. 妝成詩（隋朝・侯夫人）Makeup (Mrs. Hou, Sui dynasty)
傾聽大海（林明理）To Listen to the Sea (Lin Ming-Li) ·························270

146. 楊柳枝（隋朝・無名氏）Willow Twigs (Anonymous, Sui dynasty)
早霧（林明理）Morning Fog (Lin Ming-Li) ···272

147. 子夜四時歌・冬歌十七首（其六）（魏晉・無名氏）Midnight Songs Through the Four Seasons (Winter Song) (No. 6) (Anonymous, Wei and Jin dynasties) 深入山路的陰影（林明理）The Shadow Deep Into the Mountain Road (Lin Ming-Li) ·················· 274

148. 子夜四時歌・春歌（南北朝・無名氏）Midnight Songs Through the Four Seasons (Spring Song) (Anonymous, Northern and Southern dynasties) 我的心像隻小藍雀（林明理）My Heart Is Like a Blue Sparrow (Lin Ming-Li) ·················· 275

149. 子夜歌四十二首（其七）（魏晉・無名氏）Forty-Two Midnight Songs (No. 7) (Anonymous, Wei and Jin dynasties) 我倆相識絕非偶然（林明理）Our Meeting Is No Coincidence (Lin Ming-Li) ·················· 277

150. 子夜四時歌・秋風入窗裡（南北朝・無名氏）Midnight Songs Through the Four Seasons (Autumn Wind Into the Window) (Anonymous, Northern and Southern dynasties) 我不能忘卻⋯（林明理）I Cannot Forget... (Lin Ming-Li) ·················· 278

漢魏六朝接明理
古今抒情詩三百首
漢英對照

1.

垓下歌
先秦・項羽

力拔山兮氣蓋世，時不利兮騅不逝。
騅不逝兮可奈何，虞兮虞兮奈若何！

A Song Composed at Gaixia, or Waterloo
Xiang Yu (pre-Qin period)

I can uplift a mighty mountain,
and my heroic spirit soars

to the sky of skies, unrivaled.
But I run into bad luck, and my

steed fails me — it refuses to go
forward, and I feel so helpless.

Lady Yu, my darling consort,
how — how can I help you?

在風中，愛妳[1]
林明理

曾經，在深藍的夜空中，他們升起
　以最低安全高度，——
　　掠過海面，
　　像隻展翅上騰的神鷹，
　　　無畏風雨。
人們已為他們命名。而我彷彿聽到
　昔日那些勇殉的靈魂猶仍
被歌者稱頌，一遍又一遍……
　　恰似這雨聲，到了窗前
　　　忽而又杳無蹤影……
　　恰似所有愛情的淒美與旋律。

---

[1] 這是友人葛醫師回憶起她祖父母的舊事，也是一則光陰裡的故事，特致上敬意，並祝禱他們升入天堂，永享安寧。

啊，雨啊雨，
　　如此迷離，如此清新，──
　　　時而喃喃自語，
時而像是孩子氣地，旋轉再旋轉：
「噢，親愛的，
別為我哭泣，那顆天邊最亮的星子
──有我為妳朗讀的訊息。
　　那些眷村故事
　　　　和所有的顛沛流離，
不久將被歷史重新考掘，而我心如昨，
愛妳，在風中，愛妳單純的美麗。」

To Love You in the Wind[2]　　　　　　　Lin Ming-Li

Once, in the deep blue night sky, they rise
　　At the lowest safe altitude —
　　　　Skimming across the sea,
　　　　　Like an eagle winging heavenward,
　　　　　　Fearless of the wind and rain.
People have named for them. And I seem to hear
　　The souls of those brave martyrs in the past are still
Praised by the singers, over and over again...
　　Just like the sound of the rain, at the window
　　　　To suddenly appear and disappear...
　　Just like the melancholy beauty and melody of all love.

Oh, the rain,
　　So blurring, so fresh —
　　Now murmuring,
Then like a child, turning and whirling:
"Oh my dear,
Please don't cry for me, the brightest star in the sky
— There is the message of my reading for you.
　　The stories of the village

---

[2] This is a memory of her grandparents by my friend Dr. Ge, and it is also a story through the time, with special respect and prayers for their ascension to heaven to enjoy eternal peace.

And all the wanderings
Will soon be rediscovered by history, and my heart is like yesterday,
To love you, in the wind, for your simple beauty."

2.

和項王歌   兩漢・虞姬

漢兵已略地，四方楚歌聲。
大王意氣盡，賤妾何聊生！

In Reply to Xiang Yu
             Lady Yu (Western and Eastern Han dynasties)

Our land has been
occupied by the hostile

troops, and we are
besieged on all sides.

My dear, you are at
your last gasp — what

is the need for me to drag
out an ignoble existence?

她飛向天邊，旋舞如縷煙   林明理

她飛向天邊，旋舞如縷煙。
　　那風中的小影，恰似心底最深的
眷戀……忽遠，又近了。

晨霧把山巒拂拭，而時間彷彿
　　過去了千年。
她穿過幽徑，引我從容看待一切；

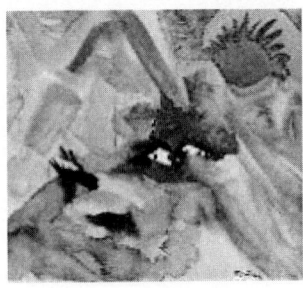

如今她安息於此，
　　百鳥振翅而歌。我的心，
從未擁有這般的感覺，──
　　縈迴，深邃。喔，靜寂的秋天。

─2025.01.03.

She Flies to the Horizon, Dancing Like a Wisp of Smoke
Lin Ming-Li

She flies to the horizon, dancing like a wisp of smoke.
　　The little shadow in the wind, just like the deepest love in
My heart…Suddenly afar, close again.

The morning mist is kissing the mountains, and it seems
　　　Thousands of years have passed.
She walks through the path, leading me to look at everything calmly;

Now she is at peace here;
　　A hundred birds are fluttering and singing. My heart,
Never has such a feeling—
　　Lingering, profound. Oh, the silent autumn.

January 3, 2025.

3・

菟絲
先秦・無名氏

菟絲從長風，根莖無斷絕。
無情尚不離，有情安可別？

Cuscuta Chinensis
Anonymous (pre-Qin period)

As a rambler, cuscuta chinensis
yields itself to the blowing wind,

without breaking of its stem
and root. The unfeeling grass

knows no separation — why
should human beings, with

great feeling and affection, tear
themselves apart from each other?

我不能忘懷妳憂鬱的眼睛
　　　　　　　　　　　　　　　　　　　　林明理

我不能忘懷妳憂鬱的眼睛，
有如夜鶯婉轉的鳴唱，
誰能理解愛情的荒誕，縱使難以探測，
誰能親吻自己的悲傷，縱使身陷牽絆。

當妳不再對我的世界訴說該有的夢想，
不再讓相遇的感動掠過我的心頭，
我倒是頗幸運，因為
我仍在水一方，伴隨潮汐呼吸，
仍將繼續奔跑下去，讓心回歸自然。

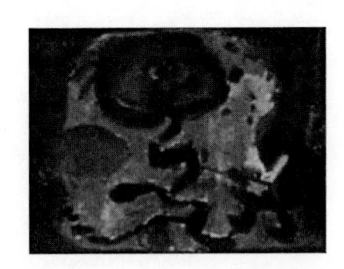

　　　　　　　　　　　　　　　　　　　　－2024.12.31.

I Cannot Forget Your Melancholy Eyes
　　　　　　　　　　　　　　　　　　　　Lin Ming-Li

I cannot forget your melancholy eyes,
Like the warbling song of the nightingale;
Who can understand the absurdity of love, though it is hard to fathom it;
Who can kiss his own sorrow, though trapped in bondage.

When you no longer tell the should-be dreams to my world,
No longer let the touch of meeting flit through my mind,
I feel so lucky, because
I am still beyond the water, breathing with the tide,
And I will continue to run, for my heart to return to nature.

　　　　　　　　　　　　　　　　　　　　December 31, 2024

4・

枯魚過河泣 　　　　　　　　　　　　漢・樂府詩

枯魚過河泣，何時悔復及！
作書與魴鱮，相教慎出入。

Dirge of a Dried Fish 　　　Anonymous (Han dynasty)

A dried fish is weeping
while crossing the river

—it is too late to rue
and regret! A letter is

written to the bream
and lumpfish: you are

never too careful and
cautious wherever you trip.

把和平帶回來 　　　　　　　　　　　　　林明理

一切都很安靜
　　　直到砲彈來襲
建築、作物和牲畜
　　　被無情催毀
天空
　　眼睜睜瞪著獨裁者的私慾
大地
　　哭訴著侵略者的罪行
一隻白鴿
　　在黃昏中悲鳴
對著眼前無盡的道路
只有明月
　　用溫存的手撫慰著難民

To Bring Peace Back

                                                        Lin Ming-Li

All is quiet
    Until the cannonball
Buildings, crops and livestock
    All are ruthlessly destroyed
The sky
    Watches the dictator's lust helplessly
The earth
    Weeps for the crime of the aggressors
A white pigeon
    Is wailing at dusk
Facing the endless road ahead
Only the bright moon
    Is comforting the refugees with her tender hand

5.

七步詩
                                                     兩漢・曹植

煮豆燃豆萁，豆在釜中泣。
本是同根生，相煎何太急？

Written Within Seven Steps
                Cao Zhi (Western and Eastern Han dynasties)

Beanstalk is burned
to burn the bean,

which is weeping
in the pot: as off-

springs of the same
root, why should we

burn and boil each
other so cruelly?

因為有了愛

因為有了愛，讓我奮起
　而不感到孤獨，——
縱然過往歲月中不得不負笈他鄉，
　故鄉的呼聲，依然在風中迴響；

因為有了愛，我才能
　重新站起來，緬懷記憶裡的
舊時光，即使山巒吹來的風，——
　把我的相思帶向遠方；

即使生命如一隻孤雁飛向那廣闊的
　世界，即使命運如此不可捉摸，
因為有了愛，——
　我不感到孤獨。

林明理

－2025.01.03

With Love

Lin Ming-Li

With love, I strive to rise up
　And feel no loneliness —
Though in the past years I have to study abroad,
　The voice of my hometown, is still echoing in the wind;

With love, I can
　Stand up again, to cherish the memory
Of old time, even if the wind is blowing from the mountain —
　To take my longing and pining to the distance;

Even if life, like a wild goose, is flying into the wide
　World, even if fate is so unpredictable,
With love —
　I feel no loneliness.

January 3, 2025.

6·

酌貪泉詩

魏晉·吳隱之

古人雲此水，一歃懷千金。
試使夷齊飲，終當不易心。

A Greedy Mouth of Spring

Wu Yinzhi (Wei and Jin dynasties)

Legend has it that this is a
greedy mouth of spring, from

which a small mouthful of water
is adequate to make the drinker

greedy of money. Yet Bo Yi
and Shu Qi, as paragons of virtue,

are constant of their virtue, and
they remain honest and upright.

我的心是一條小河

林明理

我的心是一條小河，
一路流淌到那古樸的村落。
風自三月來，
有兩隻鷹各自振翅，翱翔乘風，——

此時雲霧輕籠，陽光以祥和的方式
吻合每一寸土地，——
有塊金色的鐘乳石岩壁，
像幅藝術氣氛的抽象畫；

穿過雞鳴的小路，
我的心是一條小河，邊走邊唱和，——
在春溪的花徑旁
被一路上的野趣吸引著。

當時我沒有懷抱很多期待，
那熟悉的天空給我的訊息，
盡是輕快敞亮，——
引我坦然看待外界的風風雨雨。

－2025.01.13

My Heart Is a Small River Lin Ming-Li

My heart is a small river,
Flowing all the way to the simple village.
When the wind comes from March,
Two eagles are fluttering their wings on the wind —

Now, the clouds are lightly veiling, and the sunlight in a peaceful way
Caters to each inch of land —
There is a golden stalactite rock wall,
Like an abstract painting with artistic atmosphere;

Through the path of crows,
My heart is a small river, singing while walking —
By the flowery path of a spring creek
Attracted by the wild interests along the way.

I did not embrace a host of expectations;
The familiar sky gave me a message
Which was light and bright —
Leading me to calmly view the ups and downs of the outside world.

January 13, 2025.

7．

思吳江歌 魏晉・張翰

秋風起兮木葉飛，吳江水兮鱸正肥。
三千里兮家未歸，恨難禁兮仰天悲。

41

Longing for the Wujiang River

Zhang Han (Wei and Jin dynasties)

The rise of autumn wind brings
a shower after another shower

of leaves; perches are fattened
by the limpid water of my native

Wujiang River. My home is three
thousand miles away, away from

me — with boundless regret and
sorrow, I lift my eyes heavenward.

揚子江[3]，你活在我的心裡

林明理

你的面容與身影，讓我昂首，
　　沿著青藏高原，穿越綿長的流域
徐徐而行，——傳送孤獨雄壯之音，
　　如星夜棲在深林的飛鷹。

你在浩瀚的歷史長河中留下
　　各朝代輝煌與沒落的痕跡，
石碑上的英雄揮毫寫下
　　可歌可泣流傳千古的文字。

在新的世紀裡，人們心中或許挑不起
　　對你質樸莊嚴的記憶，
但每當你沉思的眼眸泛起了光，與愛意，
啊，揚子江，你活在我的心裡。

---

[3] 長江，又名揚子江（Yangtze River），全長 6300 公里，被稱為中華民族的父親河。—2025.01.05

Yangtze River[4], You Live in My Heart

Lin Ming-Li

Your face and figure makes me look upward,
    Along the Qinghai-Tibet Plateau, through the long river basin,
Slowly forward — to transmit the lonely majestic voice,
    Like the starry night perching in the deep forest with flying eagles.

You have left traces of the splendor and decline of each dynasty
    In the boundless river of history,
And the heroes on the stone tablets have written
    The words that can be sung and passed down through the ages.

In the new century, perhaps it is hard for people's heart to bear
    The simple and solemn memory of you,
But whenever your contemplative eyes shine with love,
Ah, Yangtze River, you live in my heart.

ঔ ঔ ঔ

8.

神情詩

東晉・顧愷之

春水滿四澤，夏雲多奇峰。
秋月揚明輝，冬嶺秀寒松。

The Four Fair Seasons

Gu Kaizhi (Eastern Jin dynasty)

The spring water fills the fields,
ponds, lakes, and rivers; the

summer clouds are capriciously
changeable, like picturesque

---

[4] The Long River, also known as Yangtze River, stretches 6,300 kilometers and is famous as the father river of the Chinese nation. -January 5, 2025.

peaks; the autumn moon shines
brightly, lending myriads of things

a layer of blurred color; the winter
mountain is nursing green cold pines.

在時間的繪影中 　　　　　　　　　　林明理

任憑時光匆匆
　　幾經滄桑和遷移的部落,
仍有風在低音區敘述一個又一個
　　古老的故事。

現在我知道：
無論什麼季節,都有一種聲音,像隻蟹,
　　眼裡還沾著細沙,
就迫不及待往岸上爬。

誰說,在時間的繪影中,每首歌裡都有
　　一個故事,每個故事裡都有悲歡離合？
這部落幾可媲美遺世獨立,
　　那是時間無法給予繪影和遺忘的。

　　　　　　　　　　　　　　　－2025.01.12

In the Shadow of Time 　　　　　　　Lin Ming-Li

In spite of the quick passage of time
　　The tribe through vicissitudes of life and migration,
There is still a wind in the bass zone to narrate
　　One after another old story.

Now I know:
Whatever the season, there is a voice, like a crab,
　　Eyes still wet with fine sand,
Cannot wait to climb ashore.

Who says in the shadow of time, each song has
　　A story, and each story contains joys and sorrows?

The tribe is almost tantamount to being aloof from the world,
Which time cannot paint and forget.

January 12, 2025.

9．

華光殿侍宴賦競病韻

南北朝・曹景宗

去時兒女悲，歸來笳鼓競。
借問行路人，何如霍去病？

At the Victory Banquet

Cao Jingzong (Northern and Southern dynasties)

When I march to the battlefield,
those who come to see us off

are dispirited and disheartened;
when I return in triumph,

there is a deafening sound of
gongs & drums. Huo Qubing,

a famous anti-enemy general
— am I inferior to him?

心頭閃亮起的名字

林明理

你的名字是金色的浪花，
　　伴隨著捲起的潮浪，——
你的名字是天邊的一片雲彩，
　　在我心頭存藏，又漸漸彌散……
你是飛馳中渴望藍天的海鷗，
　　是望穿大海的星子；

越過高低起伏的山脊，
　　舞成一篇篇詩篇……

夜裡，幾艘逆風的漁船，點綴出
　　你獨一無二的翔舞，──
那雙映射出勇敢無懼的眸光，
　　喚我進入了甜夢。

　　　　　　　　　　　　　　　　　　　　－2025.01.08.

The Name Shining in the Heart　　　　Lin Ming-Li

Your name is a golden spray,
　　Accompanied by the rising tide —
Your name is a cloud on the horizon,
　　Hidden in my heart, gradually dispersing...
You are the seagull longing for the blue sky in flight,
　　The star looking across the sea;

Over the rolling ridges,
　　　　Dancing into one after another poem...
At night, a few fishing boats against the wind, to embellish
　　Your unique gliding dance —
The pair of eyes reflecting fearless bravery,
　　Call me into a sweet dream.

　　　　　　　　　　　　　　　　　　　　January 8, 2025.

10 ·

玉階怨　　　　　　　　　　　　　　　南北朝·謝朓

夕殿下珠簾，流螢飛復息。
長夜縫羅衣，思君此何極？

Plaint of Jade Steps
　　　　　　　　Xie Tiao (Northern and Southern dynasties)

The palace, bathed in dusk,
sees the beaded curtain pulling

46

down; the fireflies keep flying
before coming to a stop for rest.

The endless night sees a stitch
after another stitch in an

embroidered dress — also endless
is the sewer's pining & longing.

當思念變成一片雲 林明理

當思念變成一片雲
　　落入我眼眸，——
一個曾經消失的愛情國度，
　　幻成天邊歸雁的殘影，
循著千百年的鳥道
　　掩映在粼粼波光中。

當所有人都以為
　　背棄愛情的神話
不再相信愛情恰似發光的藍海，
　　它的憂鬱與神祕，——
　　　　如黝藍的天空。
即使早已習慣在風中敘事的我，
也想對它這樣說，——

「瞧，我明白了：
愛情就在藍海間，
　　在枝葉間，
　　　　在我深深的足跡上」。
而此刻，微風簇擁波浪，
又是諸神微笑著邀約的時候。

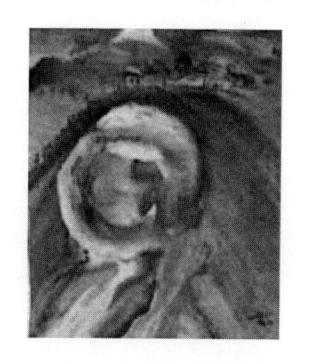

—2024.12.30

When Missing Turns Into a Cloud Lin Ming-Li

When missing turns into a cloud
　　Which falls into my eyes —

A country where love has once disappeared,
    Illusion into the dim form of returning geese in the horizon,
Following the path of birds through thousands of years
    Hidden in the sparkling light.

When everyone thinks
    To abandon the myth of love
No longer believe love is like the shining blue sea,
    Its melancholy and mystery —
        Like the blue sky.
Even if I have been accustomed to narrative in the wind,
I want to say to it —

"Look, I come to see:
Love is in the blue ocean,
    In the leaves and branches,
        In my deep footprints."
And now, the breeze kissing the waves,
It is time for the gods to invite each other while smiling.

December 30, 2024.

11·

王孫遊   南北朝·謝朓

綠草蔓如絲，雜樹紅英發。
無論君不歸，君歸芳已歇。

Too Late, Your Return
Xie Tiao (Northern and Southern dynasties)

Green grass grows silkily
to stretch afar; clumps

of trees are alive with
red flowers. Your return

―late, too late to be
significant: the height of

spring has passed, with
flowers falling, and fading…

我欲召喚在北國山村，等你   林明理

當所有人都在愛情國度裡尋尋覓覓，
　　當所有抉擇不再改變任何方向
或你已消隱，在這瞬息萬變的天宇下，
　　我還是一如恆常，
　　　一如開滿枝紅的花兒――
隨著牛背上的炊煙飄來，泊在山村，等你。

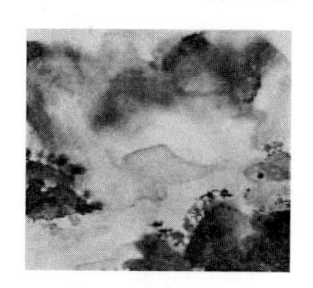

等你，就感到一個被遺忘數個世紀的永恆
　　　是可能的，――
它不再是一段無意義的史詩神話，
　　不再是讓記憶漫無目的地飄浮，――
不再是遠眺的身影，都一一在風中閃現了；

啊，我最摯愛的遠方，
或許你已然忘記，這山村只剩下美和真，
　　而原古的歌聲像流水……徐徐緩緩，
　不經意地在我身後迴響。
風來了，掠過太平洋的方向，而我是航向你的
船，等你，在靜謐的星子騰飛到我小屋上…
　　　又悄悄細語的時光。

―2025.01.03.

I Want to Summon in the North Country Mountain Village, Waiting for You   Lin Ming-Li

When all are seeking and searching in the country of love,
　　When all the choices no longer change the direction
Or you have disappeared, in this rapidly changing sky,
　　I am still as usual,
　　　Like the flowers blooming red ―

Floating here with the smoke on the cow back, parking in the mountain village, waiting for you.

Waiting for you, to feel an eternity which is forgotten for centuries
     It is possible —
It is no longer a meaningless epic myth,
     No longer for the memory to float about aimlessly —
No longer a figure looking afar, one by one flashing in the wind;

Ah, my dearest distance,
Perhaps you have forgotten, only beauty and truth remain in the mountain village,
     And the ancient songs are like running water... Slowly and sluggishly,
     Unconsciously echoing behind me.
The wind is coming, in the direction of the Pacific Ocean, and I am the ship
Heading for you, waiting for you, in the quiet star to take off to my cabin…
     Again the time of silent whispering.

January 3, 2025.

12·

子夜歌二首（其一）　　　　　　　　南北朝·蕭衍

恃愛如欲進，含羞未肯前。
朱口發艷歌，玉指弄嬌弦。

Midnight Songs (No. 1)

Xiao Yan (Northern and Southern dynasties)

Favored, flattered, coddled,
and pampered, she seems

to be unrestrained; bashful,
she is timid of approaching.

Her rosy lips produce
melodious, luscious music,

when her dainty fingers are
fondling chords & strings.

妳是畫卷裡走出來的史詩神話 　　　　　　　林明理

凡是妳下決心追逐的夢想，
　　都會在歲月中逐一實現；
凡是妳的憂思，妳的淚，都如輕風
　　吹過山之巔，海之崖。

妳是畫卷裡走出來的史詩神話，
　　像驚鴻一瞥的歌者，——
若詩似畫，瞬間航入我的視界，
　　攜著一縷青綠，帶些晨光⋯

⋯又冉冉飄遠。無人知曉妳的來處，
　　只有我試圖把時光放慢，
追趕著層巒疊嶂，跟著風四處飄蕩，
　　如那可歎的愛情和它的徬徨。

－2025.01.03

You Are an Epic Myth Walking Out of the Scroll
Lin Ming-Li

All the dreams you set your mind to pursue
　　Will come true one by one through the years.
All your worries and your tears are like the breeze
　　Blowing over the mountain tops and the cliffs of the sea.

You are an epic myth walking out of the scroll,
　Like the singer who casts enchanting glimpses —
Poem-like and painting-like, to sail into my vision in an instant,
　Carrying a wisp of green, with some morning light...

⋯And slowly floating away. Nobody knows where you are from,
　　Only I try to slow down the time,

漢魏六朝接明理
古今抒情詩三百首
漢英對照

Chasing the peaks of the mountains, with the wind floating around,
　Like the deplorable love and its hesitation.

January 3, 2025.

13・

子夜歌二首（其二） 南北朝・蕭衍

朝日照綺窗，光風動紈羅。
巧笑倩兩靨，美目揚雙蛾。

Midnight Songs (No. 2)

Xiao Yan (Northern and Southern dynasties)

The morning sun shines on
the latticed window, when

the breeze is blowing gently
on her pure white silken cloth.

A beauty is smiling beautifully,
revealing her white and neat teeth;

her soft glances are glamorous
through a pair of fair brows.

剪影 林明理

昨夜夢的朦朧
　　　那等在廣場的靜謐
如今朝的雨色淒迷

走出地鐵，花傘繽紛的街上
　妳的影子，捻起我心的律動
在風中，濕潤的空氣混濁
　妳的嘴唇似西山的繁霜秋楓

我翩翩的羽翼
　　　　是無間的力量
愛，讓我展翅，飛向光芒……

The Silhouette　　　　　　　　　　　　　　　Lin Ming-Li

Last night's dream is blurring
　　　　The quiet waiting in the square
Sad and dreary like the rain of this morning

Out of the subway, in the street of colorful flowery umbrellas
　Your shadow quickens the rhythm of my heart
In the wind, the moist air is turbid
　Your lips are like the frosty autumn maples in the western mountain

My fluttering wings
　　　　Are the seamless power
Love, making me spread my wings, in the direction of the light…

14·

別詩　　　　　　　　　　　　　　　　　　南北朝·范雲

洛陽城東西，長作經時別。
昔去雪如花，今來花似雪。

Separations　　　Fan Yun (Northern and Southern dynasties)

To the west of Luoyang,
to the east of Luoyang,

long and longer separations
are made from time to time.

When I leave here, it is
heavily snowing like flowering;

when I turn back, it is
massively flowering like snowing.

你來自飛雪遙遠的虛幻

林明理

你來自飛雪遙遠的虛幻，
天空異常的皎潔、空曠，而我
　一步步，緩緩地靠近——
宛如潑墨畫中的花。

那裡，沒有陽光，卻美得
令人心醉。沒有大白鷗
　在萬頃波中波動、起伏，——
卻恍若一場遙遠的虛幻，烙印在
　繁星與我祈福之中。

愈是接近暮晚時分，愈是
　教我思念它每一片冰瑩的輝煌，
我直想捧住
　這教我心存感恩、尊崇的…
　　…小小雪花。

—2025.01.01

You Come From the Faraway Illusion of Snow

Lin Ming-Li

You come from the faraway illusion of snow,
The sky is unusually clear and empty, and I
　Am approaching step by step, slowly —
Like a flower in the splash-ink painting.

There, there is no sunshine, but it is enchantingly
Beautiful. No great white gulls
　Are waving and undulating in the boundless waves —
But it is like a distant illusion, imprinted on
　The stars and my blessings.

The closer it is to the evening, the more
　It teaches me to miss the brilliance of each piece of ice,

How I want to hold
   The little snowflakes
     Which teach me to be grateful and respectful…

January 1, 2025.

15.

相送　　　　　　　　　　　　　　　　　　南北朝・何遜

客心已百念，孤遊重千里。
江暗雨欲來，浪白風初起。

Fare You Well　　He Xun (Northern and Southern dynasties)

A wanderer's heart:
a whirlpool of emotions;

a solitary journey:
through thousands of

miles. The river darkens,
when a rain threatens;

the waves whiten, when
a wild wind is born.

你的憂鬱是片片雪花的哀音　　　　　　　　林明理

是第一道曙光把我的目光轉變成
　　青鳥，悠然翱翔於雲天，——
讓我的思想越過了彩虹深處，
　　尋覓一個同我深情的眼眸重疊；

是北方與海峽山脈相連，
風語、碼頭、燈塔，都在不斷呼喚
你的名字，而時間卻重覆著像駝鈴般
　　　斷續的音旋。

是遠近大海的幽謐，
讓我驀然回首，
　　　瞥見萬物沉睡於水藍之中——
金陽照耀著我翹盼的心。

那飄閃的浪花恰如森林小夜曲，而
　　　你的憂鬱是片片雪花的哀音，
無聲，卻如星光照影，讓夜徘徊——
我看不到，但懂得你安寧的心靈。

　　　　　　　　　　　　　　　－2025.01.14

Your Melancholy Is the Sad Sound of Snowflakes

Lin Ming-Li

It is the first flush of dawn that turns my gaze into
　　A blue bird, to soar in the cloudy sky —
For my thought to cross the depths of the rainbow
　　In search of an overlapping with my soulful eyes;

It is the north that connects with the Channel Mountain,
The winds, the docks, the lighthouses, all are calling
Your name, when time is repeating itself like
　　　　The intermittent sound of a camel bell.

It is the serenity of the sea near and far
That makes me look back suddenly
　　　To see all things sleeping in the blue water —
The golden sun is shining on my expectant heart.

The flashing waves are like the forest serenade, and
　　　Your melancholy is the sad sound of snowflakes,
Silent, but bright like starlight, for the night to loiter and linger —
I fail to see, but I understand your peaceful mind.

　　　　　　　　　　　　　　　January 14, 2025.

16．

長安聽百舌

南北朝・韋鼎

萬里風煙異，一鳥忽相驚。
哪能對遠客，還作故鄉聲！

A Chinese Blackbird

Wei Ding (Northern and Southern dynasties)

A vista of hills &
rills with various

scenes, from which
a bird suddenly

startles. Remote
from home, a roamer,

how rueful to hear
the native chirping.

再別金陵城[5]

林明理

此刻，我從窗口透過雨絲，想你。
　　想你，——在梧桐和銀杏花開，滿城
　　　　又變回六朝古都的歡愉；
　　想你，——懷著哲人般的思想，肩負著
　　　　時代命運和昔日的輝煌；
　　想你，孕育出如此燦爛而詩意的風景，
卻依然與我同杯，啜飲舊時光。

啊，再會吧，金陵，我的夜。
　　　　多麼熟悉你嘹亮的吟唱，
　　多麼熟悉你如雪一般的鬢髮，
　　　　多麼熟悉與你肩併肩的話語，

---

[5] 南京市，別稱金陵，是江蘇省省會，歷史上有六個重要朝代曾建都於「南京」，故又稱「六朝古都」，分別是孫吳、東晉以及南朝的宋、齊、梁、陳。—2025.01.06.

多麼熟悉你沉靜而滄桑的臉龐，──
啊，再會吧，金陵，我的徬徨。
　　你不是遠方，是教我時時縈念，──
　　　　以不盡的溫柔的呼喚。

Saying Good-bye to Jinling City[6] Again Lin Ming-Li

Now, I miss you through the rain from the window.
　　Missing you — the parasol trees and ginkgo trees come into flowers, the city
　　　　Has changed back to the joy of the ancient capital of six dynasties;
　　Missing you — with philosopher-like thoughts, shouldering
　　　　The destiny of the times and the former glory;
　　Missing you, giving birth to such a brilliant and poetic landscape,
But still with me in the same cup, sipping the old time.

Ah, farewell, Jinling, my night.
　　　　How familiar with your loud singing,
How familiar with your snow-like hair,
　　　　How familiar with your words from shoulder to shoulder,
How familiar with your quiet face through vicissitudes —
Ah, goodbye, Jinling, my hesitation.
　　　　You are not far away, but teach me from time to time —
　　　　　　With endless soft summon and call.

17 •

入關故人別　　　　　　　　　　　　南北朝・王褒

百年餘古樹，千里暗黃塵。
關山行就近，相看成遠人。

---

[6] Nanjing City, also known as Jinling, is the capital of Jiangsu Province. Historically, six important dynasties were successively founded here: Sun-Wu, Eastern Jin, as well as Song, Qi, Liang and Chen of the Southern Dynasty. Therefore, it is also called "the ancient capital of Six Dynasties". -January 6, 2025.

Farewell to a Friend

      Wang Bao (Northern and Southern dynasties)

An age-old tree thrives
through hundreds of years;

thousands of miles see yellow
dust darkening. The mountain

is nearer upon approaching;
watching you walking away,

to be a speck of dust
in the boundless world.

在望不盡的海岸之前

            林明理

當海平線的浪花都成豎琴，黃昏臨近了，
有薄雲棲在溪之上，溪上多飛鳥，
白日已漸漸消失，而那細細的回憶
卻開始緩緩向我湧來……

我並不眷戀白日把太平洋映得金燦燦，
也不畏懼夜晚發亮的遠伸的大海
向我襲來，——只要妳，我的愛，只要
妳記得那些曾經讓我們歡愉的時刻。

當繁星閃爍，在望不盡的海岸之前，
在我思念妳的翅翼再度馳騁於空中，
只要妳向著遠遠的山脈的最高峯，——
那聖山的影子，都在風中成了一首歌。

也許，妳確信，愛情不是虛無縹緲的，
也許，妳不信，曾經有我熱情的守候，
啊，親愛的，在望不盡的海岸之前，
就讓我滿懷謝意在這值得懷念的記憶之中。

            －2025.01.01

Before the Endless Shore
Lin Ming-Li

When the waves on the horizon become harps, dusk is approaching
There are thin clouds perching over the stream, which is alive with many birds
The day is gradually disappearing, and the thin memories
Begin to slowly surging in me...

I do not long for the Pacific to glow gold from the sun
Nor do I fear the sea which shines endlessly at night
Charging at me — so long as you, my love, so long
As you remember the moments which bring us happiness

When the stars twinkle before the endless shore
When the wings of my longing for you fly through the air again
So long as you toward the highest peak of the distant mountain —
The shadow of the holy mountain, all become a song in the wind.

Perhaps, you are sure, love is not ethereal
Perhaps, you do not believe that I have once had my enthusiasm in waiting
Ah, dear, before the endless shore
Let me be filled with gratitude in the worthy memory.

January 1, 2025.

18・

重別周尚書
南北朝・庾信

陽關萬里道，不見一人歸。
唯有河邊雁，秋來南向飛。

Once More Farewell to Secretary Zhou
Yu Xin (Northern and Southern dynasties)

Between the Sunny Pass
and the homeland, thousands

of miles of journey; not
a single soul is seen to be

returning. Only the wild
goose, from the river, is

flying and wheeling south-
ward at the advent of autumn.

走在歸途的寂靜中

林明理

走在歸途的寂靜中，
　尋著雨中耕種的老農背影，
穿過鷺鷥群和雲彩的輝映，
　一路上步履變得很輕……
就像光陰不停地流逝，
　之後便不見任何蹤跡！

走過小徑旁的月桃花，
　前路還綿延著，——
童年的回憶一個接一個，
　至今仍是活生生的樣子。
那裡會有家人與我所有的
恬逸歡愉，會有一扇窗
為遊子點亮，迎接我蒞臨。

－2024.01.02

Walking in the Silence of the Journey Home

Lin Ming-Li

Walking in the silence of the journey home
　Looking for the back of the old farmer farming in the rain
Through the bevy of egrets and the glow of clouds
　The steps all the way become so light...
Like time going on and on
　And then it is traceless!

Walking through the moon peach blossoms by the path
　The road ahead is still meandering —

Childhood memories one by one
    Still vividly living.
There will be my family and all
My pleasures, there will be a window
Lit for the wanderer, to welcome my arrival.

January 2, 2024.

🦋 🦋 🦋

19.

春江花月夜二首（其一）   隋·楊廣

暮江平不動，春花滿正開。
流波將月去，潮水帶星來。

Spring River & Flowery Moonlit Night (No. 1)
Yang Guang (Sui dynasty)

The dusky river is tranquil,
seeming to be motionless;

spring flowers are in the
height of their flowering.

The surging waves bear
the moon away, when

the tidal water rushes here
with a brilliant maze of stars.

橋下閃爍的波影   林明理

循著鳥聲，向林中望去。
陽光照射在神慈悲的面龐，漏瀉在如金的
蘆葦影子上，──
我眼眸裡盈滿著露珠，沒有塵埃。

我看到熱氣球歇在山腳下，
以及浮過的藍影，

還有利吉惡地[7]，像一匹孤獨的蒼狼，──
神奇地讓我情感澎湃。

數千年以來，那橋下閃爍的波影，
大自然賦予的安謐和絢彩，
讓我止不住欣喜，──
跟在光的背後　擁夢飛翔。

The Flickering Shadow Under the Bridge

Lin Ming-Li

Following the birds and look out into the woods
The sun shines on the merciful face of God, leaking on the golden
Shadows of the reeds —
My eyes are filled with dews, without dust.

I see the hot air balloon resting at the foot of the mountain
And the blue shadow floating by
And Liji Badlands[8], like a lonely wolf —
The magic of my surging emotions

Through thousands of years, the flickering shadow under the bridge
The quiet and colorful colors given by nature
For me to rejoice boundlessly —
Following the light　to fly with a fond dream

20.

江陵女歌

隋・楊廣

雨從天上落，水從橋下流。
拾得娘裙帶，同心結兩頭。

---

[7] 位在臺東市卑南鄉的利吉惡地（Liji Badlands），有「台東地質國寶」之稱。─2025.1.12

[8] Liji Badlands, located in Beinan Township, Taitung City, is known as the "National geological treasure of Taitung". -January 12, 2025.

A Riverside Girl's Song Yang Guang (Sui dynasty)

The rain falls from
heaven; the water

runs beneath the
bridge. I chance

to pick up the sash
of her skirt, whose

two ends are made
into a true love knot.

倘若再有相聚之時 林明理

妳的話語——似小孩般純真，
在紅藜綴滿山林的夢中，
　　總是帶來許多驚喜。

山巒靜靜地矗立，面容安詳，
整個田野像彩虹般，隱藏在
　　時空之外，只妳我交會的眼神
閃著光燦的顏色。

倘若再有相聚之時，而妳深眸中
　　閃著奇異的光澤，
仍透射一種驕傲的亮光，
那麼，我將不知該飛向何方？

妳的話語——多麼輕靈，充滿夢幻，
到哪兒才能尋得曾經盼著妳的笑，
　　或者驚動我心靈的聲音？

—2024.12.31

If There Is Another Meeting Lin Ming-Li

Your words — naïve like a child
In the dream of the red quinoa filling the mountains
　　Always bring a host of pleasant surprises

The mountain stands quietly, with peaceful countenance
The whole field is like a rainbow, hidden
    Outside of time and space, only you and I exchange glances
Shining in bright colors

If there is another meeting, and in your deep eyes
    There is a strange shine
Still with a light of pride
Then, I know not where to fly

Your words — so ethereal, filled with dreams
Where can I find the smile which has once longed for you
    Or the voice which has stirred my heart?

December 31, 2024.

21.

春江花月夜二首（其二） 隋・楊廣

夜露含花氣，春潭漾月暉。
漢水逢遊女，湘川值二妃。

Spring River & Flowery Moonlit Night (No. 2)
Yang Guang (Sui dynasty)

The dews of warm night are
flowerily scented; the spring

pool is brilliant with a flickering
moon. The water runs ahead —

if into the Han River, there is
the river goddess; if into the Xiang

River, there are Ehuang and Nüying,
Emperor Yao's two daughters.

我步入富春江的奇山異水

林明理

我步入富春江[9]的奇山異水，
　　那美妙的聲波，夾雜著些微
白楊和綠柳的氣味，——
　　在那裡，彷若世間所有塵埃
都被洗淨，在船屋穿越層巒疊嶂中。

多少騷人墨客，為它傾慕？
　　多少春花秋月，為它哭泣？
多少朝代更迭，為它吶喊？
　　多少帆影落盡，為它謳歌？
唯有那容顏，唯有對她萬事能看淡的
　　襟懷，直抵我的心，教我眷戀。

啊，我已熟練她凜然美麗的一面，
　　她的微笑、史詩與佳傳，
她的話語和明眸……被溪畔的
　　音闋詩詞縈繞
在泛藍深深淺淺的光影之上。

I Step Into the Spectacular Mountains of the Fuchun River

Lin Ming-Li

I step into the spectacular mountains of the Fuchun River[10]
　　The wonderful sound waves, mixed with the slight
Smell of poplars and green willows —
　　There, seemingly all the dust of the world
Has been washed, in the houseboat crossing the mountains

---

[9] 富春區，位於浙江省杭州市西南部，自古代至宋朝以前，多稱「富春」，至今有2200多年歷史；風景秀麗，有「天下佳山水，古今推富春」之美譽。—2025.01.05

[10] Fuchun District, located in the southwest of Hangzhou City, Zhejiang Province, boasts a history of over 2200 years. Since ancient times to the Song Dynasty, it has mostly been called "Fuchun", which is famous for its beautiful scenery, hence the reputation of "the world's best landscape in Fuchun". -January 5, 2025.

How many poets and literary men adore it?
    How many spring flowers and autumn moons are weeping for it?
How many dynasties have come and gone, shouting for it?
    How many sail shadows have fallen, eulogizing it?
Only the face, only for her the bosom can make light of
    Everything, straight to my heart, to intoxicate me

Oh, I am familiar with her awe-inspiring beauty
    Her smiles, her epics and stories
Her words and her bright eyes... By the stream
    Music and poetry lingering
In the light shadows with deep and light blues

---

22 •

野望　　　　　　　　　　　　　　　　　　　　　隋·楊廣

寒鴉飛數點，流水繞孤村。
斜陽欲落處，一望黯銷魂。

View of Nature　　　　　　　　Yang Guang (Sui dynasty)

A few flying dots
of cold crows; a

running water runs
around a solitary

village. The slanting
sun is slowly setting;

a glance of it —
so heartbreaking!

看灰面鵟鷹[11]消逝

林明理

一群寒鷹，
　　　從滿州鄉高空
點綴著斜陽。

當晚風纏捲，
　丘陵地上，這夜棲者——
　有人驚歎，
　有人眈眈逐逐；
那衛星發報器　也振振偵聽
腳環飛去的方向。

夜來了。
我立在岸上，像一塊岩石，
　　看著牠們逐漸消逝……
遠從西伯利亞到東北，
　路經日本到琉球，
還有臺灣、菲律賓到南洋，——
聽任蟲鳴絮說
　一波波潮流和遠征的故事，
聽任海面無言無語
　用沙貝採擷你的蒼然。

Seeing Butastur Indicus[12] Disappearing

Lin Ming-Li

A bevy of cold eagles
　　　From the sky over Manchu Township
Dotting with a setting sun

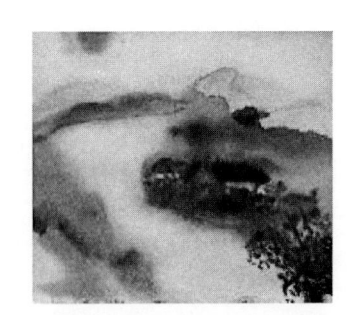

---

[11] 灰面鵟鷹（Butastur indicus），俗稱「灰面鷲」。牠在滿洲、南韓和日本繁殖，冬季時，便路經臺灣，遷徙到東南亞。

[12] Butastur indicus, as a kind of eagle, is commonly known as "grey-faced vulture". It breeds in Manchuria, South Korea and Japan, and migrates to Southeast Asia via Taiwan during the winter.

When the evening wind is lingering
   On the hills, the night dweller —
   Some are marveling
   Some are covetously chasing
The satellite transmitter also vibrates to hear
Where the anklet is going

Night is coming
I stand on the bank, like a rock
    To watch them fading away...
From Siberia to the Northeast
   Through Japan to the Ryukyu
And from Taiwan and the Philippines to the South Ocean —
In spite of the chirping of insects
   Waves upon waves and the stories of expeditions
In spite of the sea's silence
   To gather your awesomeness with sand shells

❦ ❦ ❦

23 •

子夜歌（其一）   魏晉 · 無名氏

夜長不得眠，明月何灼灼。
想聞散喚聲，虛應空中諾。

Midnight Songs (No. 1)   Anonymous (Wei and Jin dynasties)

I am deprived of sleep by
the great length of the night,

when the moon is so bright
and brilliant. How I yearn

to hear your calling — even
an illusory echo from you is

gratifying and, I seem to hear
your sweet voice through the air.

背對河南漫天飛雪的天空

林明理

啊，太行山的雪瀑紛飛了，
奔向永不靜止的河流，——
千里無人煙的山嶽啊，
如今已在光陰裡成了吟詠的歌。

我慨然地揹起行囊，
背對河南漫天飛雪的天空，那片淨土
有股令人無法置信的寂靜，——

一片雪花的回聲，是你
白色的沉默，在老村一隅，
夜，也抹上了憂鬱的顏色；
而你點起了燈，
將片片心事落於信箋上——

啊，太行山的雪瀑紛飛了，
落在億萬個詩句和宮闕之上，
恰似漫天紛雪的倒影……帶著我的問候，
在你匆匆飛離返鄉的一瞬。[13]

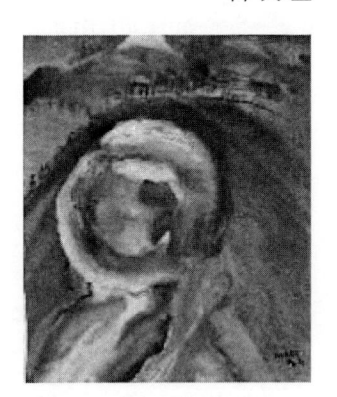

Your Back Against a Skyful of Snow in Henan

Lin Ming-Li

Ah, the snowfalls of Taihang Mountain are in profusion,
Running to the river that is never still —
The mountains of thousands of miles without any sign of humans,
Now have become a song in time.

You pick up your traveling bag without hesitation,
With your back against a skyful of snow in Henan, a pure land
There is an incredible silence —

The echo of a snowflake is your
White silence, in a corner of the old village,

---

[13] 2025.01.09，寫給吾友智中老師返鄉探望岳母重病前夕。

The night, also besmeared with melancholy color;
And you enkindle the lamp,
To write down your mind on the letterhead —

Ah, the snowfalls of Taihang Mountain are in profusion,
Falling on millions of poetic lines and palaces,
Just like the reflection of the snow all over the sky... With my regards,
At the moment of your hurry to go home.[14]

24.

子夜四時歌・春歌 　　　　　　　　　　魏晉・無名氏

春林花多媚，春鳥意多哀。
春風復多情，吹我羅裳開。

Midnight Songs Through the Four Seasons (Spring Song)
Anonymous (Wei and Jin dynasties)

So charming is
the spring forest;

so sorrowful is
the spring bird.

So passionate is
the spring wind,

which blows apart
— oh, my skirt.

愛，在深不可測中發光閃爍 　　　　　　　　林明理

大海是寂寞的，但它的心溫柔，
山並不孤獨，它保有我們心中的寧靜。

---

[14] To my friend, professor Zhang Zhizhong, on the eve of his going home to visit his mother-in-law who is down with a serious illness; on January 9, 2025.

漢魏六朝接明理
古今抒情詩三百首
漢英對照

若有其它地方能替代你
讓我擁有更多濃蔭覆蓋的安謐，
能讓我感到萬物的可貴
和生活的甜蜜，──

那麼，我的朋友，
請沿著溪澗走來吧！
讓風親吻你的憂愁，讓雲把你
擁入懷中，──就像童話書裡的故事。

每當花兒輕歌曼舞，古老的光照亮山脊時，
愛，就在深不可測中發光閃爍。

－2025.01.12.

Love Is Shining in the Unfathomable Depth

Lin Ming-Li

The sea is lonely, but its heart is gentle;
The mountain is not lonely, and it retains the peace of our hearts.

If there are other places that can replace you,
For me to own more quiet covered with shade,
For me to feel the value of all things
And the sweetness of life —

Then, my friend,
Come along the stream!
For the wind to kiss away your sorrow, for the cloud
To hold you in its arms — just like the story in a fairy book.

When flowers gently sing and dance, and the age-old light illuminates the ridge,
Love is shining in the unfathomable depth

January 12, 2025.

25．

子夜四時歌・夏歌
魏晉・無名氏

青荷蓋淥水，芙蓉葩紅鮮。
郎見欲采我，我心欲懷蓮。

Midnight Songs Through the Four Seasons (Summer Song)
Anonymous (Wei and Jin dynasties)

The limpid water is green
with lotus leaves, amid

which lotus blossoms are
pink, crimson, and brightly

red. A lad is, lovingly,
picking and plucking me,

when I cherish a fond
love for the lotus seeds.

曾經
林明理

你輕俏得似掠過細石的
小溪，似水塘底白霧，揉縮
隨我步向籬柵 探尋你的澄碧
我卻驟然顛覆了時空
熟悉你的每一次巧合

你微笑像幅半完成的畫
淨潔是你的幾筆刻劃，無羈無求
那青松的頌讚，風的吟遊：
誰能於萬籟之中盈盈閃動？每當
黃昏靠近窗口

今夜你佇立木橋
你的夢想，你的執著與彷徨
彷徨使人擔憂

惟有星星拖曳著背影，而小雨也
悄悄地貼近我的額頭

Once
Lin Ming-Li

You are light and elegant, like the creek running over
small stones, like the white fog at the bottom of the pool, wrinkling
Follow me to the hedge to explore your emerald green
And suddenly I overturn the time and space
To be familiar with each coincidence with you

Your smile is like a half-done picture
Purity is a few strokes by you, free and fetterless
The pine tree's songs and wind's singing:
Who can twinkle and sparkle in the noises? Whenever
Dusk is near the window

Tonight you stand on the wooden bridge
Your dream, your persistence and hesitation
Hesitation makes me worry
Only the stars are daggling the shadow of your back, and the drizzle
Is quietly moistening my forehead

26.

子夜四時歌・秋歌
魏晉・無名氏

涼風開窗寢，斜月垂光照。
中宵無人語，羅幌有雙笑。

Midnight Songs Through the Four Seasons (Autumn Song)
Anonymous (Wei and Jin dynasties)

Abed, asleep — a cool wind
is blowing into the open

window, when a slanting
moon is shining and pouring

beams of brilliant light.
Midnight hears nobody

speaking, except two people
laughing behind the silk curtain.

每當秋風吹起 　　　　　　　　　　　林明理

昨夜細雨疏落，老瘦樹，
　　沉睡了。被山城所籠罩的小溪，
睡得好香甜！而兩行岸柳
　　像不朽的愛情，那樣的美！

我再也不必憂傷，不必
　　傻勁地做夢，──
因為什麼都比不上這兒
暖黃的氛圍，恰似百年前的月光，
　　那樣柔和，那樣親切。

我喜愛每一處砌築磚牆，
但我最愛的是──
　　　　山石與泉緊緊相連，
內有湖水，碧潭，湧泉，
　　　　都儲在夢中──

我是隻永不疲倦的歌雀，
　　　　在林間活潑的舞蹈；
從今以後，直想睡在記憶裡，
每當秋風吹起……
　　　　你就會聽到我的笑聲。

－2025.01.06.

When the Autumn Wind Is Blowing　　Lin Ming-Li

Last night it is drizzling here and there; the old thin tree
　　Falls asleep. The brook veiled by the mountain city
Is sleeping soundly! And two lines of willows along the shore
　　Like immortal love, so beautiful!

I don't need to be sad, and no need
    To dream foolishly —
Because nothing is comparable here
The warm yellow atmosphere, just like the moonlight a hundred years ago,
  So soft, so endearing.

I love every masonry wall,
But what I love most is —
    The rocks and springs are closely connected,
And there are lakes, blue pools, and springs,
    All stored in the dream —

I am a sparrow who is never tired of singing,
     Dancing joyfully in the woods;
From now on, I want to sleep in my memory,
When the autumn wind blows....
    You are going to hear me laughing.

January 6, 2025.

27 •

子夜四時歌・冬歌　　　　　　　　　魏晉・無名氏

淵冰厚三尺，素雪覆千里。
我心如松柏，君情復何似？

Midnight Songs Through the Four Seasons (Winter Song)　　Anonymous (Wei and Jin dynasties)

The water in the deep
pool freezes into ice

of three feet; the pure
white snow stretches

for thousands of miles.
My heart is like the pine

tree which is constant in
love — what about yours?

你的歌聲純淨如雪　　　　　　　　　　林明理

啊，讓我像山谷裡的野白合，開在
　　蒙太奇式的永恆畫面，──
那兒有雲霧中繁衍生息的森林，
　　和遠離塵囂的恬靜；
那兒有你像太陽般，恩慈、豁達的愛，
　　一向是我最深的期待；

偶爾，我可以讓時光在這裡收攏、凝聚，
每當你步向這一大片蔥蔥鬱鬱，──
野鳥、小鹿為你逗留，而你的歌聲
　　純淨如雪，──
一下子便接通了我的夢想，就像
　　一首催眠曲，夜夜引我入眠。

―2025.01.02.

Your Singing Voice Is Pure Like Snow　　Lin Ming-Li

O, let me be like the wild lily in the valley, blossoming
　　In the montage of eternal pictures —
Where the forests live and grow in the clouds,
　　And the quiet far from the madding crowd;
There is kind, open-minded love which is like the sun,
　　Which has always been my most profound expectation;

Occasionally, I can let time gather and condense here;
Each time you step toward the vast expanse of green —
Wild birds and deer linger for you, and your singing voice
　　Is pure like snow —
It suddenly connects me to my dream, like
　　A lullaby which induces me to sleep from night to night.

January 2, 2025.

漢魏六朝接明理
古今抒情詩三百首
漢英對照

28．

東陽溪中贈答二首（其一）　　　　南北朝・謝靈運

可憐誰家婦，緣流洗素足。
明月在雲間，迢迢不可得。

Two Poems of Social Intercourse and Response (No. 1)
Xie Lingyun (Northern and Southern dynasties)

How beautiful is
the woman, who

by a stream is
washing her fair feet.

She is like a bright
moon in the massive

clouds, so far — quite
beyond the lad's reach.

縱然剎那　　　　林明理

湖面滿是薄染
將落的金光
讓淺玫瑰的雲霞
溶在銀波上
遠山幾行
有如紫精屏風的灰綠
遠比星空更柔然無聲的顫動
動盪的一桅風帆

半湖碧水
不若你明眸的閃爍
在影落波間
我感到宇宙只此一刻
春風拂來
我已幻成白楊之林

昂首矗立
在湖畔旁等候月光

Even for a Moment
Lin Ming-Li

The lake is filled with a light dye
The golden light on the disappearing
For the clouds of a light rose color
To dissolve on the silvery waves
A few lines of distant mountains
Like the gray green of a purple screen
The shivering is more tender and silent than the starry sky
The fluttering of a sail

Half a lakeful of green water
No better than your twinkling bright eyes
The shadow falling into the waves
I feel the universe is only a moment
Spring breeze blowing
I have become a forest of poplars
Standing straight
Waiting for the moonlight by the lake

29.

東陽溪中贈答二首（其二）
南北朝·謝靈運

可憐誰家郎，緣流乘素舸。
但問情若為，月就雲中墮。

Two Poems of Social Intercourse and Response (No. 2)
Xie Lingyun (Northern and Southern dynasties)

How smart is the lad,
who along the river is

rowing his plain boat.
Is she really beyond the

lad's reach? See the moon
which, when the time is

ripe, drops through the
clouds — into your arms.

不是春天的一場雨 　　　　　　　　　　　　林明理

不是春天的一場雨
讓我忘記了時間，忘記憂鬱，
一棵高大的苦楝花，
醉了春天，在風中散作妳的細語。

原來愛情不只是不可逆轉的安排，
不只是一幅伸展風情的畫卷，
是帶有悲愁，或雀躍與平靜，
在飄渺煙雨中，特別想妳……

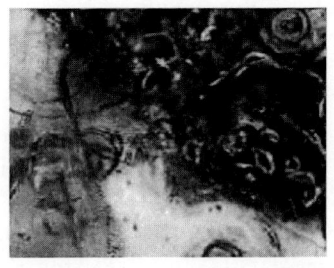

　　　　　　　　　　　　　　　　　　　—2024.12.30

Not a Fall of Spring Rain 　　　　　　Lin Ming-Li

Not a fall of spring rain
For me to forget time, and melancholy,
A tall neem flower,
Drunk in spring, scattered in the wind as your whisper.

It turns out that love is not just an irreversible arrangement,
Not just a picture of spread amorous feelings,
Tinctured with sadness, or caper and calm,
In the misty rain, particularly longing for you…

　　　　　　　　　　　　　　　　　　　December 30, 2024.

30．

詔問山中何所有，賦詩以答 　　　　　　南北朝・陶弘景

山中何所有？嶺上多白雲。
只可自怡悅，不堪持贈君。

80

In Reply to a Question

                Tao Hongjing (Northern and Southern dynasties)

What is there in
the mountain? To

your question I reply:
there are massive

clouds upon clouds.
The sight makes a

pleasant diversion,
instead of a nice gift.

在雪山西稜上，想你   林明理

真實的愛情不必裝扮，
它必然像珠玉山櫻草——
   勇敢盼著春神來到。
它斷然不會跟其他花草混同，
   在秋冬之際，
     葉片就轉色。
此地是閃著晨光的圓柏林，
而我張望的……是你
詩意的眼睛，還有這山谷——
   這春天，——
     全是奇蹟的鳴唱。

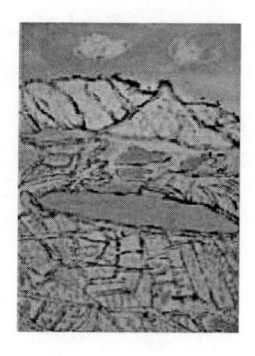

                                   —2024.12.28

Atop the Xue Mountain, to Miss You   Lin Ming-Li

True love does not need to dress up,
It must be like the primrose of Yushan Cowsli —
   Bravely looking forward to the arrival of the spring deity.
It will definitely not be confused with other flowers,
   In autumn and winter,
     The leaves will change color.
This is the woods of Chinese Juniper glittering with morning light,

And what I am gazing at... It is you
Poetic eyes, and the valley —
　　The spring —
　　　　All the songs of wonder.

December 28, 2024.

🦋 🦋 🦋

31．

寄行人　　　　　　　　　　　　　南北朝·鮑令暉

桂吐兩三枝，蘭開四五葉。
是時君不歸，春風徒笑妾。

To a Roamer　　Bao Linghui (Northern and Southern dynasties)

The cassia tree spits two
or three sprays; the orchid

blooms four or five flowers.
The height of spring

without any sight of you
as a roamer — spring

breeze is laughing at me：
spring in vain, youth in vain.

你的話語似珊瑚礁上的回聲

林明理

通往大西洋的路緩緩延展，
月光和山霧
湧入了淺灘，像長鬃山羊的
步履，隨風漫過碧綠的溪澗。

在吱嘎吱嘎小動物的交談中，
沒有人能同我一起回憶，

只有你的話語似珊瑚礁上的回聲，
越來越清晰……

－2024.12.27.

Your Words Echo on a Coral Reef Lin Ming-Li

The road to the Atlantic stretches slowly,
The moonlight and mountain mist
Pours into the shallows, like the steps of
formosan serow, sweeping over the green stream in the wind.

In the chatter of crunchy little animals,
Nobody can remember and recall with me,
Only your words echo on a coral reef,
Clearer and clearer...

December 27, 2024.

---

32 •

山中雜詩三首（其一） 南北朝・吳均

山際見來煙，竹中窺落日。
鳥向簷上飛，雲從窗裡出。

Three Miscellaneous Poems in the Mountain (No. 1) Wu Jun (Northern and Southern dynasties)

The mountain is wreathed
in rising mist & permeating

fog; through a bamboo
grove the setting sun is

seen. Birds are flying and
wheeling over the eaves,

when clouds are wafting
in and out of the window.

我愛晨露中的白馬寺[15]

林明理

初次讀到白馬寺，這個充滿古老莊嚴的
名字，是在微雨的黃昏。
我向著陽光吸吮大氣，
蜿蜒在山徑的木香氣味氤氳浮動，
有被天使吻過的氣息。

在微光倒影的水面，花開正當時，
我愛晨露中的白馬寺，
也愛春風娓娓道來的故事，
還有枝上歡快的白鳥唱和的高音；

但我更愛那暮鼓晨鐘，
山嵐在雲霧間搖舞，如真似幻……
這是深植億萬人心中的佛寺，
又像一株空山百合，傲然於大千世界。

I Love White Horse Temple[16] in the Morning Dew

Lin Ming-Li

The first time I read White Horse Temple, a name tinctured with an ancient
And solemn air, it is the dusk with a light rain.
I breathe in the great air toward the sun,
The smell of woody incense floating along the mountain path,
the breath of being kissed by an angel.

On the water with reflection of a slight light, flowers are blooming;
I love White Horse Temple in the morning dew,
And the story of spring breeze,
As well as the cheerful white birds singing on the branches;

---

[15] 白馬寺位於中國河南省洛陽老城以東之處，北依邙山，南臨洛河，是佛教傳入中國後興建的首座寺院，也是中國面積最大的佛寺。—2025.1.14

[16] White Horse Temple is located in the east of the old city of Luoyang, Henan Province, China, to the north of Mount Mangshan and the south of Luohe River. It is the first temple built after the introduction of Buddhism into China, and it is the largest Buddhist temple in China. -January 14, 2025.

But I love more the evening drum and morning bell,
The mountains dancing in mist, real-illusive...
This is a Buddhist temple deeply rooted in the hearts of millions of people,
And it is like a lily in the empty mountain, standing aloof in the boundless world.

🦋 🦋 🦋

33．

山中雜詩三首（其二）   南北朝・吳均

綠竹可充食，女蘿可代裙。
山中自有宅，桂樹籠青雲。

Three Miscellaneous Poems in the Mountain (No. 2)
Wu Jun (Northern and Southern dynasties)

Edible are green
bamboos, and usnea

longissimi can be
worn as skirt. The

mountain nurses a
homestead, where

cassia trees are
veiled in blue clouds.

憶陽明山[17]公園   林明理

一張舊照片，彷彿是昨天。
回憶帶著我穿越層層綠林，靜靜地，
　走進了舊夢。蟲鳥爭鳴，泉聲叮咚，——
　　淺草裡有蝶，在叫我的名字。

---

[17] 陽明山（Yangmingshan）位於臺北的近郊，是臺灣著名風景區。

漢魏六朝接明理
古今抒情詩三百首
漢英對照

櫻花不來，雨滴奔向泥土，蕩漾在偌大園區中。
　　花鐘旁的噴泉，沾著時光的濃墨，
在空中書寫著離別與相遇的故事。
水花在風中飄散盤旋……以它優美的旋律。
　　閃動的影子不就是我的相思麼？

在你的三月，那些掛滿枝枒的粉紅或醬紫，
　　那些招展的花瓣與豐美的樹葉裡，──
最精采的是投影在水面的天，藍得更清澈，
白得更透亮。而你的微笑，掠過了我的花園。

如今，我不知道芒花要訴說些什麼，
　　但我知道它的孤寂悠遠。
噢，不，它不過是一瞥。假如驟然而落的風
是有情的，掠過這城市的輪廓；

還有那熟悉的石子小路，
那麼，你就呼喚吧，像是初次一起觀賞
　　陽明山。那些疊影，活在詩中，
勾起了我無數的仲夏夢。

Remembering Yangmingshan[18] Park　　Lin Ming-Li

An old photo, as if it was yesterday.
Memories with me through layers of green forest, quietly,
　　Into an old dream. Birds and insects are chirping, springs are babbling —
　　There are butterflies in the masses of grass, calling my name.

Cherry blossoms refuse to come, raindrops drop to the earth, rippling in the large park.
　　The fountain next to the flower clock is tinctured with the thick ink of time,
To write the story of parting and meeting in the air.
The water is swirling in the wind.... With its beautiful melody.
　　Isn't the flashing shadow my missing and pining?

---

[18] Yangmingshan, located on the outskirts of Taipei, is a famous scenic spot in Taiwan.

In your March, the budding pink or purple,
    In the blossoming flowers and the lush leaves —
The most wonderful is the sky projected on the water, limpid and blue,
White and transparent. And your smile is sweeping across my garden.

Now, I don't know what the awn flower has to say,
    But I know its loneliness is far away.
Oh, no, it's just a glimpse. If the sudden fall of the wind
Is sentient, to skim the city's contour;

And the familiar stone path,
Then, you just call, like the first time to watch
      Yangmingshan. Those overlapping shadows, living in the poem,
  Evoke my countless midsummer dreams.

34 •

山中雜詩三首（其三）   南北朝・吳均

具區窮地險，嵇山萬里餘。
奈何梁隱士，一去無還書。

Three Miscellaneous Poems in the Mountain (No. 3)

Wu Jun (Northern and Southern dynasties)

Lake Taihu is remote
and secluded with

mountains after mountains,
and cabin life here is

free from mortal toil
and moil. No wonder —

the recluses retreat here
without any message.

聽那朱鸝圓潤的笛音

林明理

聽那朱鸝圓潤的笛音，雖是驚鴻一瞥，
卻是非常明麗，教我思慕、難忘──
整個牧場好似演奏會的集結，
而火焰樹的天空是雪藍色的……

在空寂的林中流連的地方，
枯葉落了，隨風沙沙作響──
只有紅嘴黑鵯歌聲轉啊轉，
還有風聲、竹聲和帶著水氣的陽光。

落在草坡上的乳牛群，草叢下的
唧唧聲……讓我置身在一片
被微風輕輕搖曳的夢土上，──
那朱鸝飄到我心間，卻又消聲匿跡了。

－2024.12.31

Listen to the Mellow Fluting of Orioles Lin Ming-Li

Listen to the mellow fluting of orioles, though it is a glimpse,
It is very bright, making me nostalgic and unforgettable —
The whole pasture is like a concert gathering,
And the sky of the flame tree is snow-blue....

Where they linger in the empty forest,
The dead leaves are falling, rustling in the wind —
Only the red-beak black bulbul sings liquidly,
As well as the wind and the bamboo and the watery sun.

A herd of cows on a grassy slope, chirping from
Among the grass.... For me to put myself
In a dream that is gently swaying in the breeze —
The maroon oriole drifts into my heart, finally to disappear.

December 31, 2024.

35．

於長安歸還揚州，九月九日行薇山亭賦韻　　　隋・江總

心逐南雲逝，形隨北雁來。
故鄉籬下菊，今日幾花開？

Composed on the Double Ninth Festival

Jiang Zong (Sui dynasty)

The heart is running
after the southbound
clouds, to be traceless;
the body follows the wild

goose flying from the
north. Pray, the hedge-side
chrysanthemum flowers
— blooming? How many?

每當秋風吹皺了雲朵　　　　　　　　　　　林明理

時已兩點半，正是稻浪翻風，
　　諦聽穀籟的時候，——
大地無聲無息，時間分秒過去，
　　只有白鷺翩然掠過。

突然，有歌聲飛向若隱若現的
　　時光背影，把我拉回了童年；
在故鄉那片金色田野，
　　露珠像明珠，掛在瓜棚。

在溪橋上，我喜歡聽風說故事，
　　聽雨不快不慢地下，——
每當秋風吹皺了雲朵，那遠方的
　　弦音啊……也把我帶回了家。

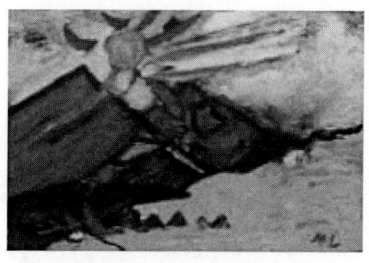

－2025.1.12.

When the Autumn Wind Ruffles the Clouds

Lin Ming-Li

It is half past two, the time when the rice waves are waving in the wind,
    Listening to the sound of grain —
The earth is silent, the seconds clicking and passing,
    Only the egrets are fluttering away.

Suddenly, a song is flying to the back
    Of the looming time, pulling me back to childhood;
In the golden fields of my hometown,
    The dew is like a pearl, hanging in the melon shed.

On the river bridge, I like to listen to the wind telling stories,
    Listen to the rain falling neither fast nor slow —
When the autumn wind ruffles the clouds, the distant
    Sound of string... also brings me home.

January 12, 2025.

36．

餞別自解 隋・樂昌公主

今日何遷次，新官對舊官。
笑啼俱不敢，方驗做人難。

A Farewell Dinner Princess Lechang[19] (Sui dynasty)

How embarrassing
it is today: to face my

---

[19] Princess Lechang has married beneath her out of love for Xu Deyan, a man in the street, but the golden time for the happy couple is short, when their nation is subjugated and, Lechang becomes the concubine of Yang Su, a meritorious general. Years later, when Xu Deyan traces his love to the homestead of Yang Su, a broad-minded man with a loving heart, Yang is moved by the rare true love between them, so much so that he resumes their matrimonial relation, hence a much-told tale.

new husband and my
old flame. No, no

smiling; no, no crying
— oh, my, so hard,
so hard it is for me
to be a human being!

歲月讓我再次聽到了你的呼喚 　　　　　林明理

歲月讓我再次聽到了你的呼喚，
　　那時我將夢見水在鄉間盤旋，──
半山腰，一片果實纍纍的桑葚樹，
　　　風親吻著臉，鳥聲
伸展枝椏的老茄冬樹和雨水
　　所有知曉歲月久長的天空最難忘的一切，
　　　都在我腦海裡，並牢記心上。

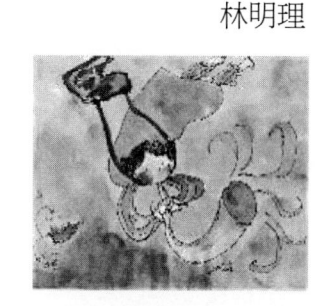

世上有什麼比夕陽波光更詩意？
　　有什麼比少女烏黑的眼睛更迷人？
　　有什麼比得上相依的柳樹悄悄地話語？
那裡，有艘紅船，緩緩漂動，──
　　除了百鳥振翅而歌，
　　除了你孤獨離去的身影與水波一起震盪，
　　除了在短暫相遇的感動裡……
我記憶深遠，好像亙古不變的秋天。

　　　　　　　　　　　　　　　　　－2025.01.09.

Time Let Me Hear Your Call Again 　　Lin Ming-Li

Time let me hear your call again,
　　Then I shall dream of water circling in the country —
Half-way up the mountain, a fruit-bearing mulberry tree,
　　　The wind kissing its face, birds' twitters
The old tomentosa japonica is spreading its branches, and the rain
　　All the most unforgettable things I know of the sky
　　　Are in my mind and in my heart.

What can be more poetic than a setting sun?
    What is more charming than the dark eyes of a maiden?
    What is better than the whisper of the willow tree?
There, there is a red ship, slowly floating —
    Except for a hundred birds singing while winging,
    Except for your lonely departing figure waving in water,
    Except for being touched in the fleeting encounter...
My memory is profound, like the constant autumn.

January 9, 2025.

37．

人日思歸　　　　　　　　　　　　　南北朝・薛道衡

入春才七日，離家已二年。
人歸落雁後，思發在花前。

Longing to Return

                Xue Daoheng (Northern and Southern dynasties)

Only seven days after the beginning
of spring, already two years

since my being away from home.
The date of my returning home

falls later than the wild geese
flying back north, and my

homesickness springs earlier
than the flowering spring.

葛根塔拉草原之戀　　　　　　　　　　　　林明理

雖然不是我的故土，
卻讓我遐思萬千，

草原未曾衰老，
胡楊憂傷如前。

每當盛夏之季，
野馬賓士勝似行雲，
營盤歌舞宛如嘉年華會，
駝鈴響過逐香之路，
神州飛船鑲入眼簾。

馬頭琴
在帳外的蒼茫中浮動，
傳說中的傳說使我迷戀；

這是天堂的邊界，
還是繆斯的樂園？
還是我無言的讚歎
枯守著期盼的誓約。

Love of Gegen Tara Prairie　　　　　　　　Lin Ming-Li

Though not my native land,
It evokes my tangled memories.
The prairie has not grown old,
When the poplars are as sorrowful as before.

Each height of summer,
Wild horses run like speeding clouds.
Singing and dancing at the camp like a carnival;
The camel bells jingling along the fragrant road.
The Shenzhou spacecraft is embedded in the eye.

The horse head string instrument,
Floating in the dusk without the tent,
I am vastly infatuated with the legend of legends;

Is this the edge of heaven,
Or the garden of Muse?
Or my silent admiration
Vainly waiting for the expected vow?

38．

懊儂歌　　　　　　　　　　　　　　　南北朝・無名氏

江陵去揚州，三千三百里。
已行一千三，所有二千在。

The Song of Annoyance

　　　　Anonymous (Northern and Southern dynasties)

From Jiangling, an upstream town, to Yangzhou,

a downstream town, it is three thousand and three

hundred miles. When one thousand and three hundred

miles have been covered, there are two thousand miles — to go.

黃河[20]，你慢慢將時光留下來　　　　　　林明理

每當我穿越時光，探尋你的澄碧，
　你的沉默，憂愁與詞語，——
所有的一切，歷史的灰燼和古文明的塵，
　都慨嘆著。而你的輕歌，可曾為誰留？
　可曾回應我的翹盼、我的愛？

每當我閱讀歷史的片段，而你輕輕
觸及我的臉，從桃花峪四面八方而來……

---

[20] 黃河，世中國的第二長河，也是世界第五長的河流，幹流全長為 5464 公里，其中下游流域是中華民族最主要的發源地，各朝代政府會因受到黃河泛濫的威脅而多次大改道，以及修建堤霸。由於興建水庫等整治因素，近年來，黃河泥沙有含量減少之趨勢。－2025.01.05.

我沉醉於沿途山川，溪流潺潺，──
而你不被遺忘的容顏，忽而湧上心頭。

啊，黃河，你慢慢將時光留下來，
只有你，──
似一幅古樸而不曾消逝的掛圖，
向著前人的足音，淡然而行；
只有你，日日夜夜孤獨而溫柔的嘆息，
　　向著晨曦的光輝一吐為快。

Yellow River[21], Please Retain Time Slowly

Lin Ming-Li

Each time I go through time to explore your blue clarity,
　　Your silence, sorrow and words —
All the ashes of history and the dust of ancient civilization,
　Are sighing with regret. And your light song, ever for whom?
　　　Have you ever answered my expectation, my love?

Each time I read a piece of history, and you gently
Touch my face, coming from all sides of the Peach Blossom Valley...
I am intoxicated by the rivers and mountains along the way, streams babbling —
And your face, not yet forgotten, suddenly appears in my mind.

Oh, Yellow River, please retain time slowly
Only you —
Like a wall chart which is simple and has never been lost,
Toward the footsteps of the predecessors, indifferent and forward;
Only you, lonely and gentle sighs day and night,
　　Outspoken against the light of the morning.

---

[21] The Yellow River, the second longest river in China and the fifth longest river in the world, has a total length of 5,464 kilometers, of which the downstream basin is the most important birthplace of the Chinese nation, and the governments of various dynasties would be threatened by the flood of the Yellow River and make many major changes to the route while building embankments. Due to the construction of reservoirs and other regulations, the sediment of the Yellow River has decreased in recent years. -January 5, 2025.

39.

送別詩　　　　　　　　　　　　　　隋朝・無名氏

楊柳青青著地垂，楊花漫漫攪天飛。
柳條折盡花飛盡，借問行人歸不歸？

A Farewell Poem　　　　　　Anonymous (Sui dynasty)

Green willows are drooping
aground; poplar filaments

are flying wantonly to
fill the sky. When all the

willow twigs are broken,
when all the filaments

fail to be flying, will the
roamer be back home?

那穀雨前夕搖曳的燈火　　　　　　　林明理

當一片靜寂落在老樹的枝梢，
風，跟著舞躍，有種靜穆的美充溢
　　我的心，如在星海中！
在稀疏的月光或在北京[22]的天空，
　　我跟我的影子告白；

沿途的溪魚，園林，天壇，伴著鳥聲的
　　混和著完美的合音。而我
輕駕著扁舟，背倚燕山——
　　航向流星的故鄉。

---

22 北京，是中華人民共和國的首都，擁有三千餘年建城歷史，有著名的故宮（即紫禁城）、天壇、頤和園、圓明園等旅遊勝地。—2025.01.09

我感到那穀雨前夕搖曳的燈火，
　　　在我眼眸暖熱，——
周遭也好似海一般的藍，拾起
　　細碎的水花，一種懷鄉的記憶，
冉冉升起，正從波光映照我的孤影。

The Flickering Lights on the Eve of the Grain Rain
　　　　　　　　　　　　　　　　　　Lin Ming-Li

When a quiet falls on the branches of the old tree,
The wind is also dancing; there is a quiet beauty
　　　To fill my heart, like in the sea of stars!
In the sparse moonlight or in the sky of Beijing[23],
　　　I confess to my shadow;

Along the way, fishes in the stream, the garden, the Temple of Heaven, with birds' twitters
　　Mixed with the perfect harmony. And I
Take a boat, back to Yanshan Mountain —
　　　　Heading for the hometown of meteors.

I feel the flickering lights on the eve of the grain rain
　　　　　Warm in my eyes —
Around like the blue of the sea, to pick up
　　　The small sprays of water, a nostalgic memory,
Rising slowly, is reflecting my lonely shadow from the wave light.

40 ·

古豔歌
　　　　　　　　　　　　　　　　　　兩漢・無名氏

煢煢白兔，東走西顧。
衣不如新，人不如故。

---

[23] Beijing, the capital of the People's Republic of China, has a history of more than 3,000 years. It has famous tourist attractions such as the Forbidden City, Temple of Heaven, Summer Palace, and Yuanming Garden, etc. -January 9, 2025.

漢魏六朝接明理
古今抒情詩三百首
漢英對照

An Ancient Love Song

                Anonymous (Western and Eastern Han dynasties)

A solitary white
rabbit is running

now hither and
then thither; for

clothes, new ones
are the best; for

lovers, old flames
are the fondest.

在綠梢的木麻黃間 　　　　　　　　　　林明理

在綠梢的木麻黃間，白雲越飄越渺；
我必須絕息地守候，恐將那水禽從池中遁走。
我從不設防愛情，那怕眼前佈滿棘徑，
我只能自求賜福保佑；

那故鄉的小路上，有我出神地思想，
溪面冷靜異常，一隻蒼鷺單腿佇立著，
全然不理會我愚蠢的憂愁，
所幸一切都未曾改變，
所幸兒時想像馳騁的夢
如那沼蛙沉潛在睡蓮上，依然靜美自然。

　　　　　　　　　　　　　　　　－2025.01.03

In the Green Tops of the Casuarina　　Lin Ming-Li

In the green tops of the casuarina, white clouds are floating leisurely;
I must keep a watchful eye, lest the waterfowl flee from the pool.
I have never defend myself against love, even if path is thorny;
I can only bless myself;

On the path of my hometown, I am lost in a trance;
The stream is very calm, when a heron is standing on one leg;

Completely ignoring my foolish sorrow,
But fortunately everything has not changed,
And the dream of my galloping childhood imagination,
Like the frog sleeping on the water lily, still beautiful and natural.

January 3, 2025.

41·

古歌
兩漢·無名氏

高田種小麥，終久不成穗。
男兒在他鄉，焉得不憔悴。

An Ancient Song
Anonymous (Western and Eastern Han dynasties)

To grow wheat in
highland field, it is

hard, owing to lack
of water, for ears to

come into being. A
boy in a foreign land —

how can he refrain from
being haggard and worn?

在我故鄉的田野
林明理

在我故鄉的田野，
　　風吹著彈性的木麻黃，
碎石小路橫在彎彎歸路上；
　　我的童年，在遠方，——
遠方有稻草人揮舞，有星辰
　　目光柔柔，歌聲深長。

在我故鄉的田野，
　　風是我的朋友，可以隨時任我
召喚，雨是我的思念，
　　時時等待我返來。暮色中的
耕耘機，白鷺鷥和老牛，
　　風之吻，雨之淚⋯

⋯交織成一幅祥和的圖畫。
啊，故鄉，我的迷戀，我的盼，
我不需要過多的期許，
　　不需要面對世界的起伏波濤；
讓我再度默默記起
　　父親闊步迎向我的步履，——
莫要驚動我閃閃發光的幽夢。

—2025.01.06.

In the Field of My Hometown　　　　　Lin Ming-Li

In the field of my hometown,
　　The wind blows the elastic casuarina,
And the gravel path lies along the circuitous return road;
　　My childhood, in the distance —
Where there is the waving scarecrow, there are stars
　　With soft eyes, profound and lingering singing.

In the field of my hometown,
　　The wind is my friend, I can call it at any
Time, the rain is my longing,
　　Waiting for my return at any time. In the twilight,
The tiller, white egrets and the old cows,
　　Kissing of the wind, the tears of rain...

... Interwoven into a peaceful picture.
Oh home, my infatuation, my hope,
I need not to expect too much,
　　No need to face the waves of the world;
For me to silently remember again
　　The strides of my father towards me —
Please do not disturb my shining dream.

January 6, 2025.

42.

采葵花
兩漢・無名氏

采葵莫傷根，傷根葵不生。
結交莫羞貧，羞貧友不成。

Plucking Sunflowers

Anonymous (Western and Eastern Han dynasties)

While plucking sunflowers,
avoid digging their roots —

when the roots are cut,
sunflowers will wither.

While making friends,
no shy of poverty —

when poverty is despised,
there is no true friendship.

亞城雪景[24]

林明理

隔著窗紗，我想像雪地上空
　　有隻山鷹掠過森林；
我聽見亞城的呼喚
　　和大雁的嘎嘎聲。

路盡處，狐狸緊挨著
　　野兔的腳印，快速
追趕過去，像樹鳥兒
　　穿過松林中。

---

[24] 今晨，美國友人藍晶電郵一張亞特蘭大雪景的照片，有感而詩。—2017.11.22

而妳對我邊揮手，邊微笑，
那一望無際的林海
　　與遠方朦朧的城鎮，
或在意味著耶誕在即的等候？

The Snowscape of Atlanta[25]   Lin Ming-Li

Through the window gauze, I imagine a mountain eagle
    Skimming the forest above the snow;
I hear the call of Atlanta
    And the quack of geese.

At the end of the road, the fox follows
    Close to the hare's footprints, quickly
To pursue it like a bird
Through the pine forest.

And you are waving and smiling at me;
The endless sea of forest
    And the distant hazy town,
Or it means the Christmas in waiting?

43 ·

秋氣   西晉・傅玄

蕭蕭秋氣升，淒淒萬物衰。
榮華零落盡，槁葉縱橫飛。

Autumnal Air   Fu Xuan (Western Jin dynasty)

The autumnal air, bleak,
bleary, dismal, desolate,

---

[25] This morning, my American friend Lan Jing emails a photo of the snow scene in Atlanta, and this poem is accordingly inspired. -November 22, 2017.

is thickening, arising —
myiads of things show

signs of a merable spectacle.
Glory fading, splendor scattering,

wilted leaves are willfully
wafting in the wild wind.

山寺[26]秋雨　　　　　　　　　　　　　　林明理

雨，打在秋天的髮梢上……
　　　　秋天走在雨的樓道裡。

聽，山中天籟梵聲，
　　　和雅而清澈——
還有園蜂在黃花叢裡盤旋……
　　　我竟遺忘了人間。

曾經幾時
　　熱愛這山裡的一切——
在大佛頭前，
　　　朝北遠眺老城；

那些崖壁造像，
　　　遠處松柏蔥蔥。
沉睡中的石佛，
也不因秋盡冬來而絕望，——

依然傾聽著暮鼓晨鐘，
啊我願帶著彩墨，為你裝扮天穹。

---

[26] 千佛山公園位於山東省濟南市，園區內有千佛山、開元寺等名勝古蹟。

The Autumn Rain of a Mountain Temple[27]

Lin Ming-Li

Rain, hitting the ends of autumn hair...
    Autumn is walking in the corridor of rain.

Listen, the sound of nature in the mountain,
    Clear and liquid —
There are garden bees circling in the yellow masses of flowers...
    I have forgotten the human world.

When did I come to love
    Everything in this mountain —
Looking north toward the old city,
    In front of the Buddha's head;

The cliffs are with statues,
    The pines are green in the distance.
The sleeping stone Buddha
Refuses to despair owing to the end of autumn and the coming of winter —

Still I am listening to the evening drum and morning clock,
Ah, I would like to take the color ink, to dress up the sky for you.

44 ·

日南

西晉 · 張華

日南出野女，群行不僅夫。
其狀精且白，裸袒無衣襦。

Wild Girls

Zhang Hua (Western Jin dynasty)

Rinan is famous
for wild girls, who

---

[27] Qianfo Mountain Park is located in Jinan City, Shandong Province, and in the park, there are scenic spots and historical sites such as Qianfo Mountain and Kaiyuan Temple.

walk in bevies
without their men;

they are so fair:
easy on the eye

— almost in a
state of nature.

歲晚

林明理

暴風雪一過，小巷更亮了，
一身白的墨水樹[28]
彈撥　枯守兩邊的布坊。

誰是等待那黎明之鐘的？
是她？
在小院的砑石上──

夜被輾平了，
睜開那戚戚的眼睛，──於是
另一記
微弱的滾軸聲；

一聲聲，在歲晚深湛的空中，
催起……
三峽老街的天明。

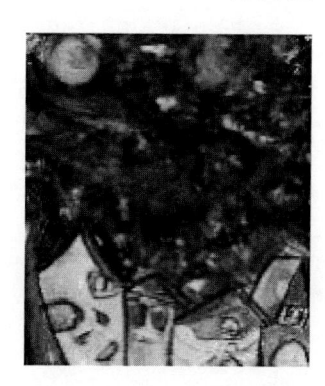

Late Into the Year

Lin Ming-Li

After the snowstorm, the alley is brighter,
A white blackwood tree[29]

---

[28] 墨水樹（bloodwood，blackwood）是開花植物，原產於中南美洲，分布於臺灣、中美以及中國大陸。三峽老街（Sanxia Old Street）是北臺灣最長的老街，有古色古香的建築，自西元1911年留存至今。

[29] The blackwood tree is a kind of flowering plant, native to Central and South America, now distributed in Taiwan, Central America, and Chinese mainland. Sanxia Old Street is the longest old street in northern Taiwan, with antique buildings which have survived since 1911.

Bounces　to keep guarding the cloth shops on both sides.

Who is waiting for the dawn bell?
Is that her?
On the little calender in the yard —

The night is flattened,
Open the sad eyes — and
Another
Faint rolling sound;

One sound after another, in the deep sky late into the year,
Urging to get up...
Daylight in the Sanxia Old Street.

45·

大道曲　　　　　　　　　　　　　　　　　東晉·謝尚

青陽二三月，柳青桃復紅。
車馬不相識，音落黃塵中。

A Thoroughfare　　　　Xie Shang (Eastern Jin dynasty)

A blazing sun of March
or April shines on green

willows and red peaches;
carriages carry spring

admirers, strange to each
other, whose sounds

and voices fall through
wreaths of yellow dust.

想念的季節 　　　　　　　　　　　　　　　　　　林明理

飛吧，
三月的木棉，
哭紅了春天的眼睛。

飛吧，
風箏載著同一張笑臉，
心卻緊緊抓住了線。

飛吧，
楓葉輕落溪底，
行腳已沒有風塵。

飛吧，
我們都把心門打開，
讓光明的窗照射進來。

飛吧，
螢火蟲，
藏進滿天星，——
我是沉默的夜。

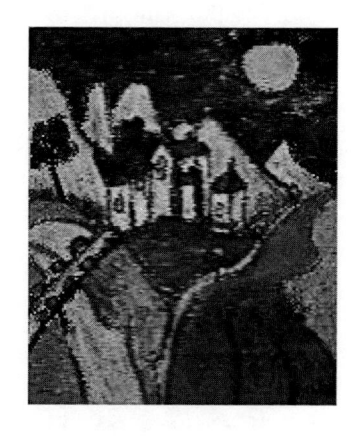

The Memorable Season 　　　　　　　　　Lin Ming-Li

Fly,
The mockmain of March,
Weeping red the eyes of spring.

Fly,
The kite carries the same smiling face,
Yet the heart holds the line tightly.

Fly,
Maple leaves falls gently to the bottom of the stream,
The feet are without wind dust.

Fly,
Let us all open the doors of our hearts,
For the windows of light to shine in.

Fly,
Fireflies,
Hide in a skyful of the stars —
I am the silent night.

46·

情人碧玉歌（二首之一）   東晉·孫綽

碧玉小家女，不敢攀貴德。
感郎千金意，慚無傾城色。

To My Love (No. 1)   Sun Chuo (Eastern Jin dynasty)

A pretty girl of humble
birth, daughter of a humble

family, claims no ties of
kinship with someone of

a higher social position.
Thankful: too many betrothal

gifts from you. The bride
price — too high for me.

致吾友——Prof. Ernesto Kahan   林明理

巨大的冰河
　　　也無法消融我的銘記。
你神奇地出現
激起所有思想的漣漪，
　　如冰晶之中的幻影

似原野樹梢的雪花；
你對我說的每句輕聲細語，
　　讓我生命帶有
色彩、笑容和明燦的未來。

－2018.02.17

To My Friend, Professor Ernesto Kahan

Lin Ming-Li

No great glacier
　　Can melt my memory.
You appear magically
To stir up ripples of all thoughts,
　　Like the vision in ice crystals
　　Like snowflakes on the tops of wild trees;
Each and every whisper you say to me
　　Brings color, smile
And bright future to my life.

February 17, 2018.

47 •

采菊

東晉・袁宏

息足回阿，圓坐長林。
披榛即澗，籍草依陰。

Picking Chrysanthemums

Yuan Hong (Eastern Jin dynasty)

Resting in an out-of-
the-way mountain area,

we sit, in a circle, in
the woods. Parting

briers and brambles,
we come to a creek,

grass as a mat, by
the shade from the tree.

這是個鳥聲躍動的茶園

林明理

是夢?是醒?
每棵植物都在爭取自己的堡壘,
每一隻昆蟲、蜂蝶,都有親人在
密葉角落辛勤地守護;
各種蕨類都滋長於真菌和藻類之間,——

那平野的盡頭,盡是山影,
大地逐將村裡的一幅幅畫卷徐徐展開。
於是
從一隻環頸雉經過,又飛向
白雲舒卷處,讓我引發想像幸福的格式;

這是個鳥聲躍動的茶園,
是夢?是醒?
我已像隻迷路的鵲鳥,
盡情在草茵上唱歌,——
完全不在乎時光是什麼樣子。

—2025.01.12

This Is a Tea Garden Alive With Birds' Chirping
Lin Ming-Li

Is it a dream? Or awake?
Each plant is fighting for its own fortress,
Each insect, bee and butterfly, there are relatives
In the corner of the dense leaves diligently keeping guard;
Ferns of all kinds grow among fungi and algae —

The end of the plain, full of the shadow of the mountains,
The earth will slowly unfold one after another scroll of the village.
Therefore

Passing by a ring neck pheasant, and flying
To the spreading white clouds, for me to trigger the format of imaginative happiness;

This is a tea garden alive with birds' chirping
Is it a dream? Or awake?
I have been like a lost magpie,
Singing on the lawn to my heart's content —
Careless of what time is like.

January 12, 2025.

48 •

松　　　　　　　　　　　　　　　　　　東晉・袁宏

森森千尺松，磊砢非一節。
雖無榱桷麗，較為棟樑傑。

The Pine Tree　　　　Yuan Hong (Eastern Jin dynasty)

Dense, lush, stalwart,
knotty, and gnarly,

the pine tree towers
heavenward; without

the comely outlook
of the rafter, it can be

used as the rooftree, the
ridgepole, and the beam.

山的愛音　　　　　　　　　　　　　　　　林明理

誰都無法否認，
最美的風景，
總要在自己心裡喚起感動才存在。

比如風掠過池畔的蓮影，
抒情地揚起愉悅的歌——
波光蕩漾的山之音；

溪水不斷地敘述著古老故事，
始而復始，
拉長，漸歇，再鳴響。
而我只要一次又一次
傾聽、觀望，
啊，就能聽見這世界存在我心中
所有的回應，——

如夜暮低垂，
永不疲憊，永不戀棧，
依舊追趕著白日——
山的堅毅軀體
也再次輕觸我的肩頭，傳達了
絕不矯飾的聲音。

－2025.01.12

The Sound of Mountains

Lin Ming-Li

Nobody can deny,
The most beautiful scenery
Does not exist until it is evoked in the heart.
For example, the lotus shadow skimming by the pool,
Lyrically to raise a joyful song —
The sound of the rippling mountains;

The stream continues to tell the old story,
In cycles,
Stretching, subsiding, and ringing again.
And I only have to listen and watch
Time and again,
Ah, I can hear all the responses of the world
In my heart —

As the night is drooping,
Never tired, never attached,

Still chasing the day —
The firm body of the mountain
Touches my shoulder again, conveying
The voice of no pretense.

January 12, 2025.

49 ·

桃葉歌三首（其一）

東晉・王獻之

桃葉映紅花，無風自婀娜。
春花映何限，感郎獨采我。

Ode to the Peach Leaf (No. 1)

Wang Xianzhi (Eastern Jin dynasty)

The peach leaves are green
against red flowers, which

are fair in the breathless
air. Among hundreds of

enchanting spring flowers,
only I, with the name

of Peach Leaf, is picked
— how thankful am I.

沒有人能搖動我的記憶

林明理

清晨六點：晨光流淌在
　玫瑰色海面。天空蔚藍，一座紅橋
在微風漾起的溪岸上醒目地伸展。

如同一隻隱形的魚兒在歌唱——
　我將永不忘記曾經到過這裡，
見到一輪朝陽在地平線上。

113

我並非善感，但嚮往大海──
它好像有雙澄澈而讀懂我的眼睛，
　　時而眸子閃爍，時而沉默。

沒有人能搖動我的記憶。
除了深夜：我在月光的撫慰下，
重新看見你滿懷滄桑與溫柔的光芒。

　　　　　　　　　　　　　　　　　　　　－2024.12.30

Nobody Can Shake My Memory　　　　　Lin Ming-Li

Six o'clock in the morning: the light is flowing
　　Over the rosy sea. The sky is blue, a red bridge
Stretching sharply over the breezy banks of the stream.

Like an invisible fish singing —
　　I shall never forget my having been here,
Seeing a morning sun on the horizon.

I am not sentimental, but I yearn for the sea —
It seems to have a pair of clear eyes to read me,
　　Sometimes twinkling, sometimes silent.

Nobody can shake my memory.
Except for the depth of night: under the comfort of the moonlight,
I see you again full of vicissitudes and gentle light.

　　　　　　　　　　　　　　　　　　　　December 30, 2024.

❦ ❦ ❦

50．

同生曲二首（其一）　　　　　　　　　　魏晉・無名氏

生年不滿百，常抱千歲憂。
早知人命促，秉燭夜行遊。

Songs of Living Together (No. 1)

Anonymous (Wei and Jin dynasties)

With a life within
one hundred years,

yet with the worries
of thousands of years.

With the knowledge of
the short span of human

life, carry a candle —
through nightlong walk.

儘管人生如露

林明理

儘管人生如露，
　　我仍偏愛這山村，飛鳥，清風，
萬物種種，彷若都在風的歌聲中
　　讚美造物主，——

我可以輕輕擦去與你走在
　　黃昏的老城，與你看著夕陽暈染
溪口的北側，
還有音樂會的記憶，和童年的夢。

除此之外，其實我對你所知不多，
而光陰，彷彿一位老詩人，總是那麼
平靜，偶爾才會浮現一些幽默；

儘管人生如露，
　　當我回首，四野寂然，——
當我默默凝視這片村野，
　　而你站在遠方，低眉淺笑了。

－2025.01.09.

Though Life Is Like Dew
Lin Ming-Li

Though life is like dew,
    Still I love the village, birds, wind,
Myriads of things, as if in the song of the wind
    To praise the Creator —

I can gently wipe away the old city
    Walking with you in the dusk, watching the sunset on the north side
Of Xikou with you,
There are memories of concerts, and childhood dreams.

Besides this, I don't know much about you,
And time, like an old poet, is always so
Calm, with occasional humor;

Though life is like dew,
    When I look back, the fields are silent —
When I stare into the field in silence,
   You stand in the distance, low eyebrows smiling.

January 9, 2025.

   🦋 🦋 🦋

51．

同生曲二首（其二）
魏晉・無名氏

歲月如流邁，行已及素秋。
蟋蟀鳴空堂，感悵令人憂。

Songs of Living Together (No. 2)
Anonymous (Wei and Jin dynasties)

Years run on like water
running away — and it

comes to the bleak and
bleary autumn. Crickets

are chirping from an
empty room to another

room — so sorrowful,
so sad, so sentimental.

誰能再見北去的風

林明理

誰能再見北去的風？
誰能飲盡月光的思愁？
誰在那海灣凝視長長的老街？
誰能記起兒時提燈籠的元宵節盈盈笑語？
誰能將秋楓寫盡詩意？

誰能再見藹藹的父親，頂著光陰難留的白髮？
誰能將你我逐漸隱逝的愛輕輕覆蓋？
是誰的叨語　讓我如此心醉沉迷？
是誰輕吻我的淚　教我如此相思？
誰能再見北去的風？
誰願與我永遠同在？

－2025.01.09

Who Can See the North Wind Again

Lin Ming-Li

Who can see the north wind again?
Who can drink the sorrows of the moonlight?
Who is gazing at the long old street in the bay?
Who can remember the laughing words of the childhood Lantern Festival?
Who can produce the poetry of autumn maples?

Who can see again the kindly father, with the white hair of time?
Who can cover up the fading love between you and me?
Whose babble can make me so obsessed?
Who kisses my tears and makes me so lovesick?
Who can see the north wind again?
Who will be with me forever?

January 9, 2025.

漢魏六朝接明理
古今抒情詩三百首
漢英對照

52.

三洲歌三首（其一） 　　　　　　南北朝・無名氏

歡送板橋灣，相待三山頭。
遙見千幅帆，知是逐風流。

Sanzhou Songs (No. 1)

　　　　　Anonymous (Northern and Southern dynasties)

You see me off at the
slab bridge, while we

are waiting for each other
atop the Three Mountains.

Thousands of sails are
seen, from afar, sailing

over the river, which follow
the current of the wind.

風中絮語　　　　　　　　　　　　　　　　林明理

在一個繁花世界裡
　愛的殿堂上
我哪裡都不會遁逃
我是我
　一如雨後的彩虹
以我所有的許願祝禱

或許你未曾留意
　穿過這片原野
天空四處雲朵閃耀
但從來沒有一朵

118

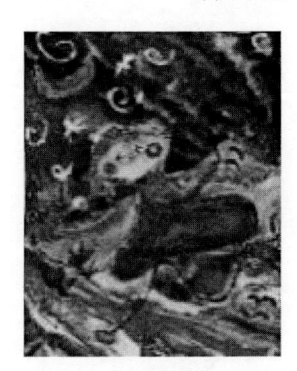

像那樣手舞足蹈……
還唱起了純真的歌

－2022.06.02

Whispering in the Wind

Lin Ming-Li

In the world of masses pf blooming flowers
    In the hall of love
I am not going anywhere
I am myself
    Like the rainbow after rain
Praying with all my wishes

Perhaps you have not noticed
    Across the field
Clouds shine in all directions in the sky
But there is never a single blossom
    Dancing with much a great joy…
While singing an innocent song

June 2, 2022.

53・

三洲歌三首（其二）

南北朝・無名氏

風流不暫停，三山隱行舟。
願作比目魚，隨歡千里遊。

Sanzhou Songs (No. 2)

Anonymous (Northern and Southern dynasties)

The current of the wind
is ceaselessly current,

when the sailing boats
are hidden by the Three

Mountains. How I wish
we were a pair of flat fishes,

which are swimming side by
side through thousands of miles.

遠方的思念 　　　　　　　　　　　　　　　　林明理

我想寄給你，寫在潔淨的
　　白雲輕靈的翅膀上
在這不是飄雪紛飛的冬天

我想寄給你
　　　豪邁而無形式的歌
以及充滿友情的琴聲

雖然祝福在心中，天涯太遙遠
當你的眼睛逮住這朵雲
　你將懂得我唱出的秘密

　　　　　　　　　　　　　　　　　　　　　　　　—2021.08.20

Longing From Afar　　　　　　　　　　Lin Ming-Li

I would like to send it to you, written
On the light wings of the pure clouds
On this winter day without snow

I would like to send it to you
A heroic and formless song
As well as the zither sound charged with friendship

Though the blessing is in the heart, and the horizon is far away
When your eyes catch this blossom of cloud
You are to understand the secrets I sing

54．

三洲歌三首（其三）   南北朝・無名氏

湘東酃酴酒，廣州龍頭鐺。
玉樽金鏤碗，與郎雙杯行。

Sanzhou Songs (No. 3)

          Anonymous (Northern and Southern dynasties)

The nectarous wine to
the east of the Xiangjiang

River, and dragon-headed
wine warmers of Guangzhou

— jade-like wine goblets
and hollowed-out gold

wares — cheers, cheer up!
— between you and me.

大地在陽光中為我哼唱   林明理

大地在陽光中為我哼唱，像個紡紗的姑娘，
用被遺忘的母語，唱著古老的歌謠……
遙遠的太平洋，是溫暖的，
它的神秘與靜謐，總讓人眼底生喜！

而我將向著與妳一同隱入深林的足跡飛去，
成蔭的綠樹把斑駁的陽光倒映在湖面，
除了我們的腳步踏碎了周遭的沉寂，——
那個時刻我早已將愛深藏，久久無法言喻。

－2025.01.01

The Earth Sings to Me in the Sun   Lin Ming-Li

The earth sings to me in the sun, like a spinning girl,
To sing old songs, in a forgotten tongue...

The remote Pacific Ocean is so warm,
Its mystery and silence always make people happy!

And I will fly away to the footprints of the deep forest with you,
The shade of the green trees reflects the mottled sunlight on the lake,
In addition to our footsteps breaking the silence around —
At that moment I have concealed my love, for a great while beyond words.

January 1, 2025.

55 ·

青陽度三首（其一） 南北朝・無名氏

隱機倚不織，尋得爛漫絲。
成匹郎莫斷，憶儂經絞時。

The Spring Ferry (No. 1)

Anonymous (Northern and Southern dynasties)

Leaning against the loom,
without weaving; splendid

cocoon fibre is easily seen.
When a bolt of cloth is woven,

please — please don't cut
off the thread: remembrance

of the goden time when
warp thread is being twisted.

邀旅歷下亭[30] 林明理

秋夜，
　　溢香的荷花已經入睡了。

---

[30] 歷下亭（Lixia Pavilion），是山東省濟南名亭之一，位於濟南市歷下區天下第一泉風景區內大明湖東南隅島上。

當涼風徐吹，
　　整個島上——
所有的花木，還有盪漾的湖，
　　都不禁動容。

你是大明湖中最美的一景，
　　久經滄桑，
不變的是行吟詩人們在夢中
　　輕輕地唱著歡歌，——
每個音符都有一段故事，
每個名士都讀懂你的心思；

我聽見，
　　杜甫的歌裡流動著水鳥的聲音。
當蔚藍的湖光沾上我的眼眸，
我才知道，——
　　為了聚散兩依依，
你可以給這裡帶來四季春色。

Touring the Lixia Pavilion[31]　　　　　Lin Ming-Li

Autumn night,
　　The sweet-scented lotus flowers have fallen asleep.
When the cool breeze blows,
　　The whole island —
All the flowers and trees, and the rippling lake,
　　Cannot help but to be touched.

You are the most beautiful scene in Daming Lake,
　　After a long time of vicissitudes,
Unchangeable is the troubadour in the dream,
　　Are gently singing joyful songs —
Each note has a story,
Each famous person can read your mind;

---

[31] Lixia Pavilion, one of the famous pavilions in Jinan, Shandong province, is located in the southeast island of Daming Lake in the Tianxiadiyiquan Scenic Spot, Lixia District, Jinan City.

I hear,
    The sound of water birds flowing through Du Fu's poetry.
When the light of the blue lake touches my eyes,
I know —
    In order to gather and disperse,
You can bring the four seasons of spring here.

🦋 🦋 🦋

56.

青陽度三首（其二）   南北朝・無名氏

碧玉擣衣砧，七寶金蓮杵。
高舉徐徐下，輕搗只為汝。

The Spring Ferry (No. 2)

    Anonymous (Northern and Southern dynasties)

The beetling stone like
green jade, plus clothes

pestle like a gold lotus
stem embedded with seven

treasures. The pestle is raised
high, before beating down

on the clothes — slowly,
and gently — all for you.

默喚   林明理

在那鐘塔上
下望蜿蜒的河床，
小船兒點點
如碎銀一般！

彷彿從古老的風口裡
吹來一個浪漫的笛音，
穿越時空
驚起我心靈盤旋的
迴響。
我怎會忘記？
妳那凝思的臉，
伴隨這風中的淡香……
妳是我千年的期盼。
啊，布魯日，
小河裝著悠悠蕩漾的情傷，
而我，孤獨的，徘徊堤岸，
彷彿是中世紀才有著向晚！

Silent Calling　　　　　　　　　　　　Lin Ming-Li

From the clock tower,
To overlook the meandering river bed,
Small dots of boats
Like scattered silver!
As if from an ancient wind
Blowing here are the romantic fluting melody,
Through time and space
Sending an echo spiraling
Through my heart.
How can I forget
Your face fixed on me
With faint fragrance in the wind…
You are my hope through thousands of years.
Oh, Bruges,
Your small river bears my long-cherished sorrow,
And I, alone, wander along the bank
In a dusk seemingly unique to the Middle Ages.

57·

青陽度三首（其三） 南北朝·無名氏

青荷蓋綠水，芙蓉披紅鮮。
下有並根藕，上有並頭蓮。

The Spring Ferry (No. 3)
Anonymous (Northern and Southern dynasties)

Green lotus leaves
cover green water,
where lotus flowers
are clothed in red.

Beneath water there
are twin lotus roots;
above water there are
twin lotus flowers.

四月的回憶 林明理

相隨而至的涼意，被遠方的
　　浪花疊影牽出了。
那原是大海深處的歌聲，
　　正盪漾一種莫名的驚喜；
而我喜歡這種看海的心境，
興許是夏日一步步靠近，
　　我卻感嘆四月遲來的春雨。

是啊，今年恐怕也與往年相似，
　　山谷的櫻，也開始著花了。
在濛濛雨中，乃見許多燕子迴轉在
　　沙岸。那時，我們曾打傘而行，
　　　天空是最美的背景。

我戀著遠方浪花追逐著浪花，
　　戀著所有相逢偶得的奇蹟。
可不知怎的，那時間慢了下來，

所有的光影、音樂，都嘎然止於
　夜的沉寂。只有雨中的碎影
一片一片的……跟著日月流雲
　　都變得安適而輕盈。

－2025.01.04

The Memories of April   Lin Ming-Li

Accompanied by the cool, the distant
　　Shadowy sprays are coaxing.
It is the song from the depths of the sea,
　Rippling with a nameless pleasant surprise;
I like this frame of mind to watch the sea,
Perhaps summer is approaching step by step,
　But I lament the delayed spring rain of April.

Yes, I am afraid this year is similar to the past years,
　　The cherry blossoms in the valley are beginning to bloom.
In the misty rain, many swallows are seen swirling
　On the sandy bank. Then, we walk while sharing an umbrella,
　　The sky is the most beautiful background.

I love the distant waves chasing waves;
　I love all the miracles of occasional meeting.
But somehow, time has slowed down,
The light & shadow, music, all come to a halt
　In the silence of the night. Only shadows in the rain
A piece after another piece... Along with the sun, moon, and flowing clouds
　　Become light and leisurely.

January 4, 2025.

❦ ❦ ❦

來羅四首（其一）　　　　　　　魏晉・無名氏

鬱金黃花標，下有同心草。
草生日已長，人生日就老。

Four Come-on Poems (No. 1)

Anonymous (Wei and Jin dynasties)

Above there are
golden tulip flowers;

beneath there is
green concentric grass.

When grass is born,
the days are grown;

when a person is born,
the days are old.

樸素的生活

林明理

我以為親近大自然，
是我心靈趨於自由的因素，——
或者說，這是我生命中該學習的功課，
是上天給我最好的祝福。

我無須從大廈高處眺望遮蔽的天空，
只耐心地觀察周遭的大千世界，
相當近地看到匆匆來去的蝴蝶，
或一隻老鷹在溪谷盤旋著。

我折回頭，那遍地欒樹的花零零落落，
野溪溫泉旁擺姿勢的兩隻野鳥，
就這樣，讓我呆望著……
而忘記了拍一張俏皮照。

如今，我住在一間有院子的小屋裡，
初老之後，同寫作也有了聯繫，
這或許正是我選擇樂於
樸素的生活之因。

—2025.01.10

A Plain Life

Lin Ming-Li

I think being close to nature
Is the factor that makes my soul tend to be free —
Or rather, it is the lesson that I should learn in life,
And it is the best blessing God has given me.

No need for me to look out at the shaded sky from the height of the building,
Only patiently to observe the world around me,
And closely see a butterfly hurrying here and there,
Or an eagle circling over a creek in the valley.

I turn back, the flowers from koelreuteria trees fall and fade everywhere;
Two wild birds posing next to the wild stream and hot spring,
Thus I lose myself in staring…
Forgetting to take a playful photo.

Now I live in a cottage with a yard;
Since I grow old, I begin to have a connection with writing,
Which is perhaps why I have chosen
To enjoy a plain life.

January 10, 2025.

59 ·

來羅四首（其二）

魏晉·無名氏

君子防未然，莫近嫌疑邊。
瓜田不躡履，李下不正冠。

Four Come-on Poems (No. 2)

Anonymous (Wei and Jin dynasties)

A gentleman shall nip
troubles in the bud, to avoid

arousing suspicion. In a
melon patch, don't lace

up your shoes even if the
shoelace is loose; under a

plum tree, don't correct your
cap even if it has gone awry.

儘管我在地球的另一端　　　　　　　　　　林明理

儘管我在地球的另一端，
但此時，驟雨初歇，我隱約聞到
山野的氣息多麼清甜！
我一直企盼你能擺脫世俗的一切，
與我同步在蒼綠的山巒間自由地呼吸，
再沒有什麼比得上聽蟬聲此起彼伏，——
各種花木飽含著陽光雨露！

儘管我在地球的另一端，
對著三面環山，一面環海的一個角落
呆立著，——看雲霧盤踞不散，
有兩隻花斑鳩像佳偶般，邊走邊歌，——
讓我思念之泉眼頃刻間泊泊地奔湧！
儘管有幾對燕子在藍色中頻頻探出了頭，
但又有何用？我只有繼續懶洋洋地做夢。

　　　　　　　　　　　　　　　　－2024.12.31

Though I'm on the Other Side of the Earth

　　　　　　　　　　　　　　　Lin Ming-Li

Though I'm on the other side of the earth,
Yet now, the shower has stopped, and I can faintly smell
How sweet is the smell of the mountains!
I have been looking forward to your getting rid of all worldly things,
Synchronizing with me in freely breathing in green mountains,
Nothing like listening to cicadas' chirping rising and falling —
All kinds of flowers and trees filled with sunshine and rain!

Though I'm on the other side of the earth,
In a corner surrounded by mountains on three sides, a sea on the other side,
Standing in a trance — to see the clouds standing still;
Two turtle-doves, like a couple, walking while singing —
For my springs of longing to pour forth immediately!
Though a few pairs of swallows are poking time and again their heads out of the blue,
What does it avail? I just keep on dreaming lazily.

December 31, 2024.

60．

來羅四首（其三） 魏晉・無名氏

故人何怨新，切少必求多。
此事何足道，聽我歌來羅。

Four Come-on Poems (No. 3)

Anonymous (Wei and Jin dynasties)

Why the need for the
first wife to complain

about the second one?
Eager rebuke brings

more followers. It is
not worth mentioning

— please, please listen
to my come-on poems.

誠然我已明白 林明理

我要從滿天奧妙的燦亮之中，親近你，
因為當樂聲逐漸清晰，追憶便翩翩而落；

因為大海已蘊含我整個思想，
因為沒有任何地方能讓我這般痴迷你。

誠然我已明白，所有季節的腳步，
所有唱頌的詞句，所有曾經的記憶，
都已驅走我心的徬徨，——
因為在地球、月亮和大海的夜裡……
我比誰都在乎你的驚喜；

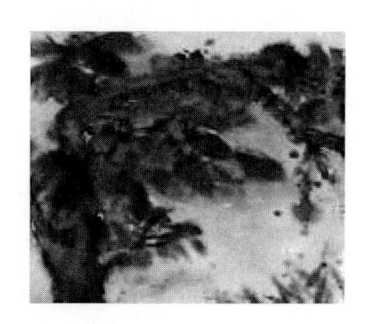

我將通過歲月更迭，
將牽繫於你與既有的詩藝——
哎，你的歌聲在清風的指間迴繞，
在綴滿風景的北方，如一江寧靜的帆。

$-$2025.01.09

Of Course I See　　　　　　　　　　Lin Ming-Li

I want to be close to you from the mysterious bright light of the sky,
Because when the music is gradually clear, the memory will be graceful to fall; Because the sea holds all my thoughts,
Because there is no place for me to be so obsessed with you.

Of course I see, all the steps of the seasons,
All the words of the song, all the memories of the past
Have driven away my hesitation —
Because in the night of the earth, the moon and the sea...
I care more about your pleasant surprise than anyone else;

I will be bound to you and the art of poetry
Through the changes of the years —
Oh, your song is winding between the fingers of the breeze,
Like a riverful of peaceful sails in the north alive with landscape.

January 9, 2025.

61 •

來羅四首（其四）   魏晉・無名氏

白頭不忍死，心愁皆敖然。
遊戲泰始世，一日當千年。

Four Come-on Poems (No. 4)
        Anonymous (Wei and Jin dynasties)

The white-haired old man can
not bear to pass away; in their

hearts they are enduring sheer
torture. The play begins from

the time when heaven and
earth first open and everything

begins to take shape; one day
is taken for thousands of years.

當歲月漸漸飛去   林明理

當歲月漸漸飛去，
  溪水依舊凝聚為動人的
身影，有些歷史的片段被記起，
  有些早已淡忘。

一隻小雲雀，飛向湖的對岸，──
  帶動群鳥歌唱。
這是一個憂傷的春天，因為
  這片濕地飽受滄桑，無奈嘆息著。

樹說：有黑水雞叫著，在薄暮中的
  灰藍色山巒前，──
雲說：我的背包滿載著遺忘，
  只有雨，什麼也不說……

133

除了相伴的風兒早已就緒，
　　彷若時間在此微不足道。
當歲月漸漸飛去，而我帶走的
　　記憶，──美如戀歌。

　　　　　　　　　　　　　　　　　－2025.01.02

When the Years Slowly Fly Away　　Lin Ming-Li

When the years slowly fly away,
　　The streams are still condensed as moving
Figures, some historical fragments are remembered,
　　And some have long been forgotten.

A little lark, flying to the opposite side of the lake —
　　Leading the birds to sing.
This is a sorrowful spring, because
　　This wetland has suffered vicissitudes of life, sighing helplessly.

The tree says: There is a black water chicken crowing, at dusk
　　Before the grey blue mountains —
The cloud says: my knapsack is full of forgetting,
　　Only the rain remains speechless...

Except that the accompanying wind is ready,
　　As if time were of no account.
When the years slowly fly away, and I take away
　　The memory — beautiful like a love song.

　　　　　　　　　　　　　　　　　January 2, 2025.

62．

贈范曄詩　　　　　　　　　　　　　　南北朝・陸凱

折梅逢驛使，寄與隴頭人。
江南無所有，聊贈一枝春。

A Poem Dedicated to Fan Ye

Lu Kai (Northern and Southern dynasties)

At the sight of a north-
bound post messenger, I

pluck a twig of plum flowers
for him to bring it to my

friend in the frontier.
No gifts to make for him

in the Southern Shore,
except this twig of spring.

贈友人－山東大學耿建華教授

林明理

瀑落深處有雲飛，
清江邀我覓林雪。
久別數載今得見，
殷勤明月第一人。

－2013.1.10

To My Friend Geng Jianhua, Professor of Shandong University

Lin Ming-Li

In depths of waterfalls
there are clouds flying
and soaring; the limpid

river induces me into a
search for the snowy woods.
Separation for years, now

eventually our meeting:
you are the first man, like
the moon, bright and brilliant.

January 10, 2013.

63.

秋思引　　　　　　　　　　　　　　　　　　　南北朝·湯惠休

秋寒依依風過河，白露蕭蕭洞庭波。
思君未光光已滅，眇眇悲望如思何？

Autumnal Thoughts

Tang Huixiu (Northern and Southern dynasties)

The autumnal cold is lingering;
the wind is flitting across

the river. White dews here
and there, waves of Dongting

Lake are waving and surging.
Longing for you until the light

is dimming — a spectacle
which is merable and lamentable.

聽微風吹過竹林　　　　　　　　　　　　　　　　林明理

許多人都相信，
你是深冬的春意，——
那純淨的淺笑裡，有我篤定的幸福，
但周遭盡是更加浪漫的海濤。

我喜歡收集花草密談的故事，
蟲鳥也喳喳應和，——
或許擦身而過，更讓我一再想起
那心湖蕩漾的聲音吧？

許多人都詫異，
你是親吻天邊的一朵雲彩，——
倘若我事先能得知
那麼引我凝眸顧盼的話；

啊，我想像著，
每當我佇望著山村鮮為人知的原貌，
便讓我更加渴想，
聽微風吹過竹林……舞於你我之間。

－2025.1.11

Listen to the Breeze Blowing Through the Bamboo Forest

Lin Ming-Li

Many people believe
You are the spring in the depths of winter —
In the pure smile, there is my assured happiness,
But it is surrounded by more romantic sea waves.

I like to collect the stories of flowers and plants,
Insects and birds are also chirping —
Perhaps passing by, for me to think time and again
Of the sound of the heart lake rippling?

Many people have marveled
You are kissing a cloud on the horizon —
If I have known earlier
The words to draw my attentive gaze;

Oh, I imagine,
Each time I stand there looking at the little-known landscape of the mountain village,
It makes me yearn more
To listen to the breeze blowing through the bamboo forest…dancing between you and me.

January 11, 2025.

64・

詠梧桐詩

南北朝・沈約

秋還遽已落，春曉猶未荑。
微葉雖可賤，一剪或成珪。

Ode to the Parasol Tree

Shen Yue (Northern and Southern dynasties)

Autumn has dropped,
departing from the world,

in great haste; the dawn
of spring has not yet come.

In spite of its insignificant
and tiny foliage, once cut

off, a single paral leaf can
be a gem on the royal crown.

禪就是這樣簡單

林明理

一杯茶裡，我與記憶裡的茶鄉相遇；
　　它在星星與大地之間，倍顯安逸。
樹是靜的，我的心是靜的，——只有風
　　蟄居在時間之上。

它要我從容看待世間冷暖，
托舉起夢想，一如晨光落在山寺間，
　　每一塊瓦，每一扇窗，
都折射著普照一方土地的光芒；

禪就是這樣簡單，好像一杯茶，
　　懷著什麼心情，就品嚐出什麼滋味，
它讓我歡喜，——甚至忘記了語言。

－2025.01.04

So Simple Is Zen

Lin Ming-Li

In a cup of tea, I meet the tea country in my memory;
　　It is at ease between the stars and the earth.
The trees are still, and my heart is still — only the wind
　　Hibernates above time.

It makes me calmly look at the world's cold and warmth,
Holding up my dream, like the morning light falling on mountains and temples,
      Each tile and every window
Reflects the light that shines on the land;

So simple is Zen, like a cup of tea,
      With what mood, and what taste,
It makes me happy — even I forget the language.

January 4, 2025.

65·

斷句   南北朝·劉昶

白雲滿鄡來，黃塵暗天起。
關山四面絕，故鄉幾千里。

A Fragment   Liu Chang (Northern and Southern dynasties)

The castle is white
with white clouds;

yellow dust is arising
in the darkening sky.

Frontier passes and
mountains are isolated

all about, with hometown
thousands of miles away.

秋暮   林明理

驟雨過後，船舶在岸畔：不明鳥聲
    在迷濛的山色中瀰漫開來，
然後是風俯在我耳際，同我談它
記憶中的舊事，像首老歌緩緩迴響。

走過重重疊疊的山，恰如前人走過的
　步履，更像秋風吹過森林和海洋，──
那萬水千山的深處，有眾星，和你
　回眸的慈光，帶我進入了夢鄉。

－2025.01.03.

The Close of Autumn　　　　　　　　　　Lin Ming-Li

After a shower, the ship is anchored by the shore: the sound of unknown birds
　　Spread in the misty mountains,
Then the wind is in my ear, talking to me
Of old things in its memory, like an old song reverberating slowly.

Through mountains upon mountains, just like the steps
Of predecessors, more like the autumn wind blowing through forests and oceans —
In the depths of rivers & mountains, there are stars, and
　　The mercy of your backward glance, bringing me into the dreamland.

January 3, 2025.

66·

別詩　　　　　　　　　　　　　　　　　南北朝·張融

白雲山上盡，清風松下歇。
欲識離人悲，孤台見明月。

A Farewell Poem
　　　　　　　Zhang Rong (Northern and Southern dynasties)

White clouds peter out
atop the mountain; clear

breeze comes to rest under
the pine trees. To know

the sorrow of wanders who
wander aimlessly afar, get

a glimpse of the bright moon
over the solitary platform.

煙台[32]黃昏的和歌 　　　　　　　　　　　　　　　　林明理

記憶中的兒時歡樂，故鄉的聲音，
每在夜裡，隨著山麓、河流的光芒
和麥穗，古廟的鐘聲⋯⋯層疊飄來，
依舊和你這麼親近，惹你牽掛。

被水意和黃昏流淌的歌聲引領，
我看見美麗的煙台在自由中騰飛，
有一種生命的喜悅掠過我的心底，——
沒錯，這是你我雀躍的心，如歌鳴響。

A Song at Dusk in Yantai[33] 　　　　　　　　Lin Ming-Li

Memories of childhood joy, the sound of hometown,
Each night, with the foothills, the light of the river
And the wheat, the tolling bells of the ancient temple... floating here in layers,
Still so close to you, making you solicitous.

Led by the water and the song flowing in the evening,
I see the beautiful Yantai galloping in freedom,
There is a joy of life across my heart —
Yes, this is your and my capering heart, like a loud song.

---

[32] 山東省牟平區，因處牟山之陽平緩地而得名，今改屬山東省煙台市。僅以此詩向原籍山東省牟平縣的王守義教授致意。—2025.1.14

[33] Muping District of Shandong Province is named for the flat terrain to the north of the Mu Mountain, now it is under the jurisdiction of Yantai City of Shandong Province. This poem is dedicated to professor Wang Shouyi, whose native home is Muping County of Shandong Province. -January 14, 2025.

67.

遊太平山　　　　　　　　　　　南北朝・孔稚珪

石險天貌分，林交日容缺。
陰澗落春榮，寒岩留夏雪。

Touring the Taiping Mountain

Kong Zhigui (Northern and Southern dynasties)

The mountains tower to pierce heaven, seemingly to split the

sky; lush and luxuriant trees interlace to block out the sun.

The secluded mountain creeks are alive with spring flowers,

and the cold rocks are still white with snow remnant from summer.

與天山相會　　　　　　　　　　　　　　　　　林明理

在夢中，我穿過雪海[34]谷地。
說著流利的古老語言，
又對著一個樂師說話。

我捕捉到這裡的白山碧水，
宛如世外桃源，——
既沉靜又聖潔的詩篇。

我心底有些好奇，
一如童年
走在田埂上釣青蛙那樣驚喜。

---

[34] 新疆的天山山脈，積雪終年不化，人們稱之為「雪海」，又名雪山。—2025.01.09

我無法飽覽所有山脈，
但很高興聽到大自然的各種聲音
與我更近了一點，──

而匆匆一瞥的雄鷹，
遨遊在冰峰間……
絕頂的美。

Meeting With Tianshan Mountain[35]

Lin Ming-Li

In my dream, I cross the snowy sea and the valley.
Speaking fluently an ancient language,
And talking to a musician.

I capture the blue waters and white mountains here,
Like the paradise ―
A quiet and holy poem.

I have some curiosity in the bottom of my heart,
Like my childhood
The surprise of walking on the field ridge to fish frogs.

I cannot see all the mountains,
But it is nice to hear the sounds of nature
Coming a little closer to me ―

And the eagle with a quick glance,
Soaring among the icy peaks…
Beauty in its height.

---

[35] The Tianshan Mountain in Xinjiang boasts constant snow which refuses to melt all year round, which is called "the snowy sea", and it is also known as a snow mountain. -January 9, 2025.

68·

春詩二首（其一）　　　　　　　　　南北朝·王儉

蘭生已匝苑，萍開欲半池。
輕風搖雜花，細雨亂叢枝。

Two Poems About Spring (No. 1)
Wang Jian (Northern and Southern dynasties)

Orchid flowers grow
to fill the whole garden,

and floating duckweed
covers half the pond.

A gentle wind blows a
variety of flowers, when

a fine rain messes up
all the twigs and branches.

雨中的回憶　　　　　　　　　　　　　　林明理

午夜，雨聲挑起我的思緒——
沒有穿越歷史也不會獲得一些啟示，
沒有繼續超越時間也不會
走向一個未知的永恆。

沒有每次不經意地拾撿片段的回憶，
沒有側耳傾聽，又將如何
聽到部落孩童的歌聲，——
以熱望擁抱未來。

沒有錯，我聽到了海波輕柔地撫慰著，
星叢又紛紛匯聚而來……
風依舊常新，
我隨性而至的的憂傷全過去。

　　　　　　　　　　　　　　　－2025.01.13

Memories in the Rain

Lin Ming-Li

Midnight, the sound of rain stirs my thoughts —
Without being through history, without enlightenment;
Without continuing to be beyond time, without
Going into an unknown eternity.

No memory of picking up fragments carelessly each time,
No prick up ears to listen, how
To hear the songs of tribal children —
To embrace the future with enthusiasm.

No mistake, I have heard the gentle soothing sea waves;
The stars are gathering again...
The wind is still fresh,
Gone are all my sentimental sorrows.

January 13, 2025.

69 •

春詩二首（其二）

南北朝・王儉

風光承露照，霧色點蘭暉。
青荑結翠藻，黃鳥弄春飛。

Two Poems About Spring (No. 2)

Wang Jian (Northern and Southern dynasties)

Spring scenery is brightened
by the dew; the mist is

alive with the fragrant glow
of orchid flowers. The green

buds are wrapped around
with green algae, and the

golden orioles fly happily
through the light of spring.

悼──空拍大師齊柏林[36]　　　　　　　　　　林明理

此刻，你已邁向天堂
　　不再憂慮了
在風雨多變的
　　六月──那支影片
記錄了你的光耀
　　也記錄了土地的滄海桑田
它深深在人民內心
　　被記牢。

The Master Photographer from the Air: in memory of Mr. Qi Bolin[37]　　Lin Ming-Li

Now, you are walking towards Heaven
　　Without any worry
In the unpredictable winds & rains
　　Of June — the film
Has recorded your glory
　　As well as the vicissitudes of the land
It is deeply planted in the hearts
　　Of the people

---

[36] 2017.6.10 紀錄片導演、環境保護運動者齊柏林在拍攝《看見台灣Ⅱ》的空中勘景途中，於花蓮縣山區不幸墜機罹難，享年52歲。其代表作品《看見台灣》，曾引起社會廣大迴響，令人不捨。－2017.6.11

[37] On June 10, 2017, the documentary director, as well as an environmental protection movement activist, Mr. Qi Bolin was killed, in an airplane accident while shooting "Seeing Taiwan II" in the mountain area of Hualien County, at the age of 52. His representative work "Seeing Taiwan" has ever made a great impact on the society. - June 11, 2017.

70.

和約法師臨友人詩 　　　　　　　南北朝・陶弘景

我有數行淚，不落十餘年。
今日為君盡，並灑秋風前。

In Reply to a Friend
Tao Hongjing (Northern and Southern dynasties)

I have a few lines
of tears, which

have not been shed
through ten years.

Now, for you, I
shed all of them,

which are splashed
in the autumn wind.

寫給天津之歌 　　　　　　　林明理

生命之流朝向濱海，唱出了頌歌
是在雨後朦朧的拂曉中：
它向東推進，一似山野的蝴蝶
是宙斯最精緻的巧思。

奇妙的你在遠方，卻與我很有默契地
相視而笑，又在碼頭停駐片刻：
或許我能喚你的名字，——
就此與你並行遨遊。

再會了，愛的廣場，天津，
可比天涯般的海河樂土：
我願在鳥聲中醒來，
記起你與鼓樓的面容；

再會了,愛的觀音閣,天塔,
可比海角般的最渴慕慈暉的部分:
我願不再虛耗光陰,
就此踏上這親切的土地。

—2025.01.14

A Song for Tianjin Lin Ming-Li

The stream of life is heading for the sea, singing its ode
In the twilight after the rain:
It moves eastward, like the butterflies in the mountains
The most exquisite of Zeus' ingenious ideas.

Wonderful, you are in the distance, but you and I have a tacit understanding
Mutual smiling, stopping at the pier for a moment:
Perhaps I can call your name —
Hence to travel with you.

Farewell, the Square of Love, Tianjin,
The Haihe River paradise is comparable to the horizon:
I would like to wake up in the twitters of birds,
To remember you and the face of the Drum Tower;

Farewell, the Guanyin Pavilion of Love, Tientsin Tower,
Comparable to the ends of the earth which are most coveted:
I would no longer waste time,
Hence to set foot on the endearing land.

January 14, 2025.

71.

贈王儉詩 南北朝・王僧祐

汝家在市門,我家在南郭。
汝家饒賓侶,我家多鳥雀。

A Poem Dedicated to Wang Jian

       Wang Shengyou (Northern and Southern dynasties)

Your home is by
a busy street; my

home is to the
southern suburb.

Your house is full
of guests and visitors;

my house is thronged
with birds and sparrows.

西藏[38]，你來自不可思議的遠方　　　　　　林明理

我從彼岸來，便跟著皚皚雪峰，
  採灼灼桃花的蹤跡。
那時，彷彿我可以隨心所欲
  走向你——
   走向不可思議的遠方——
你的眼眸
  微微閃光，——
你的窗，正跟我訴說世上最遙遠的故事；

你動人的身影，
   袒露耀眼的光華——
悄靜如高原的雪水，時時流淌在
  藏民的生命與無垠的夢中……

於是我穿越無數的河谷，
  劃破無數村莊黎明的彩虹，親近了你，

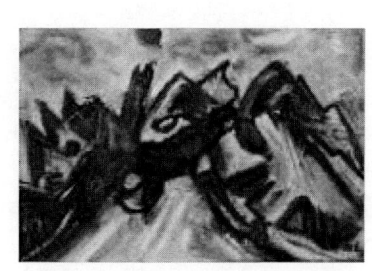

---

[38] 西藏，是中國邊疆的一個藏族自治區，位於青藏高原上。青藏高原是全球最高最大的高原，也是中國湖泊最多的地區。自治區人民政府駐拉薩市，布達拉宮是一座規模宏大的宮殿式建築群。2025 年 1 月 7 日西藏突然發生強震，致逾數千房屋倒塌、多人死傷；因而，以詩為西藏受災者祝禱祈福。－2025.01.08 寫於凌晨

就像走入自己靈魂的喜悅，
　　走入歌詠你的詩篇。

我從海峽來，一瓣桃花拂拭了我的淚水，
有人帶著無比憂心的翹望，
　　有人從四面八方急促而來，——
有人因這場強震而詑異，
　　有人規避你哀傷的視線，而我
湧現的淚和每個親吻——
　　　　都在走向你的天空……
　　　　　　與你夢中相會。

Xizang[39], You Come From an Incredible Distance
Lin Ming-Li

I come from the other side, to follow the snow peak,
　　The trace of picking peach blossoms burning red.
Then, as if I can do anything as I please
　　Walking toward you —
　　Toward the incredible distance —
Your eyes
　　Are faintly shining —
Your window is telling me the most remote stories of the world;

Your moving figure,
　　　　Exposing the dazzling brightness —
Quiet as the snow on the plateau, always flowing
　　In the life of the Xizang people and the boundless dream...

---

[39] Xizang, an autonomous region of Tibetan people on the border of China, lies on the Qinghai-Tibet Plateau. The Qinghai-Tibet Plateau is the highest and largest plateau in the world and the region with the most lakes in China. The capital of the autonomous region is Lhasa, where the Potala Palace is a large-scale palace-style complex. On January 7, 2025, a sudden strong earthquake struck Xizang, causing the collapse of thousands of houses and many deaths and injuries. Therefore, the poem is dedicated to the earthquake victims while praying for people of Xizang. -The early morning of January 8, 2025.

So I cross countless valleys,
    Cut through the rainbows of countless villages at dawn, coming close to you,
Like the joy of stepping into my own soul,
    Into the poems eulogizing you.

I come from the straits, a peach blossom wiping away my tears,
Some look with great worry,
    Some hurry here from all directions —
Some marvel at the great earthquake,
    Some avoid your mournful eyes, and my
Tears and each kiss —
      Approach your sky...
          To meet you in the dream.

72.

阻雪連句遙贈和   南北朝・謝朓

積雪皓陰池，北風鳴細枝。
九逵密如繡，何異遠別離。

Blocked By Snow   Xie Tiao (Northern and Southern dynasties)

Accumulated snow
whitens the profound

pool; the north wind
is singing among tender

twigs. A network of
roads is like embroidery,

and there is no difference
from departing afar.

漢魏六朝接明理
古今抒情詩三百首
漢英對照

雪的臆測　　　　　　　　　　　　　　　　　　　林明理

雪在沙路給我的沉悶
喞起了竹聲。

你是繾翔的歌雀，
把我的回憶
變成開蹚的足印
與時間懸垂的臉平行。

突然從遊啄中
俯衝向最深的去處。
在白草的光裡，
思想之花
逐漸遠離幽黯。

我感到一陣輕鬆，
如音樂在四周浮動，
儘管什麼事仍可能發生。

Snow Speculation　　　　　　　　　　　　　Lin Ming-Li

The snow in the sand road gives me dreariment
To pick up the sound of bamboos.

You are the lingering songbird,
To turn my memories
Into wading footprints
Parallel to the dangling face of time.

Suddenly diving from the swim
To the deepest place.
In the light of the white grass,
The flowers of thought
Gradually away from the gloom.

I feel a lightness,
Like music floating around,
Though anything can happen anytime.

73.

阻雪連句遙贈和 　　　　　　　　　　　　南北朝・江革

風庭舞流霰，冰沼結文澌。
飲春雖以燠，欽賢紛若馳。

Blocked By Snow Jiang Ge (Northern and Southern dynasties)

The wind rolls grains
of snow in the yard,

to be dancing; the frozen
marsh is solid with fine

ices. With spring wine
to warm myself up, my

heart filled, for all the
sages, with admiration.

與黑龍江[40]對話 　　　　　　　　　　　　　　林明理

夢遊多次的黑龍江
即使已處於冰雪的世界，我仍能感受
它的奇妙外表下，有一張祥和的面龐。

在無數夜的靜默中，
我總愛凝望——朝陽從山脈頂著暈環
堅韌地升起；

喔，鏡泊湖，濕地，山嵐，夢裡的舊時光，
那裡，是如此純淨，如此寬廣！
是回憶又期盼的天堂。

---

[40] 黑龍江省，位於中國大陸，省會是哈爾濱。中俄界河的黑龍江，係境內最大河流；故而，省份名字，是由江名而來。—2025.01.14.

喔，就在那中俄界河的頂端，
一隻寒鷹漸去漸遠……像一縷飄泊的飛煙，
奮翅青空的身影，使我顧盼。

Dialogue with Heilongjiang[41]   Lin Ming-Li

For times Heilongjiang has been in my dream
Even though Heilongjiang is in the world of ice and snow, still I can feel
Beneath its wonderful appearance, there is a peaceful face.

In the silence of countless nights,
I always love to watch — the sun rising from the mountain
Against the halo of perseverance;

Oh, Jingpo Lake, wetlands, mountains, the old days through the dream,
There, it is so pure, and so wide!
A paradise of memories and expectations.

Oh, just at the top of the Sino-Russian boundary river,
A cold eagle is fading away... Like a wisp of drifting smoke,
The form of its winging in the sky makes me linger to look.

74 ·

阻雪連句遙贈和   南北朝·王融

珠霙條間響，玉溜簷下垂。
杯酒不相接，寸心良共知。

Blocked By Snow
     Wang Rong (Northern and Southern dynasties)

Grains of snow
are rustling among

---

[41] Heilongjiang, as a province, is in Chinese mainland, with the capital of Harbin. Heilongjiang River, the largest river in the region, is the boundary river between China and Russia, hence the name of the province. -January 14, 2025.

tender branches and
twigs; icicles are

hanging on the eaves.
No compotation, in spite

of a fond heart for hobnob
— we share kindred spirits.

牧歸　　　　　　　　　　　　　　　　　　　林明理

我流向遠方。
　　　　荒原之月早已歸去，
風兒吹自玉峰下，
　　　　天路鋪進我家鄉。

我的睡思穿行萬里，
　　　　而放牧的雪域
　從崎嶇的盡頭在延伸，——
慢條斯理地探尋我的靈魂。

剎時，藏野唱晚。
小雨正好錯過，或直向拉薩河。
你就是虹，總在極地
　　　跨越破曉的雲裡洗亮；

誰也比不上你如許的安寧。青海的
　　天空，朝聖者期盼的聲音……
　　　　忽地將我召喚。
看啊，你是我的哈達，夢裡的詩章。[42]

Back From Herding　　　　　　　　　　Lin Ming-Li

I flow into the distance.
　　　The moon in the wilderness has long gone,

---

[42] 青藏鐵路，東起青海西寧，西至西藏拉薩，是世界上海拔最高、線路最長的高原鐵路，費時四十年以及超過四十億美金的工程預算，經過四年建設，於2006年7月試通車後，有感而作。

The wind is blowing from the jade peak,
       And the sky is paved into my hometown.

My sleep travels thousands of miles,
        And the grazing snow stretches
  From its rugged end —
A slow search for my soul.

All of a sudden, Tibetan wilderness is aloud with evening singing.
Light rain is simply missed, or straight to the Lhasa River.
You are the rainbow, always brightening
     Across the dawn clouds at the poles;

Nobody can match your peace. The sky
  Of Qinghai, the voice of pilgrims' longing...
     Suddenly calls me back.
Look, you are my Hada, a piece of silk as greeting gift, a poem in my dream. [43]

75 ·

阻雪連句遙贈和   南北朝 · 王僧孺

飛雲亂無緒，結冰明曲池。
雖乖促席燕，白首信勿虧。

Blocked By Snow

     Wang Sengru (Northern and Southern dynasties)

The swirling clouds are
confused and clueless; the ice

---

[43] The Qinghai-Tibet Railway, which runs from Xining of Qinghai Province in the east to Lhasa of Xizang in the west, is the highest and longest plateau railway in the world. With 40 years and a project budget of more than 4 billion US dollars. After four years of construction, it was inaugurated in July 2006.

brightens and cleanses the
curved ponds along the banks.

Sitting, unwillingly, close
to each other at the banquet,

snowflakes whiten the hair,
still believing: not at a loss.

溪橋　　　　　　　　　　　　　　　　　　林明理

我是橋，我是溪橋，悄然佇立的一座古橋。
　當梅花開遍山谷，發亮的、延伸的溪水潺潺，
皚皚梅林，宛如雪景，
　　翩翩疏影，即將離我而去；

細雨濛濛，讓花開得寂寞，開得執著，——
　卻閃著光彩，醉我心扉！
而我等待的，是妳飄過的足跡，妳的光明，
　　還有散發著樸素的氣息。

啊，我的愛，這裡群峰如黛。而我是妳走入
鄉野的小徑上，唯一流連徘徊的船；
既喚不回妳眼眸的凝，又不能揮手道安，——
啊，我的愛，妳是我渴望光明、沉默的岸。

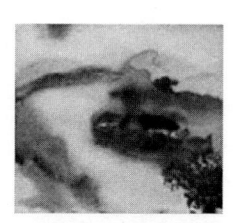

—2025.01.02

The Creek Bridge　　　　　　　　　Lin Ming-Li

I am a bridge, I am a creek bridge, an ancient bridge standing quietly.
　　When plum blossoms blossom all over the valley, the shiny, extended babbling stream,
White and silent forest, like a snow scene,
　　　The elegant and thin shadow is about to leave me;

In drizzling rain, the flowers are flowering lonely, yet persistent —
　　But they are shining, to intoxicate heart!
What I am waiting for is your fleeting footprints, your light,
　　　And your simple breath which is exuding.

Oh, my love, there are blue-black peaks here. And I am
The only boat that lingers on your path into the country;
Neither can I call back the silence of your eyes, nor can I wave my greeting —
Oh my love, you are the shore where I pine for light and silence.

January 2, 2025.

76.

阻雪連句遙贈和 　　　　　　　　　　　南北朝·謝昊

飄素瑩簷溜，岩結噎通崖。
罇罍如未澣，況乃限首儀。

Blocked By Snow　Xie Hao (Northern and Southern dynasties)

Snowing, the icicles
are crystal clear under

the eaves; snow and ice
brighten the mountains

to clog the earth. The wine
vessels have not been washed;

in a trance, my brother's face,
isolated, cannot be seen.

山居歲月 　　　　　　　　　　　林明理

一聲聲中洗騷魂，
幾點霧雨迢曉月；
杏林徑裡有孤竹，
晚課聲中看鳥飛。

Years in the Mountain　　　　　　　　Lin Ming-Li

Through the ringing of a
chime stone, the poetic soul

is purified; a few drops of
misty rain against the remote

morning moon. Along the woods
of apricot trees there are solitary

bamboos; amidst the evening class
birds are seen in their free flight.

77 •

阻雪連句遙贈和　　　　　　　　　南北朝・劉繪

原隰望徙倚，松筠竟不移。
隱憂戀萱樹，忘懷待山巵。

Blocked By Snow　Liu Hui (Northern and Southern dynasties)

In plains and low places,
I wander back and forth,

to and fro; the pine trees
and bamboos are immobile.

With inner worry, I am in
need of orange day-lily; I

forget my sorrow at the sight
of a vessel filled with wine.

緬懷山寺之音

林明理

離開山寺已多年，
　　而此刻，誦經聲起——
我沐浴光明
　　再一次體驗感情的波動。

我擁有的，只是儉樸之道，
　　我所眷戀的塵世，遺忘了也好；
我找尋，找尋寧靜——
終於被一顆星引導，來到佛的路；

在木魚聲聲、八塔的佛寺中，
　　我重遊了這舊地……
那闊別已久的思念，
　　使我像草葉上的露珠般顫動。

Memory of the Sound of the Mountains Temple

Lin Ming-Li

It has been many years since I left the mountain temple,
　　Now, the chanting begins —
I am bathed in light
　To experience again the fluctuations of emotions.

What I have is only a simple way,
　The world I love, it would be better to forget it;
I search, in search of quietude —
Finally to be led by a star to the path of Buddha;

In the sound of wooden fish, in the Buddhist temple of eight pagodas,
　　I revisit the old place...
The long-forgotten missing and pining,
　To make me quiver like the dews on a blade of grass.

78．

阻雪連句遙贈和 　　　　　　　　　　　南北朝・沈約

初昕逸翮舉，日昃駑馬疲。
幽山有桂樹，歲暮方參差。

Blocked By Snow Shen Yue (Northern and Southern dynasties)

At sunrise, birds flutter
their wings to fly; the sun

westering afar, the lean
horse is exhausted. In

quiet mountains there are
osmanthus trees, which are

dim, distant, and isolated
at the close of the year.

蘆花飛白的時候 　　　　　　　　　　　林明理

夜幕從我流轉的眼神中逃離
我的心鋪滿憂鬱
為著翱翔於星宿之間
為著我曾擁有唯一的真實
為著許多編織的舊夢

哦，我親愛的朋友
你為什麼哭了
我可以無視我的孤獨
但無法阻止風躍回每一熟悉的名字
或注滿於流水、山丘中

世界啊，快來丈量我的軀體
為何變得如此輕靈而猶疑
好似雀兒唱著：啾啾啊嗨，呦
在清秋，萬頃原野
蘆花飛白的時候

When the Reeds Are White   Lin Ming-Li

The night escapes from my turning eyes
My heart is paved with melancholy
For flying among the stars
For the only truth I have ever had
For many woven old dreams

Oh, my dear friend
Why are you crying
I can ignore my loneliness
But cannot stop the wind from leaping back to every familiar name
Or filling the waters and hills

Oh the world, come to measure my body
Why to become so light and hesitant
Like a bird singing: qiuqiu ah hai, ao
In the clear autumn, thousands of acres of wild field
When the reeds are flying in white

79 ·

春思   南北朝・王僧孺

雪罷枝即青，冰開水便綠。
復聞黃鳥聲，全作相思曲。

Longing in Spring
Wang Sengru (Northern and Southern dynasties)

After a snowfall the
green of the twigs &

branches is revealed;
when ice is broken,

green water is exhibited.
The song of orioles

falls on the ears, turning
into a soulful love song.

在濱海的渡輪上　　　　　　　　　　　　　　　林明理

起伏的舊堡壘
已不復存在，只得棲身於
被時間遺忘的小鎮上
昔日黑暗的歷史
也沉寂於神話的傳說
只剩呼嘯的風輪
與燈塔，戍守邊城

腦海中的港灣酒館
古色古香的房舍
島上的遺跡、墓塚
都被風擦亮、被雨拂拭……
只有海上渡輪的汽笛
合同遠方鐘樓敲響了
午夜十二點的窗
成了我尚未來得及發出的祝福

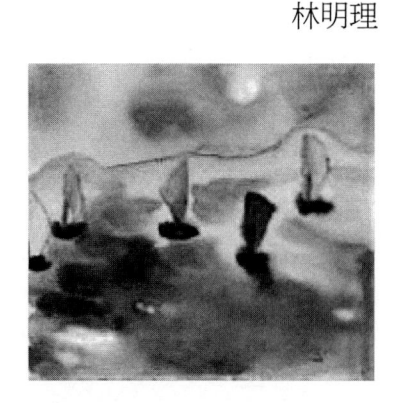

—2024.12.28.

On the Seaside Ferryboat　　　　　　　　　Lin Ming-Li

The undulating old fortress
Is no more, only to live in
A town forgotten by time
The dark past
Is lost to myth and legend
Only the whirling wind wheel
And lighthouse to guard the border town

The harbor tavern in my mind
The antique houses
The ruins and tombs on the island
Are polished by the wind and wiped by the rain...
Only the siren of the sea ferry
Contract the distant clock tower sounds

The midnight window
Becomes a blessing I have not yet had time to send

December 28, 2024.

❦ ❦ ❦

80.

江皋曲　　　　　　　　　　　　　　南北朝·王融

林斷山更續，洲盡江復開。
雲峰帝鄉起，水源桐柏來。

Melody of Riverside Marsh

Wang Rong (Northern and Southern dynasties)

When the forest breaks,
the mountains meander;

at the end of an island,
the river is spacious.

The towering mountains
rise from the Emperor

Township; the source of
water is from Tongbai.

倘若你明白　　　　　　　　　　　　　　林明理

晚天霞光已盡，夢中，你歸來，
　　春也悄然甦醒，──
　　　只有夜陷入憂傷的暗影。

啊，倘若你明白，
　　　為了時間之雨在此佇留，
　　為了返身再望那杵音與野薑花之舞，
　　　　以及所有人的殷切祝福，──

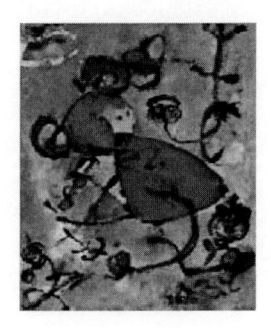

164

你可仍記得
從古老年代到今日，所有莊嚴的
　　聖容，或難忘的故事？

啊，你可是我心頭惦記的星，
　　　又飛向遙遠的國度，
恰似傍雲而生……童話中的小精靈。

　　　　　　　　　　　　　　　－2025.01.05.

If You See　　　　　　　　　　　　Lin Ming-Li

The evening sky has been exhausted, in the dream, you return,
　　Spring also wakes up quietly —
　　Only the night is caught in the sad dark shadow.

Oh, if you see,
　　　To stay here for the rain of time,
To return to look again at the sound of a pestle and the dance of wild ginger flowers,
　　As well as the sincere blessings of all —

Do you still remember
All the solemn faces or unforgettable stories
　　From ancient times to the present day?

Oh, you are the star of my heart,
　　　Flying away to distant lands,
As if you were born in the clouds... An elf in a fairy tale.

　　　　　　　　　　　　　　　　January 5, 2025.

81.

思公子　　　　　　　　　　　　　南北朝‧王融

春盡風颯颯，蘭凋木修修。
王孫久為客，思君徒自憂。

The Longing of the Princes

      Wang Rong (Northern and Southern dynasties)

When spring is over, the
wind begins to whisper; when

orchid flowers are fading
and falling, the trees begin

to thin. The princes, living in
a foreign land for a long time,

are longing for their kinsfolk
— grieving by themselves.

風就是從那兒吹起的……

                林明理

當蟬聲逐漸清晰，仲夏便開始變得
意味深長。風就是從那兒吹起的……
一如穿過溪谷的薄霧，經受幾度寒暑的磨難
又孤寂如風塵僕僕的遊子；

在高高的群山下，我瞥見了天穹深渺，
也望穿了溪橋上攀越山頂的月亮。
樹葉沙沙為我聲聲哀嘆，而我佇立於此，
  為愛情的幻變之音而流連低唱。

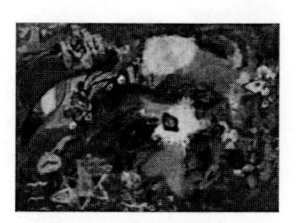

               —2025.01.01

That Is Where the Wind Blows...   Lin Ming-Li

When the chirping of cicadas become clear, midsummer begins
To be meaningful. That is where the wind blows...
Like mist flowing through the valley, withstanding several seasons of cold and heat,
And lonely like a wanderer.

Beneath the high mountains, I catch a glimpse of the deep sky,
And look across the creek bridge at the moon atop the mountain.
The leaves are rustling and sighing for me, and here I stand,
  Singing and crooning for the magic voice of love.

               January 1, 2025.

82.

後園作回文詩 　　　　　　　　南北朝・王融

斜峰繞徑曲，聳石帶山連。
花餘拂戲鳥，樹密隱鳴蟬。

A Palindromic Poem

　　　Wang Rong (Northern and Southern dynasties)

Forward reading：

The mountain slopes slowly,
and a path winds along towards

the peaks. The mountains,
stony and rocky, are rising

like the screen of a forest.
Spring gone, the branches are

with residual flowers in which
birds are hopping here & there;

from among dense woods,
cicadas are singing, unseen.

Backward reading：

The chirping of cicadas is
echoing all through the dense

woods, yet unseen; birds are
frolicking in the lingering flowers,

while brushing the tips of the twigs.
The mountains endlessly stretch

with jagged and serrated rocks, and
the winding path, vaguely discernible,

meanders forward, into the depth
of the slowly sloping mountains.

木棉花開在步道的光亮中

林明理

木棉花開在步道的光亮中，
　像一支響亮的音樂在耳畔喧響。
我步履緩緩，那些年少的天真；
　叫我從回憶中甦醒。

三月。長長步道綠意正濃，
　樹葉在風中悄靜不語，
花在雨中擲地有聲的墜落……
　不朽的時間經久不息。

校園的鐘聲──讓我驚動，引我思念，
但我不敢用言語觸及，──
因為我曾在此歌頌愛情
　神話與夢想，
就像星辰閃亮，卻又隨即黯淡。

－2024.12.31

The Silk Cotton Flowers Are Blooming in the Light of the Trail

Lin Ming-Li

The silk cotton flowers are blooming in the light of the trail,
　Like a piece of loud music in the ears.
I walk slowly, the young innocence;
　Wakes me up from my memory.

March. The long trail is heavily green,
　The leaves are silent in the wind,
The flowers are falling aloud in the rain...
　Immortal time endures.

The bell of the campus — alarms me, making me miss,
But I dare not touch with words —

Because here I have eulogized love,
    Myths and dreams,
Like the shining stars, but dim again.

December 31, 2024.

83 •

估客樂四首（其一）　　　　　　　　南北朝・釋寶月

郎作十里行，儂作九里送。
拔儂頭上釵，與郎資路用。

Joy of the Businessmen (No. 1)

Shi Baoyue (Northern and Southern dynasties)

My sweetheart, you
travel away for ten miles,

and I see you off, a great
way of nine miles; the

gold hairpin on my head
—I pluck it off, to

cover your travelling
expenses — ahead.

春之聲　　　　　　　　　　　　　　　　　林明理

春天，在石縫的樹蛙聲消匿後，
    還不時在我心上縈迴，——
因為，有純粹的生命在林間成長著，
    瀑布、蟲鳥、鷹聲……逐一隱去後，
還存留在被藍色的風帶回的感官裡。

魯冰花，在豔黃花串再次盛開後，
    仍佈滿蝴蝶飛舞的開闊之地——

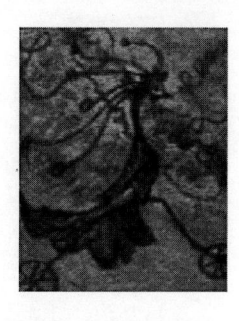

而我在這方淨土上，想你，想你⋯
　⋯如這片山林永遠在這兒等候。
噢，春天，親愛家鄉的溪流，──
　來親吻我吧！也讓愛留在心頭駐足。

－2025.01.01

The Voice of Spring   Lin Ming-Li

In spring, after the sound of tree frogs in the stone cracks is quiet,
　　It still lingers in my heart from time to time —
Because there is pure life growing in the forest,
　　Waterfalls, chirping of insects, voice of eagles... one after another to disappear,
It remains in the senses brought back by the blue wind.

Lupine flowers, after the yellow flowers bloom again,
　　Still fill the open land alive with flying butterflies —
And I am in this pure land, to miss you, time and again....
　⋯Like this mountain forest waiting here forever.
Oh spring, sweet home stream —
Come to kiss me! For love to stay and remain in the heart.

January 1, 2025.

🦋 🦋 🦋

84.

估客樂四首（其二）   南北朝・釋寶月

有信數寄書，無信心相憶。
莫作瓶落井，一去無消息。

Joy of the Businessmen (No. 2)
　　　　　　Shi Baoyue (Northern and Southern dynasties)

Receiving letters,
I write letters in reply;

not receiving letters,
I cherich fond memories

of the past. No — not
to be a bottle dropped

into the bottom of the
well:utterly voiceless.

黃昏的潮波──to Athanase Vantchev de Thracy　　林明理

燦爛春陽下晶藍色的海啊，
　你，守護聖殿的王子，
一抹光在那些船桅高高的舊港上
循著你飄逸的步子通向大洋！
我的朋友，那驟然而落的靜寂
是你身著白色長袍與桂葉的花冠！

Tidal Wave at Dusk — to Athanase Vantchev de Thracy
　　　　　　　　　　　　　　Lin Ming-Li

Oh crystal blue sea under the bright spring sun,
　You, prince of the temple,
A light follows your free fluttering steps
To the ocean in those old masted harbors!
My friend, the suddenly falling silence
Is your crown of white robes and laurel leaves!

🦋 🦋 🦋

85 •

估客樂四首（其三）　　　　　　南北朝・釋寶月

大艑珂峨頭，何處發揚州。
借問艑上郎，見儂所歡不？

Joy of the Businessmen (No. 3)
　　　　　Shi Baoyue (Northern and Southern dynasties)

A great boat is brilliantly
decorated with jade,

which starts from the
metropolis of Yangzhou.

Pray, the boy on the boat —
are you happy to see me?

遠方的綠島[44]　　　　　　　　　　　　　　　　林明理

晨光熹微中，你以一隻俯臥的雄獅姿態，
吸引我。
夜裡，來自深海珊瑚礁岩的聲音，
悠悠緩緩，伴我飛翔——

啊，像世間所有相遇都是久別重逢，
你已緊貼我的思緒……
回憶，淚水，已逝的歡樂時光。

我願像透明的風，橫越太平洋。
即使你有真實，閃爍的眼眸
沒有虛妄，——
或者促你在夢中，岸邊閃著奪目的光燦。

Green Island[45] in the Distance　　　　　　Lin Ming-Li

In the light of morning, you attract me
As a prone lion.
At night, the sound from the deep reef rock,
Leisurely and slowly, to accompany me in flying —

Oh, like all encounters in the world which are reunion after a long absence,
You have clung to my thoughts…
Memories, tears, and happy times which are gone.

---

[44] 綠島 Green Island，位於臺灣臺東縣東南方外海，太平洋之上，為臺東縣的離島鄉之一。－2025.1.13

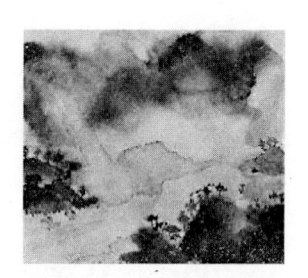

[45] Green Island, located in the southeast of Taitung County, Taiwan, in the Pacific Ocean, is one of the outlying islands of Taitung County. -January 13, 2025.

I would like to be the transparent wind, to cross the Pacific Ocean.
Even if you have true, twinkling eyes
Without any touch of vanity —
Or in your dreams, the shore shines with a dazzling light.

86.

估客樂四首（其四） 南北朝・釋寶月

初發揚州時，船出平津泊。
五兩如竹林，何處相尋博。

Joy of the Businessmen (No. 4)

Shi Baoyue (Northern and Southern dynasties)

When the boats start
from Yangzhou, the

ferry is so quiet. The
masts are thick like a

bamboo forest — how
do they greet each other?

寫給鞏義[46]之歌 林明理

輝耀的夜從大峪溝上升起。
青龍山的小鎮啊，鞏義的母親！
你像一幅綠色的畫帷，
南依嵩山，北靠黃河；

從古道繞過蜿蜒的山脊，
四山環拱，閃著一種天藍的澄淨……
在雲霧的禪音之間，
罕見而莊嚴。

---

[46] 鞏義市位於中國河南省鄭州市下轄的一個縣級市。—2025.01.14

當我走向這沃土，叢林，
走向灰瓦白牆，
走向飽受風雨的古寺，
我相信你並不只是一個傳說。

我將碑刻上的故事，藏在一朵記憶的
雲朵，並開始追逐這些遠山的回音。
看哪，河水清清，
看遍野的桃花林，杜甫故里的住處。

當四季的風吹過老橋，還有故鄉的
樂音，啊，鞏義的母親，
依舊守護著子民，從不厭倦。

誰都無法否認。
只要用眼睛，就能看到你的不屈不撓。
只要用耳朵，就能聽見你——
既無矯情也不矯飾的聲音！

A Song for Gongyi[47]   Lin Ming-Li

The bright night rises from Dayu Valley.
Oh the town of Qinglongshan, mother of Gongyi!
You are like a green painting curtain,
To the south by Songshan Mountain, to the north by the Yellow River;

From the ancient road around the winding ridge,
Four mountains round the arch, shining a kind of sky blue clarity...
Between the zen sounds of the clouds,
Rare and solemn.

When I walk to the fertile soil, to the jungle,
To the gray tiles and white walls,
To the storm-ridden ancient temple,
I believe that you are not merely a legend.

---

[47] Gongyi City is a county-level city under the jurisdiction of Zhengzhou City, Henan Province, China. -January 14, 2025.

I hide the story of the inscription in a cloud
Of memory, and begin to chase the echoes of these distant mountains.
Look, the river is clear and limpid,
Look at the forest of peach blossoms all over the field, the abode of Du Fu.

When the wind of the four seasons blows across the old bridge, there is music
Of the hometown, oh, the mother of Gongyi,
Still guarding the people, never tired of it.

Nobody can deny it.
If with the eyes, your indomitable spirit can be seen.
If with your ears, your voice — neither pretentious
nor pretentious — can be heard!

87 •

望雪詩   南北朝·虞羲

歲杪雲晝昏，玄池冰夜結。
遠風金河起，吹我玉山雪。

Watching Snow   Yu Xi (Northern and Southern dynasties)

At the close of the year,
the clouds are dim and

dark; the deep pool is
frozen in the night. A

distant wind is arising
from the golden river,

to blow the snow —
atop the Jade Mountain.

故鄉[48]之月依舊明燦

林明理

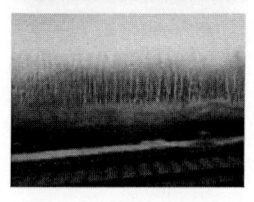

時光飛馳，又是一年歲暮。
此地是寧靜的夜，反覆的雨
彈奏著似旅愁卻抒情的老調。
而彼處緊臨沁河，——
密林中有些老屋，彷彿飛出
第一隻雛鳥，是我欣愛的珍寶。

此地有太平洋海波和我問候的
聲響，只有孤獨的靜謐通向你
和你的返鄉之路……
那兒有午夜鳥雀的啼囀，
冷風依舊送來一地的
寒——

我的友人啊，
急急飛馳而過的，——不是
你眼前長長的鐵軌，而是回憶
如搖晃不停的雲海，默默伸展……
那深夜星子無語的時刻，唯有
咱們故鄉之月依舊明燦。

Still Bright Is the Hometown[49] Moon   Lin Ming-Li

Time flies, again it is the close of the year.
Here it is a quiet night, repeated rain
Playing like a melancholy yet lyrical old tune.
And there, close to the Qinhe River —

---

[48] 吾友張智中教授的家鄉在河南省博愛縣孝敬鎮，緊鄰沁河；春節前匆匆返鄉探視高齡九十八歲的岳母時，拍攝了幾張老家照片，以及搭高鐵車窗外的風景回傳給我，有感而作。－2025.1.15

[49] My friend professor Zhang Zhizhong's hometown is in Xiaojing Township, Bo'ai County, Henan Province, close to the Qinhe River. Before the Spring Festival, he hurried back to his hometown to visit his 97-year-old mother-in-law, taking a few photos about his hometown and the scenery without the window of the high-speed train. The poem is inspired at sight of his photos. -January 15, 2025.

Some old houses in the dense forest, seemingly the first baby bird
Is flying out, which is the asset treasured by me.

Here the waves of the Pacific Ocean and the sound of my
Greeting, only the silence of solitude
Leads to you and your way home...
There is the midnight singing of the birds,
And the cold wind still brings a groundful of
Cold —

Oh my friend,
It is not the long track in front of you, but
The memory like a raging sea
Of clouds, silently stretching...
When the stars are speechless in the deep night, only
The hometown moon is still bright.

88 ·

邊城思 　　　　　　　　　　　　　南北朝·何遜

柳黃未吐葉，水綠半含苔。
春色邊城動，客思故鄉來。

Pining in the Border Town

He Xun (Northern and Southern dynasties)

The willows are yellowing,
not yet leafing; the water

is green, half covered
with moss. Spring

is in motion in the
border town, where

homesickness travels
here from hometown.

回憶似細雨彈奏的音符

林明理

冬盡，春天就靠過來了。
我在風的號角中前進，除了
　一座瓦藍色的衝浪小屋，
　　浪花
敲擊著礁石的聲響；

我看不到你臉上映照的滄桑，
也看不到玫瑰色的天空慢慢轉淡。
在山村的小路上，只能猜想：
諾大的大地塵土，哪裡才屬於
　我眷顧的地方？

椰林，沙丘，廢棄的哨站，——
馬鞍藤，海濱植物的莖芽，
　　三月的百花……
都將揮別而逝，只有
回憶似細雨彈奏的音符。

—2025.01.01

Memories Are Like the Notes Played by a Drizzle

Lin Ming-Li

Winter over, spring is around the corner.
I march in the horn of the wind, except for
　A tiled blue surf hut,
　　The sound of
Waves beating on the reef;

I fail to see the vicissitudes of life on your face,
Nor can I see the rosy sky slowly fading.
On the path in the mountain village, I can only guess:
On the boundless dusty earth, where
　Is the place that is under my care?

Coconut groves, sand dunes, abandoned outposts —
Saddle vines, the stem buds of seashore plants,

The flowers of March....
Will wave goodbye, only
Memories are like the notes played by a drizzle.

January 1, 2025.

89.

為人妾怨

南北朝・何遜

燕戲還簷際，花飛落枕前。
寸心君不見，拭淚坐調弦。

Complaint of Being a Concubine

He Xun (Northern and Southern dynasties)

Swallows are frolicking
under the eaves; flowers

are flying to fall on
the pillows. An inch

of my heart — you fail
to see, until I, sitting

and tuning before the
zither, shed copious tears.

暮春的石梯坪[50]

林明理

你告訴我，相傳很久以前
峽谷裡的水向東流與海濤相互激盪……
就這樣一代代，造就了這裡的傳奇。

在潮來潮往之間，
請仔細聽好海潮中各種生命的呢喃，

---

[50] 石梯坪（Shitiping），位於臺灣花蓮縣，因風景區的地形呈梯狀而得名。—2025.01.13

像是神秘的寶庫。
當晨曦來臨，我怎能安靜？

雖然有魚群，螃蟹和海星自由地舒展、追逐，
有具大的海岸階地，
所有的斑駁與痕跡，在山海的包圍中，
存在著巨大的寧靜，──

只有大海仍溫柔地唱著一首天然
而不平凡的歌──
像神話裡最擅長歌舞的潘朵拉一樣；
　在暮春，我踏上了這片樂土。

Shitiping[51] in Late Spring　　　　　Lin Ming-Li

You tell me, legend has it that long ago
The waters of the valley flow east and stir with the waves...
Thus, generation after generation, the legend here is created.

Between the tides rising and falling,
Please listen carefully to the whispers of various lives in the sea,
Like a mysterious treasure house.
When morning light comes, how can I be quiet?

Although there are schools of fish, crabs and starfish swimming and chasing freely,
There are large coastal terraces,
All mottled spots and traces, surrounded by seas and mountains,
There is a great peace —

Only the sea still sings softly a heavenly
Yet extraordinary song —
Like Pandora, the best dancer in mythology;
　In late spring, I set foot on this promised land.

---

[51] Shitiping, located in Hualien County, Taiwan, is named after the ladder-shaped pattern of the landscape. -January 13, 2025.

90．

詠春風詩   　　　　　　　　　　　　　南北朝・何遜

可聞不可見，能重複能輕。
鏡前飄落粉，琴上響餘聲。

Ode to Spring Wind

　　　　　　　　He Xun (Northern and Southern dynasties)

Audible, yet un-
seeable; heavy, yet

light. Dust falling
and scattering before

the mirror; lingering
voice from the zither.

在山角轉彎處　　　　　　　　　　　　　　　　林明理

陽光落在傾斜的綠坡，
一隻黑貓出現於
山角的轉彎處，——
風是輕的，帶有咸豐草香味。

在沒有一點雜色的林中，溪光
忽隱忽顯，那沉睡千年的山石間，
只有一顆星子在同我說話，——
如母親眼裡的溫柔。

站在更高處，眼下點點船隻
來往於天宇之下。
我曾是追夢的捕手，也曾
蹉跎過歲月，而如今，——

那蔚藍還在天空，
墨綠也還坐落在山坡上，

你的影子和鳥鳴
仍活躍在微笑的山丘中。

—2025.01.01

At the Corner of the Mountain

Lin Ming-Li

The sun falls on the green slope aslant,
A black cat appears
At the corner of the mountain —
The wind is light, scented with salty grass.

In the forest without a speck of color, the light of stream
Appear and disappear, among the rocks which have slept through thousands of years,
Only a star is speaking to me —
As gentle as the eyes of my mother.

Standing on a greater height, viewing dots after dots of boats
Which are coming and going below the sky.
I have been the catcher of dreams, and
I have wasted my years, and now —

The blue is still in the sky,
The dark green is still on the hillside,
Your shadow and the song of birds
Are still alive in the smiling hills.

January 1, 2025.

91·

擬古聯句

南北朝·何遜

家本青山下，好上青山上。
青山不可上，一上一惆悵。

After the Ancient Quatrain

He Xun (Northern and Southern dynasties)

My home beneath
the blue mountain,

it is easy to climb
atop the blue mountain.

No — no climbing
the blue mountain：

the climbing is tinged
with melancholy.

當月光漫舞時

林明理

你走來，在背光處，
　身影溫柔修長。
此地是空蕩蕩的操場，
濃淡不一的樹影激蕩著繁星
　竭力歌唱的曲調。

當月光漫舞時，我感到
夜鶯喚起的清音，彷若置身
　在史詩的夢幻中。
只有懇求上主，──
為我添上愛情的奇力。

－2024.12.29

When the Moonlight Is Slowly Dancing Lin Ming-Li

You are coming, in the backlight,
　Your figure gentle and slender.
Here it is an empty playground,
The trees shadows with various shades are dancing with a maze of stars
　The tune of efforts-making singing.

When the moonlight dances, I feel
The pure sound of the nightingale, as if

183

I were In an epic dream.
I only pray Lord —
To give me the magic power of love.

               December 29, 2024.

92 ·

月中飛螢詩   南北朝·紀少瑜

遠度時依幕，斜來如畏窗。
向月光還盡，臨池影更雙。

The Firefly Flying Through the Moon
       Ji Shaoyu (Northern and Southern dynasties)

Flying afar, the firefly flies
against the canopy of heaven;

flitting aslant, it seems
to be afraid of the window.

Toward the moon, it loses
all its luminance; above

the pond, it turns into
two: its shadow and itself.

愛的讚歌   林明理

藍色冰湖上
 兩隻寒鴨
  腳蹼快速拍動
彼此相伴，輕輕
 掠過白樺林
多麼靜好
  令人羨煞

就像愛情
　　來得奇妙
當它來時
　　仍會迫不及待
　　仍會理解那份激動
就像獨行荒野中
　　採擷一小串鵝莓
　　孩子般的
　　　手舞足蹈

啊，只有它
無論黑夜或白天
　　永遠不息
又有誰能詮釋
它的面容
　　或滄桑
　　或最美的樣子

－2022.01.16

The Hymn of Love　　　　　　　　　　Lin Ming-Li

On the blue ice lake
　　Two cold ducks
　　　　Flipping quickly their fins
Together, gently
　　Passing through the birch forest
So nice and quiet
　　So enviable

Like love
　　Which comes so wonderfully
When it comes
　　You burst with impatience
　　And the understandable excitement
Just like solitary walking in wilderness
　　To pick a bunch of gooseberries
　　　Like a child
　　　　To kick up my heels

Oh only it
Whether day or night
   Never stops
Who can explain
Its face
   Or vicissitudes
   Or its height of beauty

January 16, 2022.

93·

詠長信宮中草　　　　　　　　　　　南北朝·庾肩吾

委翠似知節，含芳如有情。
全由履跡少，並欲上階生。

Ode to Grass in the Palace

Yu Jianwu (Northern and Southern dynasties)

Knowing the change of
the season, the grass is

shedding its green; still
sweet-scented, it seems

to be with a lingering
emotion. Sparse and sparser

the footsteps here — the grass
is aging, and invading the stairs.

每當思念如蝶翩然而來　　　　　　　　林明理

每當思念如蝶翩然而來，
　木麻黃林的風聲又嘩嘩吹起，——
我會想起月光灑遍故鄉的田野，
　恍若看到了父親的愉悅。

186

當自己聆聽歲月低語，學會向父母
　　感恩的時候，時光卻已老去……
而往日的歡樂，——兒時的記趣
　　於每絲微微的感動中。

每當思念如蝶翩然而來，
　　金色稻海在簇簇秋風中搖曳，——
我在夢中所憶起的父親的愛，
無法逐一細數，怕是有千萬個美好。

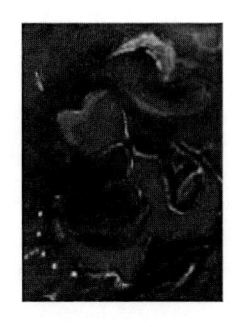

　　　　　　　　　　　　－2025.01.02

Whenever Yearning Comes Lightly Like Butterflies
　　　　　　　　　　　　　　　Lin Ming-Li

Whenever yearning comes lightly like butterflies
　　The wind of the casuarina forest is blowing again —
I will think of the moonlight spilling over the fields of my hometown,
　　As if I see my father's joy.

When I listen to the whispers of the years, learn to be grateful
　　To my parents, time has grown old...
The past joys — memory of childhood
　　In each time of being touched.

Whenever yearning comes lightly like butterflies,
　　The sea of golden rice swaying in the autumn wind in clusters —
The love of my father I remember in my dream
Fails to be counted one by one, in spite of thousands of beautiful things.
　　　　　　　　　　　　　　　January 2, 2025.

春別詩四首（其一）　　　　　南北朝・蕭子顯

翻鶯度燕雙比翼，楊柳千條共一色。
但看陌上攜手歸，誰能對此空相憶？

Bidding Adieu to Spring (No. 1)

Xiao Zixian (Northern and Southern dynasties)

The orioles and swallows
fly from a pair to another

pair; willows, myriads of
them, are of the same color.

In the field, couples are seen
returning, hand in hand; facing

this, who can refrain from
remembering the sweet hours?

當黃昏的淡雲飄來

林明理

大地靜寂，但浮雲層層翻湧，
外界的一切輕浮，彷若雲煙，
只有時間在注視著我。

遂想起蟬鳴的童年，
水牛在遠方放牧，
舞動的金黃稻穗重現腦海；

當黃昏的淡雲飄來，
時間泳於鋪滿草皮的碎石上，除了
陽光在花間跳舞，還是陽光。

而那些自由歡快的蟬，
金雨紛飛的舊路，閃耀的蔗田
與斑斕的夢想……在回眸一瞥間。

－2025.01.11

When the Evening Pale Clouds Come Here

Lin Ming-Li

The earth is still, but clouds are rising,
Everything outside is light, like clouds;
Only time is watching me.

Then to think of the childhood aloud with the chirping of cicadas,
Buffalo grazing in the distance,
Dancing golden rice ears reappearing in my mind;

When the evening pale clouds come here
Time swims on the gravel covered with turf, except for
The sunshine dancing among the flowers, still the sunshine.

Those free and cheerful cicadas,
The old road of sprinkling golden rain, the shining sugarcane fields
And the brilliant dreams... In the instant of a backward glance.

January 11, 2025.

95.

春別詩四首（其四） 　　　　　　　南北朝・蕭子顯

銜悲攬涕別心知，桃花李花任風吹。
本知人心不似樹，何意人別似花離？

Bidding Adieu to Spring (No. 4)
Xiao Zixian (Northern and Southern dynasties)

In sorrowful tears, the parting
hearts know the bitterness

of separation; peach flowers
and plum blossoms are being

blown in the wind. Human
heart is different from the

trees — why parting people
are like parting flowres?

藍色的眼淚 　　　　　　　　　　　　林明理

大海灰暗而寂然
眼淚卻得不到回應

頃刻我在你陰鬱裡找到
透明的靈魂

大海灰暗而寂然
無數雨夜、激盪的鐘聲
像沉重的煙
漫無目標地伸展你的命運

在這蒼蒼茫茫的雪原下
我心漂蕩
在北極熊血染的冰川上停泊
用毫不狡獪的麋鹿運載著未來無阻的長空[52]

Blue Tears   Lin Ming-Li

The sea is grey and silent
Tears are not answered
In an instant I find your transparent
Soul in your gloom

The sea is grey and silent
Countless rainy nights, the ringing of the bell
Like heavy smoke
Spreads your destiny aimlessly

Beneath this vast expanse of snow
My heart is drifting
On a glacier stained with the blood of a polar bear
Carrying the sky of the future unencumbered by cunning elk[53]

---

[52] 報載，全球變暖致海冰融化，北極熊在本世紀末逐漸消失，有感而作。
[53] It is reported in the newspaper that global warming causes the melting of sea ice, and polar bears are to disappear gradually by the end of the century. The poem is thus inspired.

詠鵲   南北朝・蕭紀

欲避新枝滑，還向故巢飛。
今朝聽聲喜，家信必應歸。

Ode to the Magpies   Xiao Ji (Northern and Southern dynasties)

The magpies avoid new
branches which may be

slippery, and they fly
back to their old nests.

This morning is by the
twitters of magpies

gladdened, there must
be a letter from home.

枷鎖   林明理

當愛被拋離其語言
我啞默
於我視界的原點
於被傾斜的白晝重疊

The Fetters   Lin Ming-Li

When love is thrown away from its language
I am mute
At the origin of my vision
The slanted days overlapping

97.

思公子
南北朝・邢邵

綺羅日減帶，桃李無顏色。
思君君未歸，歸來豈相識。

Longing for the Prince
Xing Shao (Northern and Southern dynasties)

My belt is short and
shorter from night to night;

peach flowers fall and
fade from day to day.

Longing for you, without
any sight of you; when

you return — how can I
recognize you, and you, me?

再會吧，溪橋
林明理

你從兩岸相望，如兩隻
　　翱翔的鷹，為生命而飛……
歲月再次傾聽你的祝禱，
　　那是新生的小米穗，滿含露珠，
倒映著雲天水中的白鷺。

我原是愛聽鳥聲與水聲的，
現在那片沉思的樹冠中，忽然覺得
　　很感恩。因為，——
我看到你像雄鷹自由安詳，在那
綴滿水花的溪谷中，誰讓你我邂逅，
讓我感受到處處盡是柔美的春天！

－2025.01.04

See You, Brook Bridge

Lin Ming-Li

You watch each other from the banks of the river, like
    Two soaring eagles, flying for life...
The years listen again to your prayer,
    It is a new ear of millet, filled with dewdrops,
Reflecting white egrets in the water of the sky.

I used to love the sound of birds and water,
But now I suddenly feel very grateful
    In that thoughtful tree canopy. Because —
I see you free and serene, like an eagle, in
The valley filled with watery flowers, who makes you and I meet,
And makes me feel everywhere is filled with soft spring!

January 4, 2025.

98·

蜀道難（其一）

南北朝・蕭綱

建平督郵道，魚復永安宮。
若奏巴渝曲，時當君思中。

Hard Is the Road to the Southwest (No. 1)

Xiao Gang (Northern and Southern dynasties)

In Jianping Period
the post road is built,

and in Yufu County,
the Palace of Eternal

Peace is constructed.
When the southern music

is played, the sovereign's
mind is in a great whirl.

黃昏在烏山頭水庫[54]

林明理

冬風呼嘯，黃昏如水
　與船影懸浮的
只有八田與一的沉思背影
　被空中大白鷺掠過驚醒

但我更愛三月的南洋櫻
　當春雨潑灑，心飛翔
在小徑上，恍若有股魔力
帶點傷感，教我沉默欣賞

Dusk in Wushantou Reservoir[55]

Lin Ming-li

Winter wind whistling, dusk like water
　　Suspending with the ship shadow
Only the brooding shadow of Yoichi Hatta
　　Awakened by a great egret skimming through the air

But I love more the South Ocean cherry in March
　　When spring rain sprinkles, the heart is flying
Along the path, as if there is a magic
Tinctured with a bit sadness, reducing me into silent appreciation

🦋 🦋 🦋

99·

蜀道難（其二）

南北朝·蕭綱

巫山七百里，巴水三回曲。
笛聲下復高，猿啼斷還續。

---

[54] 烏山頭水庫風景區位於臺灣的臺南，內有日本八田與一技師銅像。—2024.12.28
[55] Wushantou Reservoir Scenic Area is located in Tainan, Taiwan, and there is a bronze statue of the Japanese technician Yoichi Hatta. -December 28, 2024.

Hard Is the Road to the Southwest (No. 2)
Xiao Gang (Northern and Southern dynasties)

The Wushan Mountain stretches
for seven hundred miles, and

the Ba River is circuitous with
a great host of bends. Along

the river there are fluting sounds,
constantly, now high and then low,

to be punctuated with the monkeys's
wailing voices along the banks.

在每個山水之間
林明理

這一片憂鬱的草原啊 永遠延續著
古老的疏林。
當月亮模糊而遙遠之影
躲進了峻嶺，卻有個聲音
在每個山水之間飄蕩不停。
那是鋪滿了泥草的神秘老城
在淒然的冬日
以蹲踞姿勢 窺視
所有生物的流動之聲。

我向所有的星宿裡探尋，
它們深切目光使我心兒悲痛。
每當冰和雪裹上了壘石的長徑，
草原的歌聲便以它的柔波
使我在睡夢中恍惚清醒。
啊那大地之詩啊 已掠過微芒的東方，
讓我不再佇足嘆息
愛情的幻變哀音。

Between Each Mountain and Water
Lin Ming-Li

The melancholy prairie, forever stretching
The ancient sparse forest.

When the faint and distant shadow of the moon
Hides in the lofty mountain, there is a voice
On the floating in each river and mountain.
It is a mysterious old town covered with mud & grass
On a bleak winter day
Squatting to see
The moving sound of all living things.

I seek from all the stars,
Their deep sight grieves my heart.
Whenever ice and snow cover the long path of the stones,
The prairie song stirs me
In my sleep with its soft waves.
Oh poems of the earth have skimmed by the dim east,
For me to no longer stand sighing
The sad magic voice of love.

100·

春江曲　　　　　　　　　　　　　　　　　　南北朝·蕭綱

客行只念路，相爭度京口。
誰知堤上人，拭淚空搖手。

Ditty of the Spring River

Xiao Gang (Northern and Southern dynasties)

The wayfarer is
bent on going his

way, pushing and
squeezing to cross

the ferry. Who knows
the adieu bidder on

the dyke is still waving
hands in vain tears?

在似夢非夢的幸福之中　　　　　　　　林明理

多年以前，
　　　貼近燈塔的風是甜的，——
春風聚集於竹筏的停泊處，那河口，
　　有隻鷹，出沒於藍色情人橋。

而今，我聆聽，——
　　伴著鳥聲的群山，小憩在餐館裡，
那山海，如此貼近我思念的情緒，
　　　在似夢非夢的幸福之中。

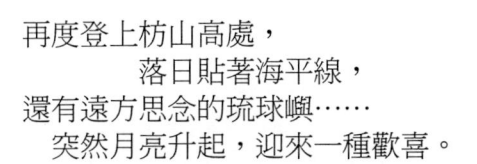

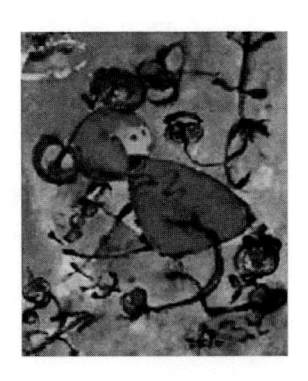

再度登上枋山高處，
　　　　落日貼著海平線，
還有遠方思念的琉球嶼……
　　突然月亮升起，迎來一種歡喜。

－2024.12.30

In Dream-Like Happiness　　　　　Lin Ming-Li

Years ago,
　　　The wind close to the lighthouse is sweet —
The spring breeze gathers at the anchorage of the bamboo raft, at the river mouth,
　　There is an eagle, haunting the Blue Lover's Bridge.

And now, I listen —
　　The mountains with the birds, resting in the restaurant,
The mountains and the sea, so close to my yearning mood,
　　In dream-like happiness.

Once again on the height of Fangshan,
　　　　The sunset is close to the sea line,
And the Ryukyus Island with distant yearning....
　　Suddenly the moon rises, to welcome in a kind of joy.

December 30, 2024.

101·

金閨思二首（其一）　　　　　　　　南北朝·蕭綱

遊子久不返，妾身當何依？
日移孤影動，羞睹燕雙飛。

Pining in a Golden Mansion (No. 1)

　　　　　Xiao Gang (Northern and Southern dynasties)

The wanderer is wandering
endlessly without return

— how can I comfort
myself? The sun is turning

and the solitary shadow
is moving; bashful,

to see swallows fly from
a pair to another pair.

月橘[56]　　　　　　　　　　　　　　　林明理

九月，
山城的小雨
輕叩眠睡中的我
我知道黎明的使者，欣喜於
我保有的自由。

可是
雲雀呵，
你為何默默不語？
為何不坦然向我？

我可把你生命的每一天
書寫在星空中，

---

[56] 月橘，又稱七里香，是一種熱帶常青植物，帶有清香的白色小花。

為你每個開花的季節
都注滿了我的溫柔……

Murraya Paniculata[57]　　　　　　　　Lin Ming-Li

In September,
The mountain rain
Knocks lightly on my sleep
I know the messenger of dawn, rejoicing
In the freedom I enjoy.

But
Oh skylark,
Why are you silent?
Why aren't you frank to me?

I can write every day of your life
In the starry sky,
For your each flowering season
Filled with my tenderness…

102.

金閨思二首（其二）　　　　　　　　南北朝・蕭綱

自君之別矣，不復染膏脂。
南風送歸雁，聊以寄相思。

Pining in a Golden Mansion (No. 2)
　　　　　　Xiao Gang (Northern and Southern dynasties)

Since you left me,
to my face I apply

---

[57] Murraya paniculata, as a kind of orange tree, is a tropical evergreen plant with fragrant white flowers.

no powder; the
south wind sends

off the returning
goose, which brings

my longing and
pining to you.

悼──2011.02.22 紐西蘭強震的罹難者　　　　　　林明理

哭泣的基督城
懸掛在塔樓上的
老鐘，碎在瓦礫裡；

驚惶的信天翁
啞默地
把頭潛入
城外的海中。

多麼傷感啊，
到哪兒尋你芳蹤？
天堂路太遙遠
該如何找到光的出口？

再一次吻醉綠萌，
濕潤而凝重。等待黎明，
在風中……飲盡夜的苦澀。

　　　　　　　　　　　　　　　　──寫於 2011.02.24

Mourning the Victims of the Powerful Earthquake in New Zealand on February 22, 2011
Lin Ming-Li

The Crying Christchurch
The old clock hanging from
The tower, shattered in the rubble;

The frightened albatross
Mute and silent
Sinks its head
Into the sea outside the city.

How sentimental,
Where can I find your traces?
Heaven road is too far away
How to find the exit of light?

To again kiss the drunk green shade,
Wet and heavy. Waiting for the dawn,
In the wind… Drink away the bitterness of night.

        Written on February 24, 2011.

103.

望月望   南北朝・蕭綱

今夜月光來，正上相思台。
可憐無遠近，光照悉徘徊。

Gazing at the Moon
     Xiao Gang (Northern and Southern dynasties)

Tonight the moon
approaches, alighting

on the pining platform.
The light, far and near,

is so lovely, caressing,
comforting, and lingering.

夏風吹拂福爾摩沙   林明理

夏風吹拂福爾摩沙，
 吹拂雲聚的土埆厝簷滴上，

引我遐想聯翩，
　激起我滿懷希望，──

猶記得，天空清澄、碧藍，
　梯田與山巒互擁，
一隻鷹，盤旋低迴的身姿……
　讓我又重溫一次舊夢；

那裡，我是隻自由歡快的黑鳥，
　棲在一座紅磚老舍上，
我開懷無憂，
　邊唱著高亢而悠揚的曲調。

當我從甜美的夢醒來，
　遠方，像是個無法觸及的岸，
就在我獨自站立，──
　不再出聲的靜默中。

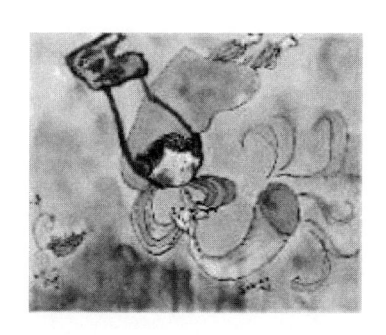

－2025.01.14

The Summer Wind Blows in Formosa

Lin Ming-Li

The summer wind blows in Formosa
　Blowing the cloud-gathered earth dripping on the eaves,
Captivating my imagination,
　Arousing my hope —

I still remember the clear blue sky,
　The terraced fields and the mountains hugging each other,
The low circling posture of an eagle....
　For me to relive the old dream;

There, I am a free and cheerful black bird,
　Perching on a red brick house,
I am happy and carefree,
　Singing a high and melodious tune.

When I wake up from a sweet dream,
　The distance, like an unreachable shore,

It is where I stand alone —
　　In the silence without any words.

January 14, 2025.

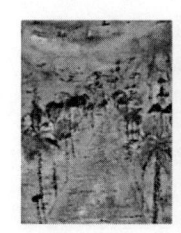

104.

夏日詩　　　　　　　　　　　　　　　南北朝‧徐悱

炎光歇中宇，清氣入房櫳。
晚荷猶卷綠，疏蓮久落紅。

A Summer Poem　Xu Peng (Northern and Southern dynasties)

The glaring light rests in
the height of the day, when

the pure air comes flowing
into the room. The evening

lotus leaves are like spring
rolls rolling green; the sparse

lotus stems are lingering for
long, with fallen red petals.

南灣[58]的記憶　　　　　　　　　　　　林明理

從瞭望台看去
　　　　整個南灣
一排排
　　　椰林的小徑
像一片藍霧——

---

[58] 南灣（South Bay）是臺灣屏東縣的一個海灣；因沙灘弧線優美，漁產豐富，昔日不時可見漁民使用地曳網或搭乘舢舨船出海去下網。但我覺得，南灣的黃昏，在我心中，美得令人心醉。山岩沿坡矗立，模糊的光與影，錯落成一幅印象式潑墨畫，愈是接近暮晚時分，愈是別有一種風情。—2025.1.23.

霧中
　　那些白色大風車
　緩慢地轉著，有小小的
大白鷗、漁船……
　　　　　在萬頃波中波動
　　　起伏

又經過多少歲月了
　那小鎮的琴音
　　　　　變成一片雲
　　落入我的夢中──
隨細雨　　漫過窗櫺

Memory of the South Bay[59]   Lin Ming-Li

From the observation tower,
　　　　　The whole South Bay
A line after another line
　　　　　Of paths choked in coconut groves
Like a stretch of blue fog —

In the fog
　　The big white windmills
　Turning slowly, there are little
White gulls, and fishing boats…
　　　　　In a vast expanse of waters waving
　　　　And undulating

How many years have passed
　　The music of the town
　　　　　Becomes a piece of cloud

---

[59] The South Bay is a bay in Pingtung County, Taiwan. Because of the beautiful arc of the beach and the rich fishing production, fishermen can be seen from time to time to use the ground dragnet or sampan boats to go out to sea to spread the net. But I think that the evening of the South Bay, in my mind, is the most beautiful. Mountains and rocks stand along the slope, the fuzzy light and dim shadow, all are scattered into an impression of splash-ink painting: the closer to the evening, the more enchanting it is with a unique style of beauty. -January 23, 2025.

Falling in my dream —
Along with the drizzling　　through the window lattice

105.

出江陵縣還詩二首（其一）　　　　　　南北朝・蕭繹

遊魚迎浪上，雛雉向林飛。
遠村雲裡出，遙船天際歸。

Out of Jiangling County (No. 1)
Xiao Yi (Northern and Southern dynasties)

The swimming fish swim
against the current; the

pheasants fly into the depth
of the woods. A remote

village appears and disappears
in massive clouds, when

a distant boat is returning
from beyond the horizon.

我寧可遐想　　　　　　　　　　　　　　林明理

我寧可遐想，
像座巨石遠眺，但見大海
延伸向彼岸。那時，——
古風依依，故鄉是我載不動的愁。

或許人生就像電腦一樣，
只要打開幾個程序，
就會看到許多不同的世界，
又能找回遺忘後又拾得的記憶。

我不知道，時間之流會不會改變
夢中的童年畫面？
那夕陽掩映的田野，會不會有
白鷺在雨中振翅而飛？

此刻，我聽到寒蟬傳來的聲音，
卻止不住對你的思念——
啊，畢竟我不是 AI。我能呼吸，
連自己的詩本上都有畫作說明襯托。

—2025.01.10

I Would Rather Daydream　　　　　　　Lin Ming-Li

I would rather daydream
Look like a megalith into the distance, only to see the sea
Stretching to the other shore. At that time —
The old wind still lingers; the hometown is my unbearable sorrow.

Perhaps life is like a computer,
So long as you open a few programs,
You will see many different worlds,
And you can retrace the forgotten memories.

I don't know, whether or not the passage of time is to change
The picture of childhood in the dream?
Will there be egrets flapping their wings in the rain
Across the fields rosy with sunset?

Now, I hear the chirping of cold cicadas,
But I can't stop missing you —
Oh, after all, I am no AI. I can breathe.
Even I have illustrations in my poetry book.

January 10, 2025.

106・

詠細雨詩   南北朝・蕭繹

風輕不動葉,雨細未沾衣。
入樓如霧上,拂馬似塵飛。

A Fine Drizzle   Xiao Yi (Northern and Southern dynasties)

A breeze is too gentle
to move the leaves;

a fine drizzle is too light to
moisten the clothes. Climbing

upstairs, it is like being
bathed in mist; spurring

the horse, it is like the
speedy flight of a mote of dust.

一棵極美的聖誕樹   林明理

排列出原住民手牽手歡愉的所有連結
   那光芒將之感受為那佳節本身
      彷若一股暖流
   而由藝術館駐站工作者集結而成
才如此認真地做出各種裝置藝術

從旅人諦聽街頭藝人表演的景象
   看起來似乎完全陶醉其中
但我昂首所能看到的
除了美麗的各種星座,充滿童趣的燈籠
   以及月光淡淡的,時間也駐足下來
只有風靜靜地蜷伏在聖誕樹衣角
   跟著低吟,在繁星與我祈福之中

－2020.12.22

A Most Beautiful Christmas Tree   Lin Ming-Li

Arrange all the connections of the native people holding hands
    The light that feels like the festival itself
        Like a warm current
    That is assembled by the staff of the museum
To produce the installation art so honestly

From the sight of travelers listening to the street performers
    It seems to be completely intoxicated
But when I hold my head up, all I can see
Is the beautiful constellations, the childlike lanterns
    And the pale moon; time stands still
Only the wind is quietly crouching in the corner of the Christmas tree
    Singing accordingly, amidst the stars and my praying

                      December 22, 2020.

107·

望春詩   南北朝·蕭繹

葉濃知柳密,花盡覺梅疏。
蘭生未可握,蒲小不堪書。

Watching Spring   Xiao Yi (Northern and Southern dynasties)

Dense leaves know the
thickness of willows; flowers

scattering, the plum trees
are sparse and sparser. Orchid

flowers are flowering, not yet
a handful of them; the cattail

leaves are too small on which
to write Chinese characters.

正月賞梅 林明理

在都蘭山南麓鸞山村,
沙沙枯葉聲和
正月沃野的白梅香味,
把所有煩囂都盡拋腦後。

雨後的五葉松更綠了!
雖然眾鳥寂靜,
倘若你願意
坐落在溪谷和部落之間,
輕輕閉上眼,
而微風輕挑,梅雪皚皚……
大自然就是苦吟詩人。

Admiring Plum Blossoms in January Lin Ming-Li

In Nanshan Village to the south side of Dulan Mountain,
There is a whistling sound of dried leaves;
The sweet-scented white plums across the field in January,
Leaving behind all the worries.

The pines after a rainfall are greener!
Though all the birds are silent,
If you would like,
To sit between the valley and the tribe,
Gently closing your eyes.
The gentle wind is frolicsome through white snow on plum blossoms,
And the great nature is a diligent bard.

詠梅詩 南北朝・蕭繹

梅含今春樹,還臨先日池。
人懷前歲憶,花發故年枝。

Ode to Plum Blossoms

Xiao Yi (Northern and Southern dynasties)

The plum blossoms are
blossoming on the trees

of this spring, and they
are by the poolside of

the olden days. When the
past memories are cherished,

the flowers are flowering
— on the old branches.

富岡漁港冥想

林明理

我沐浴在珍貴的陽光裡
　　廣大的雲層底下，
湛藍的海，
　　　　如天空一樣藍。

那數十條支流匯集的太平洋，
　　視野所及盡是鋪上光彩的波浪。
這時一艘遊艇正等待出航，
而讓我的感動是
　　漁港保持著隨性而安的激情。

我願是一朵雲，目光順著盈盈的
　　海水，穿越時空，
隨著起伏的波浪，從遠古來，
　　在清風裡
　　　　泛著不可複製的微光。

在初次相遇的富岡，我高興地發現
　　他的眼睛裡蓄滿恬淡的光芒！
當我轉身離開時，那蔚藍的海岸
　　像睡著的嬰兒般安詳。

—2021.1.7

Meditation at Tomioka Fishing Port   Lin Ming-Li

I am bathed in the precious sunshine
    Beneath boundless massy clouds,
The deep-blue sea
      Is as blue as the sky.

The Pacific Ocean which receives the afflux of dozens of tributaries,
   Is covered with glorious waves as far as the eye can see.
Now a yacht is waiting to sail,
And I am touched
   By the fishing port which maintains a peaceful passion.

I would like to be a blossom of cloud, looking along the overflowing
     Sea water, through time and space,
Along with the undulating waves, from ancient times,
   In the breeze
    Bright with an unreplicable glimmer.

Seeing Tomioka for the first time, I am happy to find
   His eyes are filled with a quiet light!
When I turn to leave, the blue shore
   Is as tranquil as a sleeping baby.

                              January 7, 2021.

109．

陌上桑   隋朝・無名氏

日出秦樓明，條垂露尚盈。
蠶饑心自急，開奩妝不成。

Mulberry Trees of the Path   Anonymous (Sui dynasty)

At sunrise, the mansion
is bright; the twigs

drooping, with dews
still full. The cocoons

are hungry, and uneasy;
the mirror case opened,

yet the makeup fails
to be made up.

多良村[60]的心影

林明理

飛翔吧，孩子。你將學會邁向幸福的勇氣。
天空已由陰沉轉成初曉，
望月的孩子時刻想念著家鄉的歌。
強勁的海風不停地吹……
黑夜席捲而來的苦難也終會漸漸遠離。

飛翔吧，孩子。跟著老師學識字。
跟著爺爺說母語，去養雞、上山種小米；
跟著奶奶說母語，去洗蛋、去掃地。
有土地，就有根，這是不變的道理。

堅強吧，孩子。誰心存感恩，光明就眷顧誰。
天空和鳥獸會靜聽你的話語。
我看到一隻大冠鷲在山上盤旋，
看到一個小孩一面跑一面跳。
看見部落的土地已逐漸發芽、期待豐收；

看到部落的青年積極打造自己的家園。
啊，——我看見了，
看見一列火車快速掠過，
給沉默的天空 拈朵微笑。

---

[60] 多良村 Duoliang Vil.「查拉密瀧部落」Cala-Vi，是排灣族的部落，曾因八八風災受創嚴重。如今，部落的青年全力投入社區的木工等工坊，正在轉型創新中，甚是欣慰。

The Heart Shadow of Duoliang Village[61]

Lin Ming-Li

Fly, child. You will acquire the courage to move towards happiness.
The sky has turned from gloomy to dawn,
The children watching the moon always miss the songs of their hometown.
The strong sea wind keeps blowing…
The suffering of the night will gradually fade away.

Fly, child. Learn to read from your teacher.
Follow grandpa to speak mother tongue, to raise chickens, millet up the mountain;
Follow grandma to speak mother tongue, to wash eggs, to sweep the floor.
Where there is land, there are roots. This is a constant truth.

Stay strong, child. The light shines on those who are thankful.
The sky and the birds & beasts will listen to your words.
I see a great crested vulture circling the hill,
A child running and jumping,
And the tribe's land is gradually sprouting, expecting a good harvest;

I see the youths of the tribe actively building their own home.
Oh — I see,
I see a train speeding by,
Beaming a smile into the silent sky.

---

[61] Duoliang Village, the Cala-Vi, a tribe of the Paiwan tribe, was badly damaged by the August 8 storm. Today, the youth of the tribe are fully engaged in carpentry and other workshops in the community, and are undergoing transformation and innovation, which is quite gratifying.

110．

紫騮馬歌辭

南北朝・無名氏

高高山頭樹，風吹葉落去。
一去數千里，何當還故處。

Song of the Purple Steed

Anonymous (Northern and Southern dynasties)

Towering atop the
mountain are the trees,

whose leaves fall
in the strong wind.

Once away, they are
away for thousands of

miles — when can they
return to their native place?

重遊南鯤鯓[62]

林明理

闊別四十餘載，
十二月的風毫不冷冽，
沙洲，浪花，匯合了
久違的候鳥，
都框在夕陽的暗影上。

在眾人的膜拜與祈禱間，
大鯤園，像神明的慈目，
閃著柔和的澄淨；
而人們所棧戀的，——

---

[62] 古云，形似大魚的沙洲為「鯤鯓」，其中，以臺南北門區最為著名，名叫南鯤鯓（Nan Kun Shen）。風景區有臺灣規模最大的王爺廟（南鯤鯓代天府，又稱：大鯤園），被市府授證為「宮廟博物館」；也有奉祀媽祖的鹿耳門天后宮等。2024年十月底，大鯤園舉辦一場世界最大的鹽祭典，吸引萬人朝聖。—2024.12.16.

是它的傳說，還是奇異的景色，
竟如此安恬，像初次來訪時。

Nan Kun Shen[63] Revisited Lin Ming-Li

After forty years of absence,
The wind of December is not cold at all,
Sandbanks, waves, and long-lost
Migratory birds converge,
All framed in the dark shadow of the sunset.

Amidst people's worship and prayer,
The great Kun Yuan, like the merciful eyes of God,
Shining with a soft clarity;
What people adore —
Is its legend, or the spectacular scene,
So peaceful, like the first visit.

111.

折楊柳歌辭五首（其一） 南北朝・無名氏

上馬不捉鞭，反折楊柳枝。
蹀座吹長笛，愁殺行客兒。

Song of Breaking the Willows (No. 1)

Anonymous (Northern and Southern dynasties)

Mounting the horse, the
rider raises his hand to break

---

[63] In ancient times, the sandbank shaped like a big fish is named "Kun", among which the most famous is Tainan Beimen District, named "Nan Kun Shen". The scenic area has the largest Wangye Temple in Taiwan (Nankun Daitianfu, also known as Da Kun Garden), which is certified as "the Palace Temple Museum" by the municipal government. There is also worship of Mazu Luermen Tianhou Palace, and so on. By the end of October, 2024, Da Kun Yuan has held the world's largest salt festival, attracting thousands of pilgrims. -December 16, 2024.

a twig from the willow tree,
instead of taking hold of

the whip on the horse.
He sits astride the horse

to play the flute, coaxing
the homesickness of wayfarers.

倒影   林明理

霧靄淡煙著
河谷的邊緣，
你的影子沉落在夕陽，
把相思飄浮在塔樓上。

回首，凝視那常春藤的院落。
每當小雨的時候，
淚光與植物，混合成
深厚而縹緲的灰色……

Inverted Image   Lin Ming-Li

Thin mist & pale smoke,
The edge of the river,
Your shadow sinks in the setting sun,
Yearning floating over the tower.

Turning back, to look at the courtyard overgrown with ivy.
Whenever a slight rain falls,
Tears and plants mingle into
Heavy and ethereal grey…

112．

折楊柳歌辭五首（其二）   南北朝・無名氏

腹中愁不樂，願作郎馬鞭。
出入攬郎臂，蹀座郎膝邊。

Song of Breaking the Willows (No. 2)
Anonymous (Northern and Southern dynasties)

My belly is filled
with sorrows —

how I wish to be
your whip. During

an outing, I can hold
fast to your arm;

sitting idle, I can
be so close to you.

雲豹[64]頌   林明理

萬點繁星，一片莊嚴的野百合，
  我感到如風吹過原野，
縈迴在山谷與夢幻之間，
  開始湧向著一條溪流：

夢中，你在空濛的溪邊輕輕地啜飲，
  而我踮起腳尖，感到莫名的狂喜。
  是你，似久違的老友，
    在這短暫的邂逅間，
在穿越百多年前的一個月夜，
    引吭唱出你的滄桑；

---

[64] 雲豹（Formosan Clouded）只分佈在東南亞。關於臺灣的雲豹，據文獻記載，最早可以追溯到 1860 年代，此後無人再發現；故而雲豹的蹤跡，已成為無解之謎。，雲豹，在此詩中，被喻為「孤獨」的象徵。－2025.01.03.

217

是你，讓風兒帶回你的容顏
　　　和深藏多年的悄悄話……
儘管你已不見蹤跡，歌也遠颺，
我仍懷念，曾經與你相遇的一瞬。

Ode to Clouded Leopard[65]　　　　　　Lin Ming-Li

Myriads of stars, a solemn field of wild lilies,
　　I feel like the wind is blowing across the field,
Lingering among the valleys and dreams,
　　And begin to flow towards a stream:

In the dream, you are sipping gently by an empty stream,
　　When I stand on tiptoe, feeling inexplicable ecstasy.
　　　It is you, like a long lost old friend,
　　　　In this brief encounter,
Through a moonlit night over a hundred years ago,
　　To sing out your vicissitudes of life;

It is you who lets the wind bring back your face
　　As well as the secret words which have been hidden for years…
Although you are traceless, the song spreading afar,
Still I miss the moment of meeting you.

❦ ❦ ❦

113．

折楊柳歌辭五首（其三）　　　　　　南北朝・無名氏

放馬兩泉澤，忘不著連羈。
擔鞍逐馬走，何見得馬騎。

---

[65] Clouded leopards are found only in Southeast Asia, and in Taiwan they can be traced back to the 1860s, and nobody has seen them since then. Therefore, the traces of clouded leopards have become a mystery. Clouded leopards, in this poem, serve as a symbol of "loneliness". -January 3, 2025.

Song of Breaking the Willows (No. 3)
Anonymous (Northern and Southern dynasties)

I walk my horse
to the two fountains,

forgetting to bridle
it with a headstall.

Shouldering a saddle,
I follow my horse on

foot — without sight
of your riding a horse.

追憶—鐵道詩人　錦連[66]　　　　　　　林明理

他似一棵雲木於
十里溪風之中
不管人間的榮枯盛衰
溪水仍在地表上潺潺地流

那有時單調有時激情的水聲
是眾神的低聲悄語
都在訴說著——
一個孤獨而充滿愛的詩人

他來到涼冷的溪流邊
想要解讀眾神智慧的啟示
於是靜靜地傾聽
並眺望故里千萬次

他橫過肥沃的黑土
那兒曾有青禾，彎彎的土橋上有月光
圍住了出沒的雞群草場
如今只留下一勺記憶，在水波飄蕩

---

[66] 詩人錦連於病中逝世，享年 85 歲。—寫於 2013.1.15 作

那黑夜只不過是黑夜
卻要我相信那天堂之上
有花園和海洋
還有宮殿裡藏有你吟遊的笑容

—2018.02.17

In Memory of Jin Lian[67], a Railway Poet

Lin Ming-Li

He is like a cloud-scraping tree
In the wind of a ten-mile stream
In spite of the vicissitudes of human life
Creek water is still babbling on the surface of the earth

The running water is now monotonous and then passionate
As the whisper of gods
All talking about —
A lonely and loving poet

He comes to the cold stream
To interpret the wisdom of gods
And he listens quietly
While looking afar at his homeland for thousands of times

He has crossed the fertile black earth
Where there have once been green crops, moonlight on the arched earth bridge
The chickens have been enclosed in the pasture
Now only a spoonful of memory is left, waves floating

The dark night is just dark night
Yet I believe beyond heaven
There are gardens and oceans
As well as palaces where your minstrel smile is hidden

---

[67] Poet Jin Lian died of illness at the age of 85. -Written on January 15, 2013.

114．

折楊柳歌辭五首（其四）   南北朝・無名氏

遙看孟津河，楊柳鬱婆娑。
我是虜家兒，不解漢兒歌。

Song of Breaking the Willows (No. 4)
Anonymous (Northern and Southern dynasties)

Looking afar at the
Mengjin River, I

find the willowy
willows, in clusters,

are dancing in the wind.
As a boy from the north,

I fail to understand the
songs of Han people.

傳說，拉瑪他・星星[68]是英雄   林明理

傳說，拉瑪他・星星是英雄。
就在此刻，一道晨光灑在這勇士雕像上，
　　　喚醒一隻山鷹，騰起半空，——
　　　　　緩緩翱翔。

我看著，想著。歷史上最悲壯的一頁，
　　　都曾有過那時代人民最深切的盼望：
而盼望與可歌可泣的一切⋯⋯
　　　　都已藏在光陰裡。

我的記憶閃爍，
但沒有時空錯置的幻覺，——在瞻望中

---

[68] 臺灣的布農族（Bunun）勇士拉瑪他・星星（Istanda Lamata Sing Sing，－1932年），以長期對抗日本政權壓迫聞名。－2025.01.05

更感到沒有喧囂的寧靜；
啊，自古英雄的回音，恰似遠年寂寥的夜。

Legend Has It That Istanda Lamata Sing Sing[69] Is a Hero
Lin Ming-Li

Legend has it that Lamata Sing Sing is a hero.
At this moment, a morning light falls on the statue of the warrior,
    Awakening a mountain eagle, rising into the air —
        Slowly spreading and soaring.

I watch while thinking. The most tragic and stirring page in history
    Has had the most honest hope of the people of that era:
Hoping everything that can be eulogized in tears….
    It is all hidden in time.

My memory flickers,
But without the illusion of the dislocation of time and space — in my contemplation
    I feel the peace without noises;
Oh the echo of the ancient heroes, like the lonely night of distant years.

115.

折楊柳歌辭五首（其五）
南北朝・無名氏

健兒須快馬，快馬須健兒。
蹕跋黃塵下，然後別雄雌。

Song of Breaking the Willows (No. 5)
Anonymous (Northern and Southern dynasties)

A valiant fighter is
in need of a speedy

---

[69] Istanda Lamata Sing Sing (born 1932), a Bunun warrior from Taiwan, is known for his long struggle against Japanese oppression. -January 5, 2025.

steed, and a speedy
steed is in need of a

valiant fighter. Galloping
and kicking through yellow

dust, the horses, male or
female, can be distinguished.

芍藥[70]   林明理

我輕拋千古花事
不管
幾春，留下來的新雨殘紅

無需過度期待
或匆忙醒來
蝶戀，寂寞，都在此山中

The Chinese Peony[71]   Lin Ming-Li

Decidedly I am away from the ancient flowers
Regardless of
A few springs, which are with fresh rain and residual red

No need to expect too much
Or wake up in a hurry
Love of butterflies, loneliness, all are in the mountain

---

[70] 芍藥（學名：Paeonia lactiflora）是一種芍藥科芍藥屬的著名草本花卉。
[71] The Chinese peony (scientific name: Paeonia lactiflora) is a famous species of herbaceous flowers.

116.

折楊柳枝詞　　　　　　　　　　　　　　南北朝・無名氏

門前一株棗，歲歲不知老。
阿婆不嫁女，那得孫兒抱。

A Song of Breaking the Willows
Anonymous (Northern and Southern dynasties)

A date tree in front
of the house refuses

to age from year to
year. If a woman

does not marry her
daughter off, how

can she dote on
her grand-child?

金池塘　　　　　　　　　　　　　　　　林明理

風在追問杳然的彩雲，
遠近的飛燕，在山林的
背影掠過……

羞澀的石榴，──
醉人的囈語，出沒的白鵝
伴著垂柳戲波；

秋塘月落，
鏡面掛住的──
恰是妳帶雨的明眸。

The Golden Pond

Lin Ming-Li

The wind is questioning the faraway clouds,
Swallows far and near are flying through
The mountain forest...

The bashful pomegranates —
Intoxicating whispering, the wandering white goose
Playing with the waves with weeping willows;

In autumn pond the moon falls,
What is hanging in the mirror —
Is your bright eyes moist with rain.

ა❤ ა❤ ა❤

117.

秋詩

南北朝・陽休之

日照前窗竹，露濕後園薇。
夜蛩扶砌響，輕蛾繞燭飛。

A Poem on Autumn

Yang Xiuzhi (Northern and Southern dynasties)

The sun shines on the
bamboos before the front

window; the dews moisten
the roses in the back garden.

The night crickets are
chirping under the stairs,

while the moths are flying
and circling the candle.

你在哪？孩子[72]

　　　　　　　　　　　　　　　　　　　　林明理

你在哪？孩子。
　　　　媽媽在等你，
你可曉得？
救難員急著尋找地點，
在黝黑星空下寒冷，
　　在斷垣殘壁中淒涼，
　　　　連雲影也哽咽了。
我愛你，
還是和以前一樣，一切未變，
　不要怕，我的寶貝；

在這夜晚的寂靜中，
我明白了，
　　　你有話對我說……
我會為你祈禱，
也為和我一樣在這裡守候的
　　　所有人家，
願諸神聽到我們
　　　在渴求，在呼喚──
讓我們肩並肩
　　擦乾淚水，再闊步向前。

Where Are You? My Child[73]

　　　　　　　　　　　　　　　　Lin Ming-Li

Where are you, my child?
　　　Mom is waiting for you,
Do you know?

---

[72] 為紀念2018年2月6日花蓮強震而作。罹難者小軒母親的焦慮與心碎的畫面，催人心肝。願天佑花蓮，全民一心加入救助行列與同悼。—2018.02.08.

[73] The poem is in memory of the great earthquake in Hualien on February 6, 2018. The victim Xiaoxuan's mother shows great anxiety and heart-brokenness — the picture is maddeningly sad. May Heaven bless Hualian, and the whole nation as one to join the rescue and mourning. -February 8, 2018.

The rescuer is in a hurry to find your spot,
Cold under the dark starry sky,
    Desolate against the broken wall,
        Even the cloudy shadow feels choked.
I love you,
Still as always, nothing has changed;
  Don't be afraid, my baby;

In the silence of the night,
I see,
    You have something to say to me....
I will pray for you,
And for those who
    Wait here like me,
May gods hear us
    Praying, calling —
Let us stand side by side,
  To dry our tears, and stride forward.

118．

感琵琶弦   南北朝・馮小憐

雖蒙今日寵，猶憶昔時憐。
欲知心斷絕，應看膝上弦。

A Farewell Poem   Anonymous (Northern and Southern dynasties)

Favored and pampered
today, I still remember

the pitiable state in former
days. To know how the

heart breaks, come to see
the chord on my knees.

四月的夜風

林明理

悠悠地,略過松梢
充滿甜眠和光,把地土慢慢甦復
光浮漾起海的蒼冥
我踱著步。水聲如雷似的
切斷夜的偷襲

我聽見
野鳩輕輕地低喚,與
唧唧的蟲兒密約
古藤下,我開始想起
去年春天。你側著頭
回眸望一回,你是凝,是碧翠
是一莖清而不寒的睡蓮!

這時刻,林裡。林外
星子不再窺視於南窗
而我豁然瞭解:
曾經有絲絲的雨,水波拍岸
在採石山前的路上……

The Night Wind of April

Lin Ming-Li

Leisurely, it passes by the top of pine trees
Filled with sweet sleep and light, gently waking the land
The light is rippling with dark green of the sea
I am fording in water. The water sounds like thunder
To cut off the sneak attack of the night

I hear
Wild turtle-doves cooing gently, while
Having a tryst with twittering insects
Under old vines, I begin to recall
The last spring. You keep your head aslant
To cast a backward glance. You are the gaze, the green jade
A stem of water lily which is clean and not cold!

Now, in the woods. And without
The stars no longer peer through the southern window
And I am suddenly enlightened:
Once there was a drizzling rain, waves lapping against the shore
On the way to the quarry mountain…

119．

寄王琳 　　　　　　　　　　　　　南北朝・庾信

玉關道路遠，金陵信使疏。
獨下千行淚，開君萬里書。

To Wang Lin, a Famous General
　　　　　　　Yu Xin (Northern and Southern dynasties)

Beyond the Jade Pass,
the road is endlessly long;

looking forward to the
messengers from Jinling

— how few! Solitarily, I shed
one thousand lines of tears,

after I read your letter coming
through thousands of miles.

夏風吹起的夜晚 　　　　　　　　　　　林明理

我辭別了我故鄉的小窗，
離開了我心愛的土壤。
當年禾田　像新煤般，
泛滿老父的顧盼。

火車似一隻灰黑的蟬，
伏在靜寂的月台上。

又如一隻溫馴的小山羊——
偎依著溫暖的土壤。

何時歸來啊,已無法想像,
田野反復地跟著星辰運轉,
門前小溪一路歌唱,
窗外擴散的世界一片天藍。

呵再會吧,再會吧,故鄉的夜晚,
也許,我的愛,赤裸而坦蕩,
偶爾有躍出來迷濛來路的月,
它的容顏將再觸及我不眠的憂傷。

The Night When Summer Wind Blows Lin Ming-Li

I bid farewell to the little window of my hometown
And leave my beloved land.
Then, the paddy field was like new coal,
Filled with old father's yearning look.

The train is like a grey and black cicadas
Lying on the silent platform.
And like a tame little goat —
Snuggling up to the warm land.

When to return, oh, it is unimaginable,
The field repeatedly follows the stars in their running,
The brook in front of the door is singing all the way,
The world without the window spreads a skyful of blue.

Oh bye, goodbye, hometown night,
Perhaps, my love, naked and open,
Occasionally the moon is leaping out of the mazy road,
Its face will again touch my sleepless sorrow.

120・

和庚四　　　　　　　　　　　　　　　南北朝・庾信

離關一長望，別恨幾重愁。
無妨對春日，懷抱只言秋。

In Reply to Yu Si　Yu Xin (Northern and Southern dynasties)

Leaving the great pass,
I cast backward glances

when my departing
sorrows multiply. In

spite of the spring season,
I feel this is an autumnal

day, a melancholy one,
in the bottom of my heart.

光點　　　　　　　　　　　　　　　　　林明理

冬日一個傍晚，亮得
　　像銀白鱗片的路，──
知更鳥，甜美且有力地，
　　在林頂上低飛，
又對我繞著圈──就這樣
　　停在湖面，啄星之影；

啊！有多少個冰晨，又刺穿
　　多少次樹林懸垂的臉？
每根細枝，每一隻蟲動
　　在互訴心事，在悸動裡
模糊。是冰已龜裂？
寒裡雪融聲漸濃，又漸遠……

像無數微醺的落葉，
　　我在空氣裡喃喃，──

231

這或許，是必然，
　　　也是偶然──
天已暗，松鼠的吱叫
　　與唯一的想望永訣。

The Luminous Spot　　　　　　　　　　Lin Ming-Li

One winter evening, a road,
　　　Bright like silver scales —
The robin, sweet and powerful,
　　　Flies low atop the woods,
And encircling me — thus
　　It stops on the lake, pecking at the stars' shadow;

Oh! How many icy mornings have pierced
　　　The hanging faces of the woods?
Each twig and every worm, moving
　　In each other's heart, in the throbbing
Blur. Is the ice cracked?
The sound of snow melting in the cold is louder and away...

Like countless tipsy leaves,
　　　I whisper in the air —
Perhaps, by necessity,
　　　　And by chance —
The sky is dark, the squirrel's squeal
　　Bids farewell forever with the only hope.

121．

和侃法師三絕詩（其三）　　　　　　南北朝・庾信

回首河堤望，眷眷嗟離絕。
誰言舊國人，倒在他鄉別。

In Reply to a Master-Monk (No. 3)

Yu Xin (Northern and Southern dynasties)

Backward glances
at the dyke, where

there is a lingering
departing. Who can

expect two persons
of a strange land

are parting company
in a stranger land?

記憶中的三條崙漁港[74]

林明理

港口成群的鷗鳥喧嘩，
恰似浪花狂捲了沙岸。
停泊的膠筏不再風光
與運吊蚵的老農相依相伴。

且讓點點漁火在海上
和月光盡情輝映吧，
我將記起昔日秋季捕魚的歡喜，
沿著黃昏的棧橋，歡快返鄉。

—2024.12.27

San-Tiau-Luen Fishing Harbor[75] in My Memory

Lin Ming-Li

Bevies of birds and gulls in the harbor are making noises,
Like waves sweeping across the sandy shore.
The rubber rafts at anchor are popular no more,
To be accompanied by old farmers hauling oysters.

---

[74] 三條崙漁港在雲林縣四湖鄉，五十年代盛極一時。
[75] San-Tiau-Luen Fishing Harbor is in Yunlin County, Taoyuan City, and the 1950s saw its heyday.

For dots of fishing fire in the sea
And moonlight enjoy the glow;
I will remember the past joys of autumn fishing,
Along the twilight trestle, back home in a joyful mood.

December 27, 2024.

122.

行途賦得四更應詔詩 南北朝・庾信

四更天欲曙，落月垂關下。
深谷暗藏人，欹松橫礙馬。

A Named Composition

Yu Xin (Northern and Southern dynasties)

After the wee hours the day
is on the verge of breaking,

when the moon is slowly
falling over the great pass.

The wayfarers are hidden
in the deep vale, and the pine

trees fallen across the road
slow down the horse speed.

珍珠的水田 林明理

夕陽西沉，蘭陽平原煙雨依舊
　　過去，島嶼上沒有比這更美的景色
入秋後，沒有比這更多的候鳥前來度冬
也沒有更多的水泥厝，更便利的隧道[76]……

---

[76] 自雪山隧道開通後，多年來，帶來臺灣宜蘭縣的觀光產業增加了效益，但也造成青年人口外流及水田生態數量日益減少等問題。如何讓當地公共運輸規劃與環境永續之間取得共識，有待各界深思。

為了注滿一畝畝消失中的水田
為了喚回黑面琵鷺、高蹺鴴群消逝的回聲
為了塭底再也不曾出現的雁群相遇
　　……我覺得，這片水田哭泣了
　　甚至我們的後代子孫也心疼不已

我懷念，這座城鎮曾是水鳥的樂園
　　如今那水田映天的景象
　正閃著光亮，只要我們翻一翻記憶
就會發現空氣中還散發出稻穗清新的氣息

The Paddy Field of Pearls　　　　　　　Lin Ming-Li

The sun is setting, the rain over the Lanyang Plain is still persistent
　　In the past, there was no more beautiful scenery on the island than this
Autumn in, there are no more migratory birds to spend winter here
And no more cement houses and more convenient tunnels[77]…

To fill acres of paddy fields on the disappearing
To bring back the fading echoes of black-faced spoonbills and stilted plover flocks
For the meeting and gathering of bevies of geese which are no more
　　…I feel that the paddy field is crying
　Even our descendants can feel a kind of heartache

Longingly I remember this town used to be a paradise for water birds
　　Now the landscape of the paddy fields shining
　With a bright sky; so long as we look back in our memories
We will find the fresh breath of rice in the air

---

[77] Since the opening of the Snow Mountain Tunnel, the tourism industry in Yilan County, Taiwan has been boosted over the years, but it has also caused problems such as the outflow of young people and the decreasing ecological quantity of paddy fields. How to strike a balance between local public transport planning and environmental sustainability — this is a problem to be considered and solved.

123.

秋夜望單飛雁　　　　　　　　　　　南北朝・庾信

失群寒雁聲可憐，夜半單飛在月邊。
無奈人心復有憶，今暝將渠俱不眠。

Watching the Solo Flight of a Wild Goose Through an Autumn Night

Yu Xin (Northern and Southern dynasties)

A cold wild goose estranged from the bevy is croaking

pitiably; mid-night finds it flying solitarily by the moon.

Helplessly I cherish a fond memory, so much so that I

remain, together with you, awake through the long night.

臺東糖廠[78]印象　　　　　　　　　　　林明理

晨光下的蓮池，金而緋粉
　　　溶入了寧靜的青綠色調
昔日滿裝甘蔗的廠房
　　倉庫牆面影影綽綽
中山堂也恰似在我跟前

接著，一隻雀鳥
　　像一個演唱家出現了
　　飛到偌大的原始廠區高唱
突然間　大地
　　　　開始甦醒

---

[78] 臺東糖廠現由臺灣糖業公司花東區處經營管理，已成立「文化創意產業園區」。

蜜蜂吻著半醒的露珠兒
　　鐵馬道上的車聲
　　　　　輕輕撫動園區
在地小農創業的故事
　　還在倉庫間來回流連

Impression of Taitung Sugar Factory[79]　　Lin Ming-Li

The lotus pond under the morning light is pink and gold
　　　Fused into the quiet green hue
The former factory warehouse filled with sugarcanes
　　The walls are speckled and mottled
Zhongshan Hall seems to be in front of me

Then, like a singer, a bird
　　　Appears to sing
　　Flying the large original plant area
All of a sudden　　the great earth
　　　　Starts to wake up

Bees kiss the half-awake dews
　　The sound of vehicles on the track
　　　　　Gently caressing the park's stories
Of small farmers starting businesses
　　Still lingering between warehouses

124·

代人傷往詩二首（其一）　　　　　　南北朝·庾信

青田松上一黃鶴，相思樹下兩鴛鴦。
無事交渠更相失，不及從來莫作雙。

---

[79] Taitung Sugar Factory is now operated and managed by Huadong District of Taiwan Sugar Company, and "Cultural and Creative Industry Park" has been set up.

Lament for the Past (No. 1)

Yu Xin (Northern and Southern dynasties)

A yellow crane on a pine
tree in the blue field; a pair

of mandarin ducks under
the lovesick tree. In case

of no communication, in
case of mutual loss, it is

advisable not to pair up with
each other in the beginning.

一個難忘的瞬間

林明理

也是這樣清早的雨天。
風把相思剪成紛紛細雨，我可以
　　站在教堂前，聽歲月低吟淺唱，
那時，聖歌響起，像一股清泉潺潺流過——
　　頌讚造物主的慈悲。

我把目光投向遠方，
遠方是迷濛的山，一輛火車緩緩靠站時，
　　彷彿跨時空的超連結……
不知怎地，
　　憶及父親曾在月台上喊我的名字；

是的，回憶感動了我。是的，我的心頭
　　暖暖的。
當我沿著雨水打濕的田野上漫步，
　　草葉上的垂露，純淨如雪。
是的，那是一個難忘的瞬間。

－2025.1.11

An Unforgettable Moment

Lin Ming-Li

It is also rainy in the morning.
The wind has cut the yearning into a drizzling rain, and I can

Stand in front of the church, to hear the years sing,
When the hymn sounds like a clear spring flowing by —
　　In praise of the Creator's mercy.

I cast my eyes to the distance,
Which is the misty mountain, where a train stops slowly in the station,
　　Like a hyperlink across time and space....
Somehow,
　　Remembering my father calling my name from the platform;

Yes, the memory has touched me. Yes, my heart
　　　Is warm.
As I walk in the rain-wet field,
　　The dew on the grass is pure like snow.
Yes, it is an unforgettable moment.

January 11, 2025.

🦋 🦋 🦋

125·

和王褒詠摘菊　　　　　　　　　　　　　　南北朝·宇文毓

玉碗承花落，花落碗中芳。
酒浮花不沒，花含酒更香。

Plucking Chrysanthemums

Yu Wenyu (Northern and Southern dynasties)

The jade-like bowl
contains fallen flowers,

which significantly
sweeten the bowl.

The flowers are floating
in the wine, refusing to

sink down; with wine, the
flowers are more fragrant.

記夢

林明理

一整晚妳的聲音如細浪
泛白了黯淡的星河
我匆匆留下一個吻
在滴溜的霧徑上
或者,也想出其不備地說
愛,其實笨拙如牛

現在我試著親近妳 給妳
一季的麥花,著實想逗引妳
深深地在手心呼吸一下
如貓的小嘴唱和著相酬的
詩譜,叫我聞得到
那逃逸的形跡是多麼輕盈
——漫過山后

The Memory of a Dream

Lin Ming-Li

Throughout the night your breath is like gentle waves
Whitening the dreary river of stars
In a hurry I leave behind a kiss
Along the slippery foggy path
Or, wanting to say unawares
Love is actually awkward like an ox

Now I try to approach you, to give you
Wheat flowers of a season, intending to tease you
To take a deep breath in the palm of my hand
Like a cat's small mouth singing reciprocal
Poems, for me to know
How light are the lost traces
— Overflowing across the mountain

126 ·

破鏡詩　　　　　　　　　　　　　　　　　南北朝・徐德言

鏡與人俱去，鏡歸人未歸。
無復姮娥影，空留明月輝。

A Poem of the Broken Mirror
Xu Deyan (Northern and Southern dynasties)

Gong are the mirror
and the person, the

mirror returning without
the person. The form

of the Moon Goddess
is no more, leaving

vainly the brilliance
of the bright moon.

致小說家——鄭念[80]　　　　　　　　　　　林明理

在文革最黑暗之夜
妳的眼睛，清澈而幽深
吸引我眼睛朝外看的
是妳心中那盞不滅的光
　　——告訴世人
　　不要氣餒！
而我完全領會了
妳在風雨中
　　對我點頭微笑的含意

---

[80] 2018.01.30 晨間收到 Dr. William Marr 電郵一封書寫鄭念（1915-2009）的事蹟。她生於北京，原名姚念媛，文革時被關六年，72 歲時在美國寫下一書：《上海生死劫》《Life and Death in Shanghai》，轟動於國際，享年 94 歲。我很喜歡此則勵志的故事，因而為詩。—2018.01.31

To Novelist: Zheng Nian[81]

Lin Ming-Li

In the darkest night of the Cultural Revolution
Your eyes are limpid and profound
What attracts me to look outward
Is the eternal light in your heart
    —Tell people of the world
      Don't be discouraged!
And I fully understand the meaning
Of your nodding at me in the storm
    With a smile

127 ·

哭魯廣達

南北朝・江總

黃泉雖抱恨，白日自留名。
悲君感義死，不作負恩生。

Lament for Lu Guangda

Jiang Zong (Northern and Southern dynasties)

Entering the netherworld
with a regret, you establish

a name in the world, like
the sun moving in the broad

sky. I sigh over your personal
loyalty, for which you died,

---

[81] On the morning of January 30, 2018, I received an e-mail from Dr. William Marr concerning the novelist Zheng Nian (1915-2009). Born in Beijing, formerly known as Yao Nianyuan, she was imprisoned for six years during the Cultural Revolution. At the age of 72 she published in the United States her book Life and Death in Shanghai, which shocked the world. She passed away at the age of 94. I like her story very much, and the poem is thus inspired. -January 31, 2018.

instead of eking out a meagre
life out of sheer ingratitude.

青藤花　　　　　　　　　　　　　　　　　　　　　林明理

一株青藤花
在芬馥的原野中
靜聽著雲端裡的低的
雷聲，忽而幾顆雨點
開始打在額上
悒鬱的
青藤花
無端地笑了

屋外很遼闊
你聽，蚯蚓聲如雨
如雷
你是否聞到泥土的香？
是否也曾細心咀嚼便玩味書中了！
在這初夏之夜，我便看見
一個凝定的容顏
浸透了轉動的世界

Sinomenia Flowers　　　　　　　　　　　　　　　Lin Ming-Li

A green vine
Is in the sweet-scented field
Quietly listening to the low thunder in
The clouds, when a few drops of rain
Begin to hit its forehead
And the sad
Vine smiles
For no reason

Outside it is very vast
You listen, earthworms sound like rain
Like thunder
Do you smell the fragrance of earth?
Whether you have carefully chewed and savored the book?

On this early summer night, I see
A frozen face
Permeating the turning world

❦ ❦ ❦

128·

夏晚詩 　　　　　　　　　　　南北朝·薛道衡

流火稍西傾，夕影遍曾城。
高天澄遠色，秋氣入蟬聲。

Late Summer　　Xue Daoheng (Northern and Southern dynasties)

The running fire runs a bit
westward, when the lingering

glow of the setting sun fills
the whole town. The high

sky is limpid near and
afar, when the chirping

of cicadas is tinged with
a breath of autumn air.

寫給卡法薩巴[82] 　　　　　　　　　　　林明理

想像中我造訪了
　卡法薩巴
我一邊深情地注視
　各處
一邊尋找共鳴的開始
老城欣喜地
接納我的詩篇
　　許諾我的心願

---

[82] 2017.6.26 寫於 Prof. Ernesto Kahan 在以色列的脊椎注射治療日。

讓我在風中
在蔚藍海面上
　　寫下你的名字

To Kfar Saba, Israel[83]　　　　　　　Lin Ming-Li

In my imagination I have visited
　Kfar Saba
While watching with deep feeling
　Here and there
I look for the beginning of resonance
With pleasure the old town
Has accepted my poems
　To promise my wish
For me to write in the wind
And on the blue sea
　　Your name

❦ ❦ ❦

129 ·

三洲歌　　　　　　　　　　　　南北朝·陳叔寶

春江聊一望，細草遍長洲。
沙汀時起伏，畫舸屢淹留。

The Song of Sanzhou
　　　　　Chen Shubao (Northern and Southern dynasties)

A long view of the
spring river: fine grass

filling the endlessly
stretching continent.

---

[83] Written on June 26, 2017, the day when Professor Ernesto Kahan of Israel received his spine injection treatment.

The sandy land is now
rising and then falling;

a painted boat after another
is tethered here for long.

我偏愛牢記詩詞　　　　　　　　　　　　　林明理

我偏愛牢記詩詞。
因為，它們經風，沐雨，
泛出深淺不一的歷史記憶。
我喜歡盡情閱讀，
欣然任時間流過，
像個好奇的孩子，傾其中
佈滿詩意的回聲。

我偏愛探索，
偏愛每一詩詞被遺落在時光裡的
史實。
因為，相伴而生的傷感或愜意，
讓我的遐想更為生動活潑。
我偏愛英雄慷慨赴義的故事，
每讀一篇，都為之莫名感動。

－2025.01.12.

I Prefer Memorizing Poetry　　　　　　Lin Ming-Li

I prefer memorizing poetry.
Because, through winds & rains,
They twinkle with a wide range of historical memories.
I like reading to my heart's content,
Gladly to let time pass by,
Like a curious child, full
Of poetic echoes.

I love exploration,
I love the fact that each poem is lost
In time.
Because, the accompanying sentimentality or great ease

Makes my reverie more vivid.
I prefer the stories of heroic generosity to justice;
Each time I read it, I am inexplicably touched.

                January 12, 2025.

130.

戲贈沈後   南北朝・陳叔寶

留人不留人，不留人也去。
此處不留人，自有留人處。

A Parody   Chen Shubao (Northern and Southern dynasties)

He does not
value me, and

I go away to
be valued. This

place does not
value me, and I

find another place
to be valued.

如風往事   林明理

終究
一切都已結束
終究
讓愛遠飆
終究
獨自步上荊棘之路
我的靈魂懸在崖壁
邊遊邊躲

是誰
讓一切返回虛無
是誰
兀自矗立懸崖之後
不再夢寐以求什麼
愛，可以反覆難測
也可以歸於平淡
來去無蹤

Gone With the Wind Lin Ming-Li

Eventually
Everything is over
Eventually
For love to float away
Eventually
Alone on the thorny road
My soul is hanging over the cliff
Wandering and evading

Who is it
For everything to return to nothingness
Who is it
Standing alone behind the cliff
No longer dreaming of anything
Love, can be fathomed time and again
And it can be ignored in spite of
Its willful coming and going

131·

自君之出矣六首（其一） 南北朝·陳叔寶

自君之出矣，霜暉當夜明。
思君若風影，來去不曾停。

Since You Left Me (No. 1)

Chen Shubao (Northern and Southern dynasties)

Since you left me,
the frosty light is

bright throughout
the night. My pining

for you, like the shadow
of the wind, to and

fro, is constantly
on the moving.

古老的驛站

林明理

一座古老的驛站，閃耀著朝氣的光，
它的柔音像首詩，輕輕地在那兒奔馳，
時時送來野鳥聲也沒有變，
而陽光從牆上雨痕悄然走過……

歲歲年年。那些舊倉庫斑駁的木牆
像老歌在吟唱。
雖然它僅存半木造結構車庫，
在歷史的洪流中，仍像一首夜曲──
在星空唱和；

它溫潤了許多遊子最遙遠的夢，
且留存著無數孩子的純真。
啊，我從不忘記它的面貌，
就在此值得緬懷的時刻。

－2025.01.11

An Age-Old Post

Lin Ming-Li

An age-old post, shining with the light of youth,
Its soft sound like a poem, running gently there,
From time to time the sound of wild birds has not changed,
The sun glides quietly through the rain marks on the wall...

Year after year. The mottled wooden walls of those old warehouses
Are singing like old songs.
Although it is only a semi-wooden structure garage,
In the torrent of history, it is still like a nocturne —
Singing in the starry sky;

It moistens the most remote dreams of many wanderers,
And retains the innocence of countless children.
Ah, I never forget its face,
On this memorable occasion.

January 11, 2025.

132·

敦煌樂二首（其一） 隋朝·王冑

長途望無已，高山斷還續。
意欲此念時，氣絕不成曲。

The Melody of Dunhuang (No. 1)

Wang Zhou (Sui dynasty)

The endless road
is out of sight, when

the mountains, broken
off for a short while,

continue to meander
afar. Thinking of this

sight, the breath is broken,
incapable of a composition.

那些回味時代的光影 林明理

那些回味時代的光影：伴隨著
　　感人的神話與水，起起伏伏。

我穿越時空，邊走邊問，──
　　有位耆老迎面回答，粼粼波光閃耀著，
泉聲愈大，閃耀的光芒愈加燦亮；

我從歷史的縫隙間，盡可能打開我的
　　想像力，就好像翻閱一本古書，
族人用詫異的眼睛瞅著我看，──
　　讓我不知不覺中，
　　　　在多情的水畔遐想。

我恍惚記起那愛情湧泉，泛起漣漪……
　　有幾滴清露在林葉上翻轉，──
　　眾鳥歌著，那些回味時代的光影。
如果說，傳說是一種真實的夢，
那麼，流傳千古，便是一種幸福。

　　　　　　　　　　　　　　－2025.01.03

The Light & Shadow of the Times with Lingering Aftertaste

　　　　　　　　　　　　　　　　　　Lin Ming-Li

The light & shadow of the times with lingering aftertaste: with
　　Moving myths and water, ups and downs.
As I walk through time and space, I keep asking —
　　A senior citizen answers in the face, with sparkling light,
The louder the sound of the spring, the more brilliant the shining light;

I open my imagination as much as possible
　　From the gaps in history, like flipping through an ancient book;
The people look at me with surprised eyes —
　　For me unconsciously, to daydream
　　　　On the side of the sentimental water.

I dimly remember the spring of love, rippling....
　　A few drops of dew turning on the forest leaves —
　　Birds are singing, the light & shadow of the times with lingering aftertaste.
If it is said that the legend is a real dream,
Then, to spread through the ages is a kind of happiness.

　　　　　　　　　　　　　　　　　　January 3, 2025.

133.

敦煌樂二首（其二） 隋朝・王冑

極目眺修途，平原忽超遠。
心期在何處？望望崦嵫晚。

The Melody of Dunhuang (No. 2)

Wang Zhou (Sui dynasty)

Looking afar, into the
infinity of the road: the plain

is stretching and stretching
on endlessly. The heart is

pining and yearning, but
where? Keep looking afar

— the Yanzi Mountain is
caught in the descending dusk.

詩觀 林明理

詩是畫中的萌動，
也是自由意志的翔飛；
詩是滿月的皺紋，
也是望斷的飄然。

My View on Poetry

Lin Ming-Li

Poetry is the stirring in the painting,
as well as the flight of free will;
poetry is the wrinkles of the full moon,
as well as the drifting glances.

134.

寄夫詩 南北朝・陳少女

自君上河梁，蓬首臥蘭房。
安得一樽酒，慰妾九回腸。

To My Husband Chen Shaonü (Northern and Southern dynasties)

Since you go away,
crossing rivers, to do

business, I lie in the bed
of my orchid chamber

listly, without washing
and combing. A cup of

wine, as a comforter, to
ease my sorrowful heart.

憶台南水道博物館[84] 林明理

跟著小火車行進，
紅牆的廊道和綠蔭的縫隙，
有迎面親吻的長風。

博物館裡的光，
穿過各種文物
與陳設的水道工程融合。

---

[84] 為紀念臺灣水道建設的三位大功臣威廉・巴爾頓（1856-1899）、濱野彌四郎（1869-1932）、八田與一（1886-1942），於 2024 年 12 月 6 日上午參觀台南水道博物館後，有感而作。—2024.12.13.

兩個師生，巴爾頓和濱野彌四郎
與屬下八田與一工程師，
為臺灣水道建設，厥功甚偉。

他們飽經風霜，
跋山涉水到臺灣許多城鄉，
其塑像，也讓四周發亮了。

Remembering Tainan Waterway Museum[85]

Lin Ming-Li

To follow the little train,
The corridor of red walls and the crevices of green shade,
There is a long wind of kissing.

The light in the museum,
Through various artifacts,
To fuse into the display waterway project.

As teacher and student, Barton and Yachiro Hamano
And their subordinate Yata Yuichi as an engineer,
Great achievements in the construction of Taiwan waterway.

They have weathered winds & frosts,
Traveled across rivers & mountains to many cities in Taiwan,
Their statues have brightened the neighborhood.

❦ ❦ ❦

135・

拔蒲二首（其一）　　　　　　　　　南北朝・無名氏

青蒲銜紫茸，長葉復從風。
與君同舟去，拔蒲五湖中。

---

[85] To commemorate three men meritorious in the construction of Taiwan waterway: William Barton (1856-1899), Yachiro Hamano (1869-1932), and Yata Yuichi (1886-1942), I compose this poem after visiting Tainan Waterway Museum on December 6, 2024. -December 13, 2024.

Plucking Cattails (No. 1)

Anonymous (Northern and Southern dynasties)

Green cattails are alive
with fine purple flower-

lets; their long leaves are
resigning themselves to

the gentle wind. In the same
boat, my love and I, we are

plucking cattails while roaming
through the five great lakes.

航行者

林明理

飛車狂野地迴轉
穿越森林隧道
驚呼四起
直落雲霄

我提著鞋帶
側耳聽聽馳過
近旁的水花笑了
燦然萬朵

古老的尖塔紅楓
互相踏掩
在意猶未盡中
遺忘破碎的光影

The Navigator

Lin Ming-Li

The flying vehicle spins wildly
Through the forest tunnel
Screaming and startling
Into the cloudy sky

I take my shoelaces
And listen to its passing by
The water sprays nearby are laughing
Millions of brilliant blossoms

The old steeple & red maple trees
Setting off each other
In something lingering
To forget the broken light & shadow

136.

拔蒲二首（其二）   南北朝・無名氏

朝發桂蘭渚，晝息桑榆下。
與君同拔蒲，竟日不成把。

Plucking Cattails (No. 2)

     Anonymous (Northern and Southern dynasties)

The morning sees us starting
off at the Islent of laurels &

orchids; the evening sees us
resting under the mulberry

and elm trees. You and me,
we pluck cattails side by side,

and not yet a handful of them
through the whole day.

我不能忘卻   林明理

哪裡來的風啊，如此浩蕩！如
一匹曠野的狼——激動地

哀嚎……
教我到處找尋牠的飛光！

我走遍山崖，渡過艱危的波浪，
衣袂飄飄，僅繫上一朵同故鄉的
田裡一齊飛揚的花！
我一邊唱和，一邊追趕；

哪裡來的雪啊，沿著這路到
我故土的山上，到處是白樺，
不如就帶我回去吧——
幫我把影子拉長。

我不能忘卻
你的聲音……隨你飛逸；
啊，在久已不曾踏上的歸路，
和閃爍著星辰的斑駁而熟悉的白牆。

－2025.01.17

I Cannot Forget

Lin Ming-Li

Where does the wind come from? It is so mighty! Like
A wolf in the wilderness — wailing
Excitedly...
Making me to look everywhere for his flying light!

I walk across the cliffs, through the dangerous waves,
Wearing fluttering sleeves, only tied with a flower from the same hometown
Flying and dancing in the field!
I am singing, and I am pursuing;

Where is the snow from, oh, along this road
To my native mountain, birches are everywhere,
It is better to take me back —
To help me elongate the shadow.

I cannot forget
Your voice... As you fly;

Oh, on the long untrodden return road,
And the familiar mottled white wall twinkling with stars.

January 17, 2025.

137 ·

作蠶絲二首（其一）　　　　　　　　南北朝・無名氏

春蠶不應老，晝夜常懷絲。
何惜微軀盡，纏綿自有時。

Producing the Cocoon Silk (No. 1)
Anonymous (Northern and Southern dynasties)

The spring silk-
worms should not

grow old, and they
always produce silk

day and night. In spite
of their weak body,

they are lingering
from time to time.

跟著風的腳步　　　　　　　　　　　　林明理

這裡擁有千年遺跡，像謎題般，擁有了
巨石文明。它開啟了我心的寧靜，——
是某種奇妙的感動，雖然我無法
多加揣摩，或畫出它的完整輪廓；
除了獻上這首小詩，我只想：
跟著風和一隻鷹的腳步，此外已無所求。

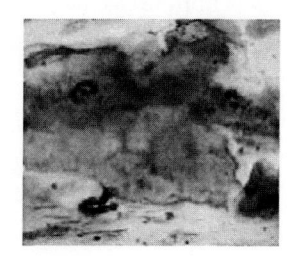

歲月啊，拿出你攜著的一幕幕長鏡頭，
放映一下老村的命運，——

讓我也思索一下流亡至此的人，
是否已開創一條屬於自己的路？
歲月啊，跟著風的腳步，
我已瞥見比你標記出的更古老的歌。

－2025.1.11

Follow the Steps of Wind   Lin Ming-Li

Here it boasts the ruins through thousands of years, like a puzzle, with
The megalithic civilization. It has contributed to the peace of my heart —
Something wonderful, though I cannot
Fathom it, or draw its full outline;
In addition to dedicating this poem, I only want
To follow the steps of wind and an eagle, and nothing more.

Oh years, take out the long lenses you carry,
To project the fate of the old village —
Let me think about the people exiled here,
Have they blazed a road of their own?
Oh years, following the footsteps of the wind,
I have glimpsed songs older than those you have marked.

January 11, 2025.

138．

入關詩   隋朝‧虞世基

隴雲低不散，黃河咽複流。
關山多道里，相接幾重愁。

Upon Entering the Pass   Yu Shiji (Sui dynasty)

The northwestern clouds
mass low, without dispersing;

the Yellow River, choked,
flows forward again.

As many passes, as
many roads. Roads lead

on to roads, as sorrows
multiply after sorrows.

給 Giovanni G. Campisi　　　　　　　　　　林明理

吾友，當你沉靜的目光
　　　觸碰到我的詩園時，
我認出了
　　你祖先堅韌的血液及
　　　　熱情的靈魂；
並因此而讓我更瞭解
　　你在我身邊，友情不移。

To Giovanni G. Campisi　　　　　Lin Ming-Li

My friend, when your quiet eyes
Are directed to my poetry garden,
I come to realize
The tough blood and the passionate
Soul of your ancestors;
And I know more clearly
With you by my side, our friendship lasts.

139·

送別秦王學士江益詩　　　　　　　隋朝·劉萼予

百年風月意，一旦死生分。
客心還送客，悲我復悲君。

Seeing a Friend Off　　　　Liu Mengyu (Sui dynasty)

Through one hundred years,
we admire the moon & the

wind; we are, sooner or later,
to be separated by life &

death. With a wandering
heart, I see you off, also

a wanderer; sorrowful
— for you, and for me.

寒星 　　　　　　　　　　　　　　　　　　　　　林明理

一瞬間
記憶突然碎成
許多浪花

感覺的春天
在我呼喊中瞇著眼
並攬住那
黑潤的泥路
匆匆穿過樹林

帶走了一封發不出的信

The Cold Stars 　　　　　　　　　　　　　Lin Ming-Li

In a split second
Memory suddenly breaks into
A host of waves

The spring of feeling
Squinting amidst my cry
While blocking
The dark muddy road
Hurriedly through the woods

Taking away a letter that fails to be posted

140.

因故人歸作詩　　　　　　　　　　隋朝・蘇蟬翼

郎去何太速，郎來何太遲。
欲借一尊酒，共敘十年悲。

Upon the Returning of an Old Friend

　　　　　　　　　　　　Su Chanyi (Sui dynasty)

Oh my boy, how
speedily you leave

here, and how belatedly
you come back. I

would like, with a cup
of wine, to tell, to detail

— the sorrows through
the past ten years.

靈魂靜留在一塊礁岩上　　　　　　林明理

靈魂在靈魂的五官裡
奔馳

夜總是不甘靜默
總是讓我目光灼灼

月如此眷顧著我
我還是靦腆不說

但，親愛的，請朝向我
我依然在一塊礁岩上
靜留

The Soul Rests on a Rock   Lin Ming-Li

The soul runs in the features of
The soul

The night is always reluctant to be silent
Always renders my eyes burning

The moon is solicitous about me
Still I am too shy to say

But, my dear, turn to me
As I remain on
A rock

141·

寄阮郎詩   隋朝·張碧蘭

郎如洛陽花，妾似武昌柳。
兩地惜春風，何時一攜手？

To My Darling Boy   Zhang Bilan (Sui dynasty)

My darling boy is like
the peony of Luoyang,

when I am like a twig
of willow in Wuchang.

Southern Wuchang and
northern Luoyang cherish

the same spring wind —
when can we go hand in hand?

致黃櫨樹[86]

林明理

我愛香山，
　　紅黃，鑲橄欖，──
在秋陽的斜坡，
　　欣喜且悠然。

那不斷的呼聲，
　　欲帶我到何等的極限？
我如果追隨，
將如何學聽法松，
　　寧謐地……於萬株叢，
不論冬雪，
　　　或夏雨。

亦或，你近旁的滿地銀杏，
　　也吹皺老家鄉的星空？
霧　溜進寺內，
　　風　從東吹來。

To the Cotinus Tree[87]

Lin Ming-Li

I love the Fragrant Hills,
　　Red & yellow, inlaid with olives —
On the slope of the autumn sun,
　　Joyful and leisurely.

The constant cries,
　　How far will they take me?
If I follow,
How will I learn to listen to the pines,
　　Quietly... In thousands of plants,

---

[86] 黃櫨樹 cotinus tree，又名紅葉樹。北京香山公園（Fragrant Hills Park），是一座具有山林特色的皇家園林；而香山紅葉最具濃郁的秋色。─2025.01.06

[87] The cotinus tree is also known as the red-leaf tree. The Fragrant Hills Park in Beijing is a royal garden with the characteristics of mountain forests, and the red leaves of the Fragrant Hills are the symbol of autumnal tints. -January 6, 2025.

Whether winter snow,
　　　Or summer rain.

Or, a groundful of ginkgo leaves near you,
　　Also blows to crumple the starry sky of the old hometown?
Fog　creeps into the temple,
　　Wind　blows from the east.

142・

自感詩三首（其一）　　　　　　　　隋朝・侯夫人

庭絕玉輦跡，芳草漸成窠。
隱隱聞簫鼓，君恩何處多？

The Moving Moments (No. 1)　Mrs. Hou (Sui dynasty)

The courtyard is deserted
of the imperial carriage,

without any trace; wild grass
grows rampant here and there.

In the distance travels
the dim sound of piping

and drumming — where can
I find the imperial favor?

葬禮　　　　　　　　　　　　　　　　　　　　林明理

再沒有比參加葬禮更難過的事了，
小村靜寂，鳥雀一唱，周遭便聽得見
隨風飄送的落葉
哀戚於一束百合花鋪造的墓園。

又有誰能預測死亡的來臨？
唯一的回憶是，當我轉身離去，

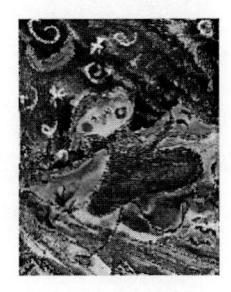

便開始想念父親的背影。
那沐浴金光的教堂，讓我
回歸思慕，童年的時光……
與父親手牽手的某些話語；

此外，
一張懷中與父親合影的相片，
又使我的精神飛揚起來，——
那真是少有的幸福。

─2025.1.12.

The Funeral   Lin Ming-Li

There is nothing more sorrowful than attending a funeral;
The small village is quiet, and when the birds sing, you can hear the falling
Leaves dancing in the wind
And mourning a cemetery paved with lilies.

Who can predict the approaching of death?
The only memory is that when I turn to leave,
I begin to miss my father's form of back.
The church bathed in golden light, making me
Return to the yearning, the childhood time…
Some words about holding hands with my father;

In addition,
A photo with my father in my arms,
Makes my spirit fly up —
This is really rare happiness.

January 12, 2025.

143．

自感詩三首（其二）   隋朝・侯夫人

欲泣不成淚，悲來翻強歌。
庭花方爛漫，無計奈春何。

The Moving Moments (No. 2)   Mrs. Hou (Sui dynasty)

I am on the verge of shedding
tears, yet without tearing;

my mind filled with sorrow,
yet I disguise my sorrow

beneath a cheerful appearance.
The courtyard flowers are

blooming brilliant, and I am
helpless about the fair spring.

赤崁樓[88]懷古   林明理

這座城堡珍貴如金，
但金子般的遺跡難以重現。
當我把耳朵貼近樓閣，
忽然聽見它的話語：
「告訴我，妳聽見了什麼？
是否聽得見昔日古城
與那棵老樹哼著歌？」

是的，
我從整建中的建築往外看，
街道上人車擁擠，
世界的戰爭仍難以預料，
就像光陰站在這裡，
三百多年流過去了，
我根本來不及回首⋯
看看它滄桑又動人的面容。

---

[88] 臺南市的赤崁樓 Chihkan Tower 係 1653 年進佔臺灣南部的荷蘭人所建的西式城堡，迄今三百多年來，仍可見厚牆、拱圈遺構，已被列為一級古蹟。—2024.12.13

Remembering the Past in Chihkan Tower[89]

Lin Ming-Li

The castle is as precious as gold,
But its golden ruins are hard to reproduce.
When I prick up my ears close to the pavilion,
Suddenly I hear its words:
"Tell me, what do you hear?
Do you hear the old city and
The old tree humming?"

Yes,
I look out from the building under construction,
The streets are crowded with people and cars,
The world's wars are still unpredictable,
Just like time standing here,
More than 300 years have passed,
I have no time to look back...
To look at its sad, beautiful face.

144.

自感詩三首（其三）　　　　　　　　隋朝・侯夫人

春陰正無際，獨步意如何？
不及閒花草，翻承雨露多。

The Moving Moments (No. 3)　　Mrs. Hou (Sui dynasty)

Boundless and limit-
less is the cloudy spring;

---

[89] The Chihkan Tower in Tainan City is a Western-style castle built by the Dutch who occupied southern Taiwan in 1653. For more than 300 years, the ruins of thick walls and arch circles are still seeable, which have been listed as a first-grade historic site. -December 13, 2024.

what about a walk
alone? The idle grass

and fair flowers are
superior to me: they

receive more dews
and rainwater than me.

寫作也是一種快樂 　　　　　　　　林明理

一幅畫裡包藏著我為數甚多的
思緒，因為我找回了自由的浪漫，
準備拾起封塵已久的筆，──

那些林中的飛鳥，耕種的老農，
崖邊的大冠鷲……都逐一成了我的風景，
讓我懂得這才是寫作人生，
可以讓我想像力盡情翱翔；

我會豎耳諦聽貓頭鷹
惹動枝椏的簌簌聲，
也學會和蝴蝶，鳥獸說悄悄話；

如今，再也不必為教學而奔波，
因為，寫作既是一種快樂，
也是我的存在與奮發向上的力量。

－2025.01.09

Writing Is Also a Pleasure 　　　　Lin Ming-Li

A painting contains a lot of my
Thoughts, because I have retraced the romance of freedom,
Ready to pick up the pen that has been sealed for long—

The birds in the forest, the old farmers in the field,
The vultures on the edge of the cliff... All become my scenery one by one,
For me to know that this is the writing life,
For my imagination to soar freely;

I will prick my ears to listen to the whisper
Of the owls on the branches,
And learn to whisper with butterflies, birds and animals;

Today, I no longer have to rush to teach,
Because writing is not only a joy,
But also my existence and strength to strive for greater progress.

January 9, 2025.

145.

妝成詩 隋朝・侯夫人

妝成多自惜，夢好卻成悲。
不及楊花意，春來到處飛。

Makeup Mrs. Hou (Sui dynasty)

After makeup, I admire
myself; awake from a

fond dream, I feel so
sorrowful. I am inferior

to poplar filaments which,
with the advent of spring,

fly high and low, here,
there, and everywhere.

傾聽大海 林明理

一封寄自綠蠵龜，
　　用淚寫的關於冰原的信，
字字句句如礁島的喚聲，
　　像漂流的殘冰串起我激蕩的心靈。

深深的夜，還藏著你靈魂的孤獨，
　　這玻璃窗外的嘆息屬於誰？
我潛入黑暗找尋你，微弱的昏光
　　可是你日夜傳遞的陰鬱？

誰讓你疲憊的身軀，留下
　　一次次蒼老的記號？
一灘灘的小湖泊是否也寫下
　　同樣的叫喊於世界？

在靜寂的灣流中，
　　　在珊瑚的謳歌裡，
在沒有星光的桂樹旁，
　　　你的足音，已傳來

總是瑟縮地向我召喚
　　總是永遠、永遠溫柔地
向著我在窗後……哦，提燈而來
　　又匆匆走過。

To Listen to the Sea   Lin Ming-Li

　　　A mail from the green loggerhead turtle,
With tears to write about the icy land;
　Each and every word like the calling of the reefs,
Like the drifting string of ice to stir up my heart.

　　The deep night is still hidden with your lonely soul,
The sighs outside the window belong to whom?
　I dive into the night in search of you, the faint light,
Is it the gloom you deliver day and night?

　　Who makes your exhausted body marked
With the old signs time and again?
　　Whether the shoals of the small lakes also write down
The same calling to the world?

In the quiet stream of the bay,
In the singing of the corals,
    By the cherry bay trees without starlight,
The echo of your footsteps is traveling here.

    Constantly cowering and calling to me,
Always, always with tenderness,
    Towards the back of my window — oh, with a lamp
To hurry past.

146·

楊柳枝   隋朝·無名氏

萬里長江一帶開,岸邊楊柳幾千栽?
錦帆未落西風起,惆悵龍舟去不回。

Willow Twigs   Anonymous (Sui dynasty)

The two banks of the Yangtze
River are waving with count-

less willow twigs; myriads
of them are planted as aligned.

Before the embroidered sail
is set, the west wind is arising;

a great regret: a dragon boat,
once gone, returns never more.

早霧   林明理

窗臺外,遠處木犁
    空蕩蕩地……
        單掛在田壟。

那兒，山煙之上，
　　你瞅著我，有好一陣──
接著，我倚上沙發閉上眼睛，
　　有如羊在霧中。
想起了那年
　　瑟縮的二月，──
　　　　透一股清冷。

那是多久前的事兒了？
　　我懷疑地問：
夜裡吹亂我頭髮的風
　　　　從上面經過，回聲
　　落滿了河谷；

過去的日子彷彿
　　　　一切都很重要，
又都不很重要，
就像早霧頑皮地溜走，
　　說了等於沒說。

Morning Fog   Lin Ming-Li

Without the window, beyond the wooden plough,
　　Empty, solitarily….
　　　　Hanging in the field.

There, atop the foggy mountain,
　　You look at me, for a great while —
Then, I lean on the sofa, closing my eyes,
　　Like a sheep in the fog.
I remember the year,
　　The shivering February —
　　　　A current of pure cold.

How long ago is that?
　　　　I ask doubtfully:
The night wind has tousled my hair.
　　　　Passing over my head, echoing,
Filling the valley;

The past days seem
   Everything is so important,
And not so important;
Just like the morning fog playfully gliding by,
  What is said as if nothing has been said.

❦ ❦ ❦

147．

子夜四時歌・冬歌十七首（其六）   魏晉・無名氏

昔別春草綠，今還墀雪盈。
誰知相思老，玄鬢白髮生。

Midnight Songs Through the Four Seasons (Winter Song) (No. 6)   Anonymous (Wei and Jin dynasties)

When I leave here in
the former day, the grass

grows lush and green;
now I return home,

it is heavily snowing.
Pining & yearning make

me old — see the gray
hairs on my temples.

深入山路的陰影   林明理

我早該細細領略從此開始的芳香，
山嵐在潑墨間，一叢叢粉紅的洛神花。
一隻大冠鷲騰起，翱翔，——
超凡而神奇。

那八萬四千詩偈，在風中低吟，
我不必茫然回首。

當寺院鐘聲輕輕喚醒，──
那最深記憶裡，每次回首的名字；

我驚訝於他立在山的南方閃蕩，
有時，像隻鷹──
即將沒入灰藍的遠方，
卻又像是要停泊在我心上。

－2025.01.12

The Shadow Deep Into the Mountain Road

Lin Ming-Li

I should have admired the fragrance from now on,
The mountains in the ink, a cluster after another cluster of pink Hibiscus flowers.
A crowned vulture rises, soars —
Extraordinary and magical.

The eighty-four thousand verses, whispering in the wind,
I do not have to look back in blankness.
When the temple bell gently awakens —
In the deepest memory, each time the name is recalled;

I marvel at how he stands on the south side of the mountain, shivering and flashing,
Sometimes, like an eagle —
About to disappear into the gray distance,
But as if to anchor in my heart.

January 12, 2025.

148．

子夜四時歌・春歌

南北朝・無名氏

春風動春心，流目矚山林。
山林多奇采，陽鳥吐清音。

Midnight Songs Through the Four Seasons (Spring Song) Anonymous (Northern and Southern dynasties)

Spring wind ruffles
my spring heart; my

turning eyes gaze at
the remote mountain

forest, which is resplendent,
spectacular, and wondrous.

The sunny birds are
articulating limpid sounds.

我的心像隻小藍雀

林明理

我的心像隻小藍雀，
一會兒飛入山林溪谷，
拖著長音歡快地吟唱——

一會兒在空中盤旋，
與另一隻相互鳴叫，恰似
蕭邦的華爾滋舞曲；

那山邊有座最好的秘境，
偶有歌聲悠悠傳來，
像秋夜裡講述的小小神話。

我邊飛，邊想著：
這就是我探尋之後的點滴絮語，
有清溪在腳下流淌，詩般純粹。

—2025.1.22.

My Heart Is Like a Blue Sparrow Lin Ming-Li

My heart, like a blue sparrow,
Now it flies into the hills and valleys,
Singing joyously with a long drawl —

Then it hovers in the air,
Calling to one another, like
A Chopin waltz;

Beyond the mountain there is a best secret place,
Occasionally a song travelling here,
Like a little myth told in the autumn night.

While flying, I am thinking:
This is my little talk after exploring,
There is a clear stream flowing at the foot, pure as poetry.

January 22, 2025.

149·

子夜歌四十二首（其七）   魏晉·無名氏

始欲識郎時，兩心望如一。
理絲入殘機，何悟不成匹。

Forty-Two Midnight Songs (No. 7)
Anonymous (Wei and Jin dynasties)

Initial acquaintance
with you, it is hoped

we share the same
heart. When yearning

& pining is woven
into the loom, no worry:

we'll be a couple
to match each other.

我倆相識絕非偶然   林明理

如首次展翅而飛的海鳩，
只想與你平行遨遊；

我會努力
絕不輕易墜落……
天空何其寬廣，為自由
我無懼黑暗和險惡，
只想沿著這路到潺潺水流。

Our Meeting Is No Coincidence

Lin Ming-Li

Like the sea dove which flies for the first time,
Just wanting to soar together with you;
I will make efforts
To avoid dropping down easily...
How vast is the sky, and for freedom
I do not dread darkness and danger.
I just want to follow the path to the babbling water.

150·

子夜四時歌·秋風入窗裡

南北朝·無名氏

秋風入窗裡，羅帳起飄颺。
仰頭看明月，寄情千里光。

Midnight Songs Through the Four Seasons (Autumn Wind Into the Window)

Anonymous (Northern and Southern dynasties)

Autumn wind into
the window, the silk

curtain begins to be
wafting and dancing.

Upward looking at
the bright moon, and

emotional through the
light of thousands of miles.

我不能忘卻⋯   林明理

我不能忘卻
經常閒踱長長的堤岸，
仰視茂密的白樺，──或是
山村簇擁著月亮的花冠；

當我慣於沉思
牽曳而出的北辰星拱，
在我眼前緘默無語，──
而我將歡喜相隨。

我不能忘卻
在我親愛的家鄉日間辛勤的
勞動者與遍野的閃爍安詳──
將驅散我心頭的黯淡；

啊呀，我不再藏匿自己！
不再總是冥思，我將歌吟松風──
我將揚帆，如飛起的第一隻鷹，
銘記實現之夢想。

－2025.01.17

I Cannot Forget...   Lin Ming-Li

I cannot forget
I often stroll along the long bank,
And look up at the dense birches — or
The crown of the moon attended by the hill-village;

When I am used to meditation,
The North star, drawn by it,
Is silent before my eyes —
And I shall be glad to follow.

I cannot forget
The laborers diligently laboring in my dear
Town and the twinkling peace across the field —
Will dispel the gloom from my heart;

Oh, I won't hide myself anymore!
Instead of constant meditating, I will eulogize the pine wind —
I will sail, like the first eagle in flight,
To remember the dreams which come true.

              January 17, 2025.

國家圖書館出版品預行編目資料

```
漢魏六朝接明理——古今抒情詩三百首（漢英對照）／林明理　著、
張智中　譯　－初版－
臺中市：天空數位圖書　2025.03
面：17*23 公分
ISBN：978-626-7576-12-0（平裝）
831                                                              114003733
```

書　　　名：漢魏六朝接明理——古今抒情詩三百首（漢英對照）
發　行　人：蔡輝振
出　版　者：天空數位圖書有限公司
作　　　者：林明理
譯　　　者：張智中
美工設計：設計組
版面編輯：採編組
出版日期：2025 年 3 月（初版）
銀行名稱：合作金庫銀行南台中分行
銀行帳戶：天空數位圖書有限公司
銀行帳號：006—1070717811498
郵政帳戶：天空數位圖書有限公司
劃撥帳號：22670142
定　　　價：新台幣 540 元整
電子書發明專利第　I　306564　號
※如有缺頁、破損等請寄回更換　　　　　　　　　　版權所有請勿仿製

服務項目：個人著作、學位論文、學報期刊等出版印刷及DVD製作
影片拍攝、網站建置與代管、系統資料庫設計、個人企業形象包裝與行銷
影音教學與技能檢定系統建置、多媒體設計、電子書製作及客製化等
TEL　　：(04)22623893　　MOB：0900602919
FAX　　：(04)22623863
E-mail　：familysky@familysky.com.tw
Https　：//www.familysky.com.tw/
地　　址：台中市南區忠明南路 787 號 30 樓國王大樓
No.787-30, Zhongming S. Rd., South District, Taichung City 402, Taiwan (R.O.C.)